P9-BUG-678

SHADOW
OF WAR

Based on the Journal of

Daniel Kippelstein

James Slocum

Grand Marais

Publishing

Shadow of War

Copyright @ 2010 by James Slocum

All rights reserved under International and Pan-American Copyright Conventions. No part of this book may be used or reproduced in any manner whatsoever without written permission except in the case of brief quotations embodied in articles or reviews.

Published in the United States by Grand Marais Publishing, Pasadena, California. grandmaraispublishing@gmail.com

Although based on Daniel Kippelstein's journal, because all names (other than well known historical figures) and places have been changed, any resemblance to real persons living or dead is a coincidence.

ISBN 978-0-615-43796-7

Printed in the United States of America

Cover Art by Andrew Behr

Dedicated to

David and Daniel Kippelstein

Foreword

For me the saga of *Shadow of War* began in 1991 with Frank Daniel. Mr. Daniel was an Academy Award-winning Czech filmmaker who headed the Prague Film School. After run-ins with the Communist regime, Mr. Daniel emigrated to the United States, where he headed the Film School at Columbia University and later was Dean of the University of Southern California's Film School. It was there that we became friends and he advised me on my thesis. During his days in Prague, Frank (he preferred being called by his first name) had made the acquaintance of David Kippelstein, whose father, Daniel Kippelstein, had authored a journal on the war-torn Czechoslovakia of 1939. Frank had me read a translation of Daniel Kippelstein's journal. I was impressed with the story the journal told and thought it would make an outstanding film. Frank introduced me to David Kippelstein and I began to write a screenplay.

Soon it became apparent that the journal would also make the basis of a fine book. Eventually, after much time and deliberation, I myself was enticed to write the book. Well, perhaps "enticed" isn't quite the right term; no one else would do it, and in a leap of blind optimism, I agreed to try. I had fallen in love with the story of Daniel Kippelstein and wanted to do it justice. I don't know if I have, but I have given it my all.

One thing I must make clear: this is a work of fiction. While based on Daniel's journal, you will see in the story that after his stay in Bratislava, Daniel recopied the journal and changed the names as well as locations in case it was confiscated by the Nazis. The original at that point was destroyed. By the time of Daniel's death in 1987, he had not changed back the names and locations so as to accurately reflect the facts of history.

Furthermore, Daniel's journal recounted the events he witnessed in the spring of 1939 with immediacy but without much detailed description. Clothes, architecture, how people looked and behaved, what people said, many of these details had to be researched and added. They are thus fiction.

David Kippelstein's sensitive occupation further complicates matters. He works for a security agency in eastern Europe. That's all he will tell me. I can only speculate on whom he works for and what he does. Frank Daniel has vouched for him and I know of no reason to doubt his integrity. But David refuses to compromise his current work situation for the sake of this book. After discussing my issues in regard to factual accuracy with him, he agreed with my position that this must be called a work of fiction. But that said, I know of nothing that disputes the main elements of Daniel's story. Therefore, until someone proves to me otherwise, I believe the journal to be true. And I leave it to readers to decide for themselves.

Acknowledgements

There are numerous people to thank. First and foremost is Daniel Kippelstein, for showing such courage and tenacity in the light of overwhelming odds. To his son David, for having such trust in me and sticking with me despite so many obstacles. To Frank Daniel, for thinking of me as the right person to get this story to a wider audience. To Robyn Elliott Logelin, whose editorial guidance and good cheer were indispensable. A special thanks to my editors, Elizabeth Weinstein and Peter Skutches, whose skill, effort and enthusiasm improved this book tremendously. Lastly, to my family, who read numerous drafts and were unbelievably supportive.
A heartfelt thank you.

James Slocum

SHADOW of WAR

1

The End of Time

April brought cold winds and a fine sleet to the gray cobblestone streets of Prague. Stray drops fell from rooftops and overhangs. Black puddles gathered in gutters and dotted the roadway and sidewalk. A biting gust stabbed through all but the heaviest wool. It was winter's final gasp, and thankfully so. The winter of 1939 had been one Czechoslovakia and all the world would not soon forget.

While the days were growing noticeably longer and spring was waiting just offstage, the sun had set at least a half hour before Solomon Kippelstein usually quit work, at 6:30 or 7:00 in the evening, and walked the hundred steps to his home next door. Solomon Kippelstein was dark-haired and slender and moved with an absentminded grace. His short sideburns revealed the slightest flecks of gray, and unlike more Orthodox men, he was clean-shaven. His left eyelid drooped just slightly, sometimes giving the impression he was calm and perhaps a little slow mentally, which was not the case. He ran the Kippelstein Watch Works, a business established by his great-grandfather and passed along through generations to him. April was a comparatively quiet time of year for the business. Eighteen- and twenty-hour days were common for him in August, September, and October when Christmas inventories were being built and shipped. About 45 percent of the company's sales were made at Christmas, the rest being spread throughout the year.

A Kippelstein watch was arguably one of the finest and most reliable east of Switzerland. It was nothing for a fifty-year-old Kippelstein watch to be brought back to the factory for a new crystal face, which had broken due to some odd accident, while the watch itself, if wound properly, had never missed a single second. In fifty years! Solomon's pride in the company and its products was fierce beyond words and exceeded only by his pride in his family.

The Kippelstein home and the Watch Works were located on the fringes of the Old Town section of Prague. Here, the streets were narrow, leading to many a tiny courtyard with narrower alleys between ancient, frescoed tenements. The rooftops were a rust-colored brown and steeply angled to prevent winter snows from piling up too high. Some of the buildings dated back to the ninth century. The factory was in a twelfth-century edifice that had been modernized considerably. Their home was of more recent vintage, rebuilt after a mid-nineteenth-century fire destroyed a previous structure. Esta Kippelstein sat with her nine year-old son Jacob in the kitchen, enjoying a milk and kolachy break. Esta had pale white skin and jet-black hair the consistency of steel wool. Her nervous energy could, at times, put others on edge. But her smile was disarming and her gray eyes often shined with mischief when they weren't furrowed with worry. Despite having borne three children, she barely tipped the scales past 110 pounds. Nearby, Vlasta, the Kippelstein's cook and

housekeeper, peeled potatoes for their dinner. Esta calmly corrected
Jacob's hurried stuffing of kolachys down his throat as if he were a
starving bird.

"Please, Jacob. One at a time and slowly, or you'll choke to
death."

His love of kolachys, as well as most food, made Jacob slightly
pudgy in build. His dark, wiry hair repelled all combs. His eyeglasses
were constantly slipping down his nose and just as constantly he pushed
them back in front of his eyes. Vlasta, a big-boned peasant girl of great
strength and joyous laughter, was famous in the neighborhood for her
culinary skills and kolachys, a round, doughy pastry filled with poppy seed
or with apricot or prune preserves, were one of her specialties.

It was a little after six when Esta noticed that fifteen-year-old
Anna was late returning from her piano lesson. Her other son, fourteen-
year-old Daniel, was a full-time student at St. Jude's, a boys' school on the
southeast side of Prague. Esta went to the living room window, which
faced the street, and nervously spied out. No Anna. She unconsciously
twirled her hair into tight locks like unraveled watch springs. Before the
Nazi invasion just a month ago, Esta would not have given Anna's absence
a second thought. But now with Prague under martial law, German
soldiers were everywhere, and the tension was palpable.

This tension was of little concern to Anna right then. As the
dark, heavy clouds of the day began to slowly breakup, Anna detoured
through the Old Town Square and down the main shopping avenues. Anna
had long, light brown hair and blue eyes with the warm luster of pearls,
belying a playful side to her serious demeanor. She had a fine linear nose
and a smile that, when she chose to exhibit it, could brighten a room. She
wore a dark gray wool skirt that flowed to mid-calf and a white blouse that

buttoned down the back and had lace around the collar. Her stylish but rather thin navy blue jacket was often unsuccessful at keeping the wind and cold out. She didn't care. She sensed spring was near, and it elated her.

So Anna dilly-dallied, looking at the luminous treasures beckoning from the store windows. One displayed elegant women's clothing; one jewelry and fine crystal; another men's shoes and belts; still another, kitchenware. This evening she lingered outside Melnik's, a small store that sold children's clothing and toys. Her attention was caught by an intricately fashioned dollhouse, its back open to the street, fully decorated with tiny furnishings and tiny people.

Most captivating of all, the dollhouse contained a miniature modern bathroom, complete with shower. Daniel had told her all about the group showers at St. Jude's, and despite his disdain for them, she yearned to try a shower bath. Naturally St. Jude's facilities lacked the privacy of this luxurious dollhouse's creation, which Anna thought must be like bathing in a warm summer rain.

Anna was a dreamer. For her, a dollhouse behind the dusty window of Melnik's became more than a plaything. She placed herself inside it, in her mind's eye applying deep red lipstick at the Art Deco dressing table, wearing a white silk and marabou trimmed robe, pinching her lips, just like the movie star Jean Harlow, preparing for a date.

Books could also whisk Anna off into whatever world had been created on the page before her. She liked to imagine herself in the story and unselfconsciously created elaborate additions to the works featuring herself as heroine. She read everything she could get her hands on, sometimes neglecting math problems and biology assignments in favor of fiction. That evening, along with her piano music, she clasped two books:

a collection of Hans Christian Andersen stories and a copy of Mark Twain's *Huckleberry Finn*. She had been instantly smitten with Huck and the mighty Mississippi. The boy, about her age, with his beguiling innocence and honesty and the verdant open spaces of mid-nineteenth century Missouri, all seemed so different from the cold, gray, armed camp that Prague had become. As a result, lately her mind wasn't in her hometown, harassed by Nazis and curfews, but transplanted to America, where she'd go calmly rafting down the majestic Mississippi River. She could almost smell the massed wood violets at the great river's shore, hear the suck of the pole as it pulled free from the muddy bottom, feel the bump of the channel catfish nosing about the raft.

A German soldier on a motorcycle sped loudly past Melnik's. Reluctantly Anna shook off her reverie and left the shop window. She realized they might be worried about her at home. She knew the occupation had changed things irrevocably. She began to head back.

Esta and Solomon had witnessed from afar the Germans invasion of neighboring Austria in March the year before and saw the viciousness with which the Nazis dealt with Jews, Communists, and anyone else they decided they didn't like. They had heard about Mauthausen, the first concentration camp outside of Germany, constructed near Linz, and rumors flew about the frightening number of executions and general deplorable conditions (prisoners forced to mine with no tools, just bare hands). But they were just rumors; things couldn't be that bad, could they? There was no denying that after the Anschluss in Austria, Czechoslovakia was now surrounded on three sides by the Third Reich. Austrian Jews were being forced to hand over their wealth and property to the Reich in exchange for permits to leave Austria. Those Jews without wealth were being shipped to Mauthausen.

Many Jews in Prague, aware of what was happening, had fled their homeland that summer. On the other hand, the Kippelsteins, along with many others, felt that Austria was the end of the line in the Nazis' plans for expansion (the Austrian population was mostly German, after all), that the Germans wanted nothing to do with Czechoslovakia and besides, the other European nations would never stand for another German invasion. But in late September Hitler set his sights on the Sudetenland, a small region in northern Czechoslovakia that bordered Germany and had been cut away from the Fatherland after World War I as part of the armistice.

On September 30, 1938, under threat of German invasion, Great Britain and France agreed to let Hitler take over the Sudetenland from Czechoslovakia and allowed the Germans first to dissolve the elected government in Prague and then to install Supreme Court Chief Justice Dr. Emil Hacha, who was sixty-five years old and in the early stages of senility, at the head of a puppet government. To Solomon and Esta's complete astonishment, all the major European powers, including Great Britain's Prime Minister Neville Chamberlain, subscribed to Hitler's claims that the Sudetenland was really part of Germany and Czechoslovakia was still under Czech control. The United States stood by quietly and proclaimed its neutrality. With Hacha's foggy mental condition, Czechoslovakia was on the verge of chaos within six months. On March 15, 1939, Hacha went to Berlin and Hitler made him sign a declaration allowing the German Army to overrun the remainder of the country "to protect" Czechoslovakia.

The Kipplesteins, as well as nearly all of their countrymen, awaited the world's outrage and prompt military response to the invasion. But none came. Unarmed and with no army of their own, the Czechs could only watch as the German SS was sent in to terrorize politicians and intellectuals, take over the press, and dehumanize Jews. New rules appeared. No Jews on trolleys. No Jews in theaters. No Jews allowed on the streets from 8 P.M. until 6 A.M. Jews could shop only from noon to 4 P.M. Solomon and Esta had read in the Czech newspapers with deep concern about the Krystalnacht that had occurred in Germany just five months before, where Jews' property was seized or destroyed and the Germans rescinded any remaining civil rights the Jews hadn't already lost since the Nazis came to power in 1933. Now the Nazis were completely in charge in Czechoslovakia, and with their control of the Czech press, there was little or no coverage of the Germans' murderous campaign of terror.

Solomon immediately began to plan his family's escape. It took a week for the Czech borders to reopen slightly for the purposes of commerce. He sent Anton, his most trusted employee, to Zurich on the pretext of picking up watch screws and other parts. There Anton opened up an account in the company's name at the Union Bank of Switzerland with a wad of cash (just over $1000 worth) sewn into the lining of his leather satchel. Solomon raised further cash by closing one bank account (before it was frozen and confiscated) and pawning a gold necklace, some hand-painted Venetian glassware with gold leaf he and Esta had received as a wedding present, and two sterling silver candelabras. The items only brought a third of what they would have prior to the invasion, but it was money. In the next two weeks at the first opportunity, the Kippelsteins would escape south to Hungary, their eventual goal being Switzerland. Not a word was mentioned to the children.

At 6:15 that evening, about the time Anna tore herself away from Melnik's store window, the Kippelsteins' back door flew open, and

Solomon ran in, panting heavily, with no hat, his shirt partly untucked, his black wool coat unbuttoned and flowing like a cape. He slammed the door shut behind him. Esta jumped up, knowing something was amiss because Solomon never came in the back door and rarely came home even a few minutes early.

"Sol! What has happened!" she cried anxiously.

"Hurry. There's no time. Where is Anna?"

"Anna's at her piano lesson but she'll be back soon. Solomon, tell me, what's wrong?!"

Catching his breath, he supported himself against the staircase newel post. "The Germans. They're at the factory, looking for me. I ran out the back. They'll be here anytime now. Hurry! Put all your jewelry in a valise. We can use it to buy passage. We must run now. We'll fetch Daniel from school and then make for the border."

But it was too late. Heavy footsteps stomped on the walk and up to the front door. A booted foot kicked it open.

Esta and Solomon watched in disbelief and horror as the hated storm troopers entered their home. Solomon pushed his wife back into the kitchen and then stepped forward to confront the Nazis.

An SS colonel in jet-black uniform stepped through the broken door and five soldiers dressed in mouse gray followed. Their breeches bagged at the thighs and their black boots rose to the knees. Each man wore a scarlet band with a black and white swastika on the left arm. The colonel had a Ritterkruez, or Knight's Cross, at his neck and a First Class Iron Cross on his left breast pocket. His hat with visor bore the dreaded Totenkopf, or death's head, worn only by the SS, and above that a silver German eagle with spread wings held a swastika in a wreath. His left collar had a black rectangle with three silver diamonds; his right collar two

SS lightning bolts. He wore a black leather belt with cross strap and side-arm holster. Two soldiers carried 9mm MP-40 submachine guns.

"You broke our door. Why didn't you just knock?" Solomon asked, his voice quavering more from anger than fear.

The tall SS colonel dismissed the words as if they had never been uttered.

"You are Solomon Kippelstein?" asked the colonel.

"Yes. What do you want?" Solomon again was ignored.

"Take him outside," the officer commanded. Two of his men took Solomon by the arms and dragged him out the door.

"Find the rest of them," the colonel barked to the other three troops.

In the kitchen Esta frantically pulled Jacob to his feet, as he stuffed one last kolachy into his mouth. "Quick, upstairs!" she said under her breath.

"Why?!" he cried.

"Hurry!" she countered with quiet determination.

They ran up the back stairs.

Vlasta watched dumbfounded. She had heard the whispered stories. Now they were here for the Kippelsteins. Still holding a wooden spoon caked with kolachy dough, she stood frozen with fear.

The men marched into her kitchen, and glancing at the half-empty glasses of milk on the table, their leader demanded, "Where are they?"

"Who?" she retorted, feigning ignorance.

"The wife, the children, you stupid Slovak! Where are they?!"

"Gone," Vlasta answered.

"Search upstairs," he commanded a private.

Anna turned the corner to her street, but stopped in her tracks as if her feet were suddenly encased in cement. A German car and canvas-covered truck were parked before her house. Petrified, she managed to back into a doorway and watch. What did it all mean, this black car, these SS troops, this truck with its sinister swastika on its side? Gathered out front, a curious crowd of a dozen people made it difficult for Anna to have a clear view.

Suddenly two soldiers emerged from her house, carrying her father by his arms. He attempted to escape their hold. One soldier cracked him across the head with the butt of a pistol, which knocked Solomon into semiconsciousness. Too frightened to weep, too fearful to move, Anna crouched into the doorway and tried to disappear into the building's bricks.

The soldier roughly threw her father against the side of the truck and held him there. From this vantage point she could see half of his face was dark with blood. Anna bit the back of her hand so hard that hours later teeth marks remained.

Three more Gestapo troops emerged from the house, pushing her weeping mother and Jacob before them at gunpoint. Her parents managed to touch hands briefly, as Esta and Jacob were forced into the back of the truck.

There was a heated discussion among the soldiers. Suddenly, the colonel tired of the debate, raised a pistol to her father's head, and fired. A spray of blood and brains hit the side of the truck as the bullet exited, and Solomon's body fell to the ground in a crumpled heap.

The small crowd stood in shocked silence. No one moved.

"Let this be a lesson to all filthy Communist Jews who defy the Reich! We will cleanse Czechoslovakia just as we are cleansing

Germany!" shouted the Nazi colonel who had just murdered Anna's father.

The assembled onlookers were stunned, afraid to flee, afraid to move, for fear of meeting the same fate as their neighbor. The colonel then turned with an arrogant huff, as if he were wasting his breath on such ignorant vermin, and got into his car.

Anna heard her mother's pitiful, muffled screams; then things began to go black. Her knees buckled, but she clung to the wall and remained on her feet. She watched as life as she knew it was stamped out like a spent cigarette and casually tossed in the gutter. She wanted to run to the crowd of people in front of her house and beg them for help, but whom could she trust? She didn't recognize any of her family's friends among them. The SS had Mother and Jacob. They would surely want her too.

Her father's lifeless body was thrown onto the truck as if it were a sack of flour. The other officers calmly got into their sedan and sped away, leaving nothing behind but eerie stillness and the scent of fresh diesel fumes.

Once the Nazis departed, the crowd began to react excitedly to the tragedy. Some women wept, while most others simply stood clucking their tongues like a flock of chickens, sure that somehow Kippelstein had deserved the wrath of the Gestapo. Events had spun out with such speed that none of the Kippelstein's Jewish neighbors had had time to gather or witness them. They would learn of the treachery secondhand. Just then everyone's attention was drawn upward. They pointed and cried out. The dark sky pulsed with an ugly orange glow. The Watch Works was on fire!

A teenage boy ran off towards the nearest firebox to summon the fire brigade, while the rest stood helplessly and watched the flames leap about in a ghastly dance behind the ancient leaded glass windows. As the heat grew more intense, the glass shattered and sent a rain of deadly splinters down upon the rough cobblestones below. The crowd had to retreat to a safer distance. Transfixed, Anna watched, and heard the approach of sirens. But it was too late; nothing could save the factory now.

She stumbled away from the doorway. Her mind spun with fierce speed, like a top that was about to wobble out of control and shoot across the floor. Daniel. She had to find her brother. Perhaps together they could figure out what to do. The crowd of neighbors, distracted by the fire and still gabbing like magpies over the events leading to the murder of Solomon Kippelstein, did not notice Anna slip away, running, bound for St. Jude's school.

2

St. Jude's

Due to the late hour of the attack, no newspaper the next morning reported the incident. That afternoon Daniel Kippelstein and his classmates were listening inattentively to Father Pothan, his lecture on scientific theories proving to be about as absorbing as the droning of the flies that emerged with the lengthening days and warmer weather. Father Pothan, a round, bald man four decades in age, was of medium height with short arms and thick fingers and a disposition as mild as a clear spring day. Only rarely did his disposition grow dark, and when it did, it usually involved Germans and Nazis. Today the Nazis' views on science were the catalyst. Dressed in a black cassock under a bulky priest's robe, with a black cincture around his bulging waist and a clergy tab collar at his neck, Father Pothan had rolled up his sleeves. For Daniel this was a clear sign to pay attention, because this matter was likely to be on an upcoming test. Daniel's note-taking stepped up.

Anna had arrived outside St. Jude's earlier that morning. She had slept four hours beneath a park bench in a square a half mile from the school before making the final leg of her trip just after daylight. She stood across the street, near a hickory tree in case she needed to duck behind something fast. There wasn't much traffic– a few cars, bikes, motorbikes. Daniel's school was located next door to St. Jude's Cathedral, an ornate baroque church with an ostentatious bell tower topped by a cross. The school building looked like an afterthought; smaller, architecturally much simpler, as if it were a poor stepchild of the great church. Eight stairs led up to the school's large, arched oak door stained a coffee-bean brown. When Anna had visited on family Sundays, the door was open and the place appeared welcoming. With the imposing dark door closed, the school looked forbidding.

Just inside the front door was a three-story courtyard crowned by its own bell tower, but it housed no bell. Overlooking the courtyard, the second and third floors had balustrades ringing them. She knew there was a wide stairway just to the right on the inside and that most of the classrooms were on the second floor while most of the living quarters were on the third. She knew exactly where on the third floor Daniel's bed was located, but there was no way for her to find Daniel without being seen by his classmates or the priests and arousing some suspicion. She recalled there was a city park behind the church and school where Daniel had said the boys used to play football and other sports. Her family had picnicked in the park several times on visiting days. She decided to make her way there and wait for her opportunity to meet Daniel alone.

Father Pothan could rattle on about science all he wanted; at this moment hardly any of it would sink in. Only one thing was on the boys' minds. Football. It wasn't pouring rain for a change, the ground was dry in places, and the grass was bursting greenly forth after a long cold season's dormancy. Everyone was ready to get outside.

Daniel was shorter than most of the other boys and had a slender, angular build that, even with the help of a belt, seemed barely able to hold up his trousers. He had wavy dark brown hair and serious attentive eyes. Above his upper lip had appeared the slightest wisp of the beginnings of a mustache, which he secretly inspected daily for the tiniest evidence of growth. He wasn't what you would call handsome; on the other hand, he wasn't homely either. Once, when he had asked his mother, "Am I handsome?" she replied, "You're handsome enough for me." That seemed like faint praise to Daniel, but it is one of those questions which, no matter how it's answered, a parent cannot win. "Handsome enough," though, was remarkably accurate.

By virtue of the alphabetical seating chart, Daniel happened to be seated next to Josef Czerny, nicknamed Donkey Boy. While one might assume otherwise, it was not a nickname of derision, but rather of respect. Josef was bigger than the other boys in height and muscle. With sandy brown hair, finely carved cheekbones, and blue eyes, Josef definitely fell into the category of handsome. A smile and wink from him could lift almost anyone's spirits and usually meant a practical joke was afoot. Talkative and boisterous, he was a natural leader. Athletic grace came to him as easily as it did to a leopard. At the same time, Josef was about as conscious of his own grace as the Eiffel Tower is of hers. Furthermore, rumor had it that Josef's family was one of the wealthiest in northeastern Czechoslovakia. All this wrapped up in one person was a grating annoyance to Daniel, who had few if any of these advantages and hated acknowledging them in Josef.

Daniel had started at St.Jude's just seven months ago. Being the new student, the other boys looked appraisingly upon him, like hyenas crouching on the savannah sizing up potential prey.

Daniel's first day had begun smoothly. After classes, Daniel and the other boys played football for an hour and a half, getting sweat-drenched in the warm September sunshine. None had been particularly friendly to Daniel, but there had been no overt hostility either.

Supervising football was Father Pothan. He called out as gym time expired: "All right, boys. Showers! You stink to high heaven!"

Daniel was not only about to take the first shower of his life, but a group shower at that. His house was equipped with only a bath. Few residents of Prague, for that matter, had been exposed to this modern convenience.

St. Jude's had installed the showers the previous fall as a means of saving water. That fact was obvious from the anemic trickle that came dripping out of the nozzles. A hot water heater was deemed an unnecessary luxury by the spartan fathers, leaving the water temperature tepid at best, glacial at worst. In fact from December through March the water was so icy, the showers were used only for punishment. But this was September, so the boys undressed and, naked, formed a line behind Father Pothan to enter the showers. Their pale, bony bodies resembled half-melted snowflakes, but in one case, suddenly a strange freak of nature was discovered.

All eyes were fixed on Daniel. On Daniel's nether region, to be more precise. He was the only one of two dozen boys who had been circumcised.

Daniel, until this moment, had never really thought a penis might be fashioned any other way. He had attended numerous brises but had never considered that the practice set Jews apart from Gentiles. Now, he was harshly confronted with compelling evidence that he was different and, perhaps, not quite normal. The shock of discovery gave way to widespread pointing and rude laughter. Unaware of the reason for the commotion, Father Pothan shouted, "Enough chatter! *Move* before the water runs out!"

The shower room, which had been converted from a storage area adjacent to the boys' sleeping quarters, was large enough for eight spigots, four on one wall and four opposite them. Due to the water temperature, showers were brief. No sensible person would linger even a second longer than necessary. There were at least three boys under each dribbling showerhead. Once he was wet enough, Daniel lathered up with a bar of soap.

One of the boys who shared Daniel's spigot stared, puzzled, at Daniel's lower region and then raised his gaze until he met the uncomfortable look in Daniel's eyes. Then he burst out laughing. And started to chant, "No-Tip Kip! No-Tip Kip!"

After cascades of riotous laughter, the other boys chimed in like a chorus of harpies. The chant reverberated endlessly, endlessly, endlessly off the stone walls. Daniel was so mortified, he wished the drain would widen and he could simply disappear with the scummy, dirty water. He thought about punching the leader of the chants. Unfortunately the boy was much bigger, and his well-defined biceps indicated he was far stronger too. Daniel later learned the name of his phrase-turning tormentor: Josef Czerny.

Silent, confused, Daniel quickly finished showering. As he dried himself off in the area outside the showers, he felt the sharp sting of a wet towel across his buttocks. As a newcomer, he'd have suffered this initiation in any case, but the hazing had added cruelty when combined with the shame of his oddball male organ.

The blows grew in strength and fury until Father Pothan returned. Then the whipping abruptly ceased, and the perpetrators, led by Josef, assumed expressions of angelic innocence. The only outward evidence that remained was Daniel's reddened, smarting behind. Inwardly, however, he burned with humiliation.

Daniel never gave them the satisfaction of a single tear or whimper, but late that first night he covered his head with his pillow and quietly wept until he fell into a sleep of disordered dreams. The initial excitement of his arrival at St. Jude's had turned to ashes. Why had his parents sent him to this horrible place? Why did he look different from everyone else? How would he survive another day, much less the rest of the school year?

Daniel had begun keeping a journal during the summer of 1938, just before starting at St. Jude's. While he tried to make daily entries, time and circumstances would conspire against him; he found he wrote on average about once a week. At St. Jude's his journal entries were made even more difficult because day and night he was around other boys whom he felt certain would mock and ridicule him should the journal be discovered. So he wrote entries while seated in the water closet and hid the journal pages carefully in his arithmetic book, which he determined was the least likely place any one would look.

He added pages as needed, so the color and texture of the pages varied somewhat. He started off using ink, which he preferred because, unlike pencil lead, it didn't smudge. Using ink though, which involved dipping the fountain pen into a bottle of ink while in a water closet, sitting on the throne, writing on the uneven surface of his thigh, proved impractical. As a result, the pencil became Daniel's tool of choice. Combining a pencil's tendency to smudge, Daniel's small writing, and the less than ideal conditions under which he wrote, the reading of the journal later was a challenge. Eventually though, he could always figure out what he had scribbled. And very often what he had scribbled revealed he was terribly, terribly homesick; he couldn't wait for Sunday when his family would visit or he could go home for the afternoon.

One aspect of home he especially missed was the comfort of his big, airy bedroom, shared only with Jacob, a comparatively sweet-smelling nine-year-old. At St. Jude's, sleeping quarters were a large hall with high timbered ceilings, which held twenty-six beds, thirteen on each side of the room, with a trunk at the foot of each bed for a boy's clothes and belongings. In short, no privacy whatsoever.

Food at St. Jude's also was not a strong point. The boys' diet consisted of a monotonous parade of sauerkraut and sausage. Any straying from this menu (like an occasional roasted chicken) was cause for a minor celebration among the boys. Kosher food for the single Jewish boy was never even considered. Daniel vowed never to eat the sausage but, due to extreme hunger pangs, twice broke his vow. Both times he silently said a prayer beseeching forgiveness. Daniel didn't know for certain if prayers actually worked, but his stomach felt markedly better.

Given the boys unrelenting diet of sauerkraut and sausage, the results were consistent and predictable. There was always some acutely obnoxious offense to the nostrils emitting from one or more of the twenty-six boys. There were times when even Daniel himself kept his bed cover tucked firmly under his chin, to prevent his own foul wind from reaching his nose.

The most disgusting odor of all arose when the boy assigned to the bed next to Daniel's, none other than Josef Czerny, removed his shoes and socks prior to bedtime. Daniel was not alone in his estimation, for the other boys would dramatically pinch their nostrils, collapse on their beds, and beg for gas masks. If Daniel's feet had been the villains, they surely would have brought additional scorn upon him. But in Josef's case, the stench only added to his cachet.

For Daniel, Josef's feet were only minor offenses compared to the bigger boy's bullying. Josef had street wiles, but school was not his strong suit. Since Daniel immediately had established himself as one of the best students and his bed was so close, Josef took full advantage of the situation by being a constant pest about their assignments. It was easier to poke Daniel in the ribs and ask, "Hey, Kip, what's the answer to this problem?" or "What did Brother Tomas mean by this assignment?" or "What's this question all about?" than to actually apply his own brain to the matter.

And Daniel usually helped, since Josef could be annoyingly persistent. Better to cave quickly and get him off my back, was Daniel's reasoning. But never once did Josef thank him. Prima donna that he was, Josef took such aid as his rightful due from a loyal subject. He wouldn't even admit that he needed help in the first place. Once Daniel supplied the necessary information, Josef smugly acted as though he had known all along and was simply checking up. Such arrogance irritated Daniel like some irremovable pebble in his shoe dogging his every step.

One day Daniel decided to teach Josef a lesson. He fed Josef some obviously wrong answers, hoping henceforth to be left alone. In geography class the next day, Brother Tomas called upon Josef.

Daniel snickered to himself, thinking, Perfect! At last Josef will drink from the well of public humiliation.

"Josef, in what part of the world is Sao Paulo located?" asked Brother Tomas, a lanky, sandy-haired man of thirty years.

"Portugal," replied Josef confidently.

The class snorted with laughter.

Brother Tomas waved his pointer at a wall map in the general direction of South America and asked dryly, "Can you be a little more accurate?"

"Southern Portugal?" Josef tried again, with less certainty.

The laughter grew.

"I mean *northern* Portugal," Josef corrected himself, fully regaining his confidence.

This was followed by absolute screams of laughter. Josef turned and glared significantly at Daniel, who shrugged innocently until he too surrendered to the general hilarity. Even after Brother Tomas restored order, occasional bursts of quiet laughter punctuated the rest of the class period. Seemingly oblivious, Josef remained straight-faced throughout.

Nothing more was said about the incident until that night when the boys were undressing for bed. Just as Daniel had peeled down to his underwear, Josef suddenly seized him like a fox pouncing on a hen and carried him to a towel hook on the wall. Despite Daniel's futile struggles, Josef easily hung him up by the back of his drawers. The fabric got painfully wedged up the crack between his buttocks, and his testicles felt like they were being compressed into pancakes. Any effort to free himself only increased the torture.

The boys gathered around and cackled with unmerciful laughter at the plight of the helpless Daniel. After a few minutes the underpants, unable to take the strain of his 108 pounds any longer, shredded, and he dropped to the floor in a naked heap. He quickly bounded up, raced to his bed, and put on a new pair.

It was the last time Daniel ever gave Josef a wrong answer. But it was hardly the last time Josef thoroughly annoyed Daniel. Mail day usually brought such an opportunity. Letters arrived at the school three days a week—Mondays, Wednesdays, and Fridays—and were eagerly anticipated. Even though most of the boys' families lived in or near Prague, receiving mail (for there were no phones) meant that someone was thinking of them, that they were still a vital part of the family. If a boy didn't receive any letters, no one made any comment, but it hardly went unnoticed.

Since Daniel's family always visited on Sundays, he rarely received mail on Mondays. There would have been nothing new to report. But Wednesdays and Fridays always brought letters, and occasionally packages. Either Mother or Father would write, usually so would Anna, and sometimes even Jacob would pen messages in his careful script matter-of-fact sentences about mundane events at school or on the playground. Mail sporadically came from distant relatives he barely knew. Any letter, even one from the most irritating of cousins, was savored like a fine Swiss chocolate.

After mail was distributed, each boy took his own back to his bed and read it, sometimes sharing excerpts if they were funny or newsworthy.

Best of all were the letters from girls. Josef Czerny seemed to get more than his share of those, and he delighted in reading them aloud in a breathless fashion, insinuating all sorts of wild activity.

One letter smelled so heavily of perfume that Daniel wondered if it had been pickled in it. The second Josef opened the envelope the dorm was permeated with the odor, which temporarily masked the smell of cooked cabbage that had been omnipresent for centuries. Josef delicately drew out the letter (written on pale pink paper, of course) and held it to his nostrils, sniffing like a dog in heat. As if he couldn't smell it clear across the room anyway, thought Daniel balefully.

The boys put down their own letters; weather reports and updates on Uncle Anton's rheumatism could wait. All expected a dramatic reading, and Josef did not disappoint.

"My dearest Jo-Boo-Boo," he began. The boys hooted with delight, egging him on.

"I miss you so much. I miss your"—he paused for dramatic effect as his audience fairly drooled—"big limbs"—his voice, throbbing with erotic implications, elicited yet more excited yelps—"wrapped around me!" This one sentence, which said nothing at all, yet offered everything a hormonally over-charged adolescent imagination could invest in it, had the boys nearly in a frenzy. As Josef skimmed the remaining scandalous paragraphs, his eyes popped open wide in exaggerated shock, then rolled heavenward. He carefully folded the letter and tucked it inside his shirt. "Sorry, I can't read any more," he apologized. The bad news was met with frustrated groans, the boys' vicarious enjoyment unconsummated. Gradually they went back to their own letters, occasionally glancing enviously at Josef and sniffing the air with appreciation.

Not all of Josef's letters were from lusty girls scattered across the Czechoslovakian countryside. Letters from home demonstrated (as if there had ever been any doubt) the wealth and importance of the Czerny family. One such missive began, "The new wing on the house is finally finished. Finally! But times are hard. We've had to cut back the field workers from 125 to just under 100."

The boys went, "Aww, must be tough," in mock sympathy. Even Mr. Kippelstein's thriving business had only forty people on the payroll. Josef continued, 'Having dinner with the Prince of Bohemia tomorrow night.'

"Wooo!" came the sarcastic jeer, hiding the fact they were deeply impressed.

'I'll tell you all about it in my next letter. Love, Father'

With that, a pillow came flying through the air, scoring a direct hit on Josef's head. All hell broke loose as pillows were launched from every bed, seams breaking and feathers clouding the air in a blizzard of goose down. Brother Tomas heard the riot and ran in to quell the mayhem.

Once the outbreak had simmered down and relative calm was restored, Daniel took out his copybook and began work on math problems. He had trouble concentrating, for although Josef wasn't actively bothering him at the moment, his presence alone was an intrusion. The pillow attack was a form of worship and adulation from the other boys, and Josef, in his boundless conceit, knew it.

Daniel had trouble fathoming this adoration. To him, Josef was simply odious: a bully who flaunted his wealth and bragged about his sexual conquests. How was it possible, Daniel thought, that the most vile, most obnoxious, and least intelligent boy in the school can manage to be the most popular?

Not everything at St. Jude's was objectionable. The academics were strong, although the students were not nearly as competitive as at Daniel's previous schools, and the result was that he rocketed from the middle of the pack to the top of his class. Daniel also discovered singing. St. Jude's had a boys' choir.

His previous schools had no such thing. The closest thing the Jewish schools had were Hebrew chants, which were rather monotonous and unpleasant to the ears. As a matter of course Daniel was brought in to the cathedral to audition for Father Pothan, who himself could barely sing a note but was a decent pianist and so he headed the choir. Daniel could read music easily and when handed a choral piece, he unselfconsciously began to sing. It was "Ave Maria." His pitch was perfect and his tone so clear and pure that Father Pothan's neck tingled. As Daniel continued, a large lump rose in the priest's throat; had he been asked to speak at that moment, he could not have. As Daniel's singular voice echoed around the marvelous acoustics of the cathedral, tears rose to the Father's eyes. Sound this wonderful surely must come directly from heaven. When Daniel held the last note superbly and then halted and the sound reverberated throughout the cathedral before dying away, Father Pothan had to sit down and gather himself. Finally the priest managed to say barely audibly, "Daniel, you are in the choir."

Daniel loved choir too, although since choir music was not highly valued in his community he never mentioned it to his family. The words were mostly in Italian or Latin and so he barely had any idea what they were singing about, but he adored the sound. He hated when the boys slacked off or grew tired and hit more flat notes than correct ones. But when their harmonies converged perfectly and all their voices sang as one, his whole body would get goose pimples; the pleasure was so intense it felt like his spirit had ripped free of his body and was floating ecstatically above everyone.

Father Pothan gave him occasional solos to sing at Sunday morning mass that were electrifying. Yet the other boys hardly noticed; their priorities were football and girls. To them choir was a necessary requirement, nothing more. The priests noticed, though, and would discreetly inquire of Father Pothan when Daniel might be singing again. They didn't make more out of it because, after all, the boy wasn't Catholic. Daniel was oblivious to most of this; to him choir was his joy and quiet, guilty pleasure.

3

Daniel's Discovery

At last, the clock made its tedious way to the hour for sports, Father Pothan's science lecture mercifully ended, and the boys raced up to the third floor to change. Daniel enjoyed football. He was moderately good at it, his lack of height an advantage in dodging between the bigger boys and sneaking in for the goal.

The score was tied 1-1, and he was dribbling the ball down field, when Mikael came out of nowhere, knocked him down, and stole the ball. A blatant foul.

Brother Milo, a squat, black haired priest with inch-thick spectacles, who was supposed to be refereeing, had about as much interest in football as the boys had in his botany class. He had wandered off to observe some of the spring's first and most adventuresome flowers. The result? The boys were on their own. Daniel cried, "Foul!" He would have loved to have emphasized his point with a right hook to Mikael's jaw, but this was not prudent. Mikael was built short and stout, like a keg of beer. His stubby arms and legs, thick, flat nose, and squealing voice seemed to imply that a pig was secretly weighing down a prominent limb of his family tree.

Mikael snorted back, "You shut your little pipsqueak mouth!"

Honor now required that Daniel punch him. His face flushing with anger, he prepared to attack (knowing full well that Mikael would hit him back with considerably greater force), when something unprecedented happened. Josef Czerny stepped into the fray.

"Shut up, Mikael! It was an obvious foul. Anyway, if you want to fight, pick on someone your own size."

"Like you, Donkey Boy?" squealed Mikael. "Why don't you mind your own business?"

"It *is* my business. He's on my team. You pick on him, you pick on me."

"Oh, I didn't know you were such a Jew-lover!" hissed Mikael, his hog-like nose flaring. "Why don't you go kiss the Jew, you Jew-lover!"

Josef's face took on a menacing look Daniel had never seen before, and he thought he'd seen all the moods of Josef Czerny: bullying, self-aggrandizing, mocking, threatening. Mikael had obviously struck a nerve. Josef wound up and took a powerful swing.

Luckily, Mikael ducked.

Unluckily the punch landed squarely in the eye of the boy standing behind Mikael. Who happened to be Daniel. He hit the ground like a load of bricks.

Going as fast as his squat legs and cassock would allow, Brother Milo ran up to see what the fuss was all about. All at once everyone was shouting contradictory explanations, until he closed his eyes and raised his hands high with frustration. "Okay, that's enough. End of game. Everyone inside."

Amidst much grumbling and protest, the rest of the boys trudged away to take showers. Meanwhile Josef offered to help Daniel up. Impatiently Daniel shook off his assistance, and gingerly felt his eye. It would be black and blue in no time, a beautiful shiner. Thinking he had been set up and that Josef was the instigator, Daniel turned to Czerny and with as much hostility and sarcasm as he could marshal said, "Thanks for all your 'help.'"

In this instance Josef was utterly innocent of any treachery, guilty only of poor aim, and hardly responsible for Mikael's ability to dodge a punch. So without picking up on Daniel's distrust, Josef simply laughed in his usual cocky way and shrugged, then turned and jogged off to catch up with the group.

Daniel started to straggle after them, but was stopped by a familiar voice calling his name.

"Daniel!" He halted as if suddenly realizing he was about to step into a pit of quicksand.

"Daniel!!" It was his sister Anna, calling out to him, partially obscured by a patch of dogwood bushes a few feet from the field's end line.

What on earth was she doing here, alone, in the middle of the week? Instantly he knew something was dreadfully wrong.

Anna thought she had wept so many tears on her trek across Prague that she could never cry again, but her relief in seeing Daniel was so intense that they poured forth afresh. Her sobbing was sufficiently violent that she couldn't talk. Daniel guided her behind the bushes so no one would see them. The football field was now deserted. A cool wind quietly ruffled the leaves. The great city seemed to melt away. Daniel took her shoulders in his hands.

"Anna! Anna! What's wrong? Please calm down and tell me."

At last she steadied herself and reported the horrors of the previous evening in a staccato voice, punctuated by gasps for breath as a result of her crying. As she spoke, Daniel's skin grew cold in the warm afternoon sunshine. A glacial chill seized his soul.

"Father is dead?" he said in disbelief.

She nodded.

"You're sure?" he asked, almost pleading.

She returned his gaze, eyes red, tears still on her cheeks, and didn't have to answer.

He put his fingers to his forehead and massaged deeply, as if that might rid him of the facts he had just heard. Anna concluded by telling him how the Germans had set fire to the Watch Works.

"I-I had to find you as soon as I could. Daniel, do you think they'll take us away? Like they took Mother and Jacob?"

"I don't know. But we have to go back," said Daniel grimly.

"It's too dangerous!" exclaimed Anna.

"If everything you say is true, the SS has done their work. They won't still be around. Besides, I have to see. I have to see what they did."

It wasn't a matter of not believing her report; he simply needed to see it for himself. In a strange way Anna felt she needed to go back too. Somehow the whole frightening ordeal would not be truly real until Daniel, always the more pragmatic one, saw the scene and convinced her that it wasn't some nightmarish hallucination. Although Anna was exhausted, she nodded her agreement.

Their home and the watch factory were on the northwest side of the city, by foot a very long way from St. Jude's. The trek had consumed most of the previous night, although Anna had stopped frequently, managed a few hours sleep, and, because of the curfew in effect since the invasion, taken a circuitous route to avoid major streets and squares. They set out by the power of their own two feet.

Back at St. Jude's bunk room, Josef peeled off his sweaty football jersey and joined the others in the shower. Mikael attempted to get some more mileage out of the fight he'd started on the field. Josef merely let the frosty trickle of water stream over his face and ignored his taunts.

Father Miklas, a tall, soft-spoken man with thin blond hair and wire-rimmed spectacles, entered the locker room. "Josef, please come with me. Father Beneš wants to see you."

"Was my geography test that bad?!" Josef asked in half-hearted jest, knowing the summons had nothing to do with his grades.

The boys teased, "Uh-oh, you're in trouble now! Don't cry when he whips you! Boo-hoo-hoo!"

Mikael growled, "Serves him right. The donkey. Hee-haw! Hee-haw!" In the midst of all this, no one noticed that Daniel had not returned from the field.

Josef dried himself off and finished dressing, then followed Father Miklas upstairs to the headmaster's office. Father Beneš had dark hair, and although clean-shaven, he looked like the sort who could grow a full beard in the course of an afternoon. His eyes were quite large and bulged from his head like a grasshopper's. As the leader of St. Jude's, he had every right to be stern and fussy and sour as a lemon; in fact, he was nothing of the kind — smiling often, laughing loudly, he was a true friend to the boys. Wearing a black suit with a nine-button vest that ended snugly at his white priest's collar, Beneš was working at his desk when they entered his office. He looked up from his work and said gently, "Sit down, my son."

Both Josef and Father Miklas rapidly crossed themselves in the presence of the crucifix mounted on the wall behind the headmaster, then took their seats.

Father Beneš sighed as he began. "Josef, have you had any word from your family?"

Josef bit his lower lip and shook his head.

Beneš and Miklas shot each other subtle looks that silently communicated their concern. They could only speculate on what might have happened to Josef's family, but considering the times, it was serious.

Beneš continued. "We haven't heard from your parents in over five months."

"If they don't write, it's because they're busy," Josef said, unsuccessfully trying to hide his anxiety. Then, "Even my uncle hasn't sent any money?" Josef asked, practically pleading, yet knowing if the answer was positive, he would not be sitting there at that moment.

"Josef ... we've made a few inquiries, and can't get any kind of information. We think you ought to make a visit back home to be sure your family is all right."

Josef objected vigorously. "I'm first string! We have a football game against St. Vitus this Saturday! Besides," he asked in an uncertain tone, "how would I get there?"

"We've purchased a return ticket for you," Father Beneš assured him. "Brother Tomas will accompany you. You'll depart tomorrow on the one-forty train to Zabreh. No matter what the trouble is, you are welcome to return to finish this semester, regardless of the tuition problem." He handed Josef an envelope that held a train ticket.

"Thank you, Father," mumbled Josef. "I guess I'd better pack."

"Josef—why don't you wait until morning, when the other boys are in class. Just pretend all is well tonight."

"Sure," he agreed. "I can pretend." He got up, crossed himself again, and left the study, the ticket home clutched tightly in his hand.

Anna and Daniel barely spoke during their cross-town trek. The Nazis, just ten days after their arrival, had decreed that cars would no longer travel on the left side of the street, as was the practice in Prague, and would henceforth travel on the right side of the street, as in Germany. Out of ingrained habit the children still looked right first, whenever approaching a street, even though the traffic was immediately coming from the left now. Since the invasion auto traffic on Prague's streets had fallen off drastically. Thankfully, the two did not have to cross any of the bridges over the Vltana, since the Germans had stationed a soldier with a machine gun on a tripod at each end of every one. When they arrived in their neighborhood, it was well past sundown. Glancing warily about them and alert to the sound of any footsteps, constantly aware they were in violation of the curfew that began at dark, they kept to the shadows. If seen by patrolling German soldiers, they could be taken into custody. The curfew also kept their neighbors in their houses, neighbors who could easily identify them and perhaps turn them in.

Daniel had no idea what time it was, since his watch was back at school. He never wore it while playing sports for fear of breaking it. Now that the sun had set, they both grew chilled, Anna in just her light jacket and Daniel in his athletic uniform.

Their house was dark, the front door nailed shut. Anna pointed to a spot on the cobblestone street, dimly illuminated by the street lamps overhead. A pool of blood had dried like black ink, marking the place where their father had fallen. In a crevice a foot away lay a shiny object. Daniel picked it up. While he had never seen one before, instinctively he knew the object's identity: a spent bullet casing.

He was suddenly and violently seized by a wave of nausea, and he would have vomited if he'd had even a thimbleful of food in his empty stomach. He silently put the shell in his pocket: a memento of his father's murderers, a tangible reminder of his hatred and a goad to vengeance.

They peered inside the factory, now a charred, smoking ruin. The street was empty and a funereal quiet reigned. A car, its headlights blazing, suddenly turned down the street and barreled toward them. They quickly ducked down an alley. The car streaked by them. When it was again quiet, they took one more look at the blackened, smoke-scarred Watch Works and at the house that was closed to them forever. The street seemed unfamiliar and remote; yet just a scant few hours ago it was their lifelong home. Now they felt like aliens from another world set down in this dark, strange place, utterly alone.

"What do we do now, Daniel?" asked Anna.

Usually it was she who would issue orders. Like most older sisters, she could be bossy, but the spirit had gone out of her. He shrugged. "We can't risk being found on the street after curfew, so I don't think we should try to make it all the way back to St. Jude's tonight."

Anna rubbed her chilled arms and hands.

Daniel looked around. "We need to find a place, out of the wind. If we huddle up together, we can keep warm."

They turned in a direction that took them deeper into the Old

Town, encountering no other people, no soldiers. Daniel had been as familiar with the area as his own house, having explored it exhaustively since the age of five. But in the dark and in his dislocated state of mind, it was an entirely different landscape; familiar landmarks were obscured by shadow and made sinister in the harsh lamplight. Just outside the Stavovske Theater, they heard the roar of an approaching motorcycle and ducked into the shadows of the theater's overhang. Peering out from behind the square column, Daniel saw a German soldier's back as the cycle hurtled by. He led Anna to an alley that dead-ended behind a sweatshop which manufactured ladies' dresses. As usual, it was heaped with rubbish awaiting scavenging rag pickers.

They carefully arranged a few crates to form a low wall, then piled fabric scraps and tail ends of yarn goods behind it to make a nest. Weary from their hike, they curled up together like stacked spoons and managed to fall asleep.

They abruptly awoke to the raucous outcry of resident sparrows greeting the dawn. After picking lint and threads out of each other's hair, they returned across the city to St. Jude's. Even in the early light of day, they were vigilant, wary of any passerby who looked at them too long. They passed the Jewish Cemetery, and through the wrought-iron fence they could see the jammed forest of tombstones, tilting at odd angles after many centuries of winter freezes and spring thaws. It looked chaotic and crazy, and the quiet made it frightening. Without saying a word, they picked up their pace to a trot until they were by it. They passed the Church of the Holy Savior, where a large statue of a priest clad in vestments and holding a gold holy cross looked down on them, as if he were blessing them. But they did not feel blessed. Nor looked after. In fact, they felt they were being hunted, and they hoped Father Beneš might be able to tell them what to do next. Daniel looked forward to changing into some warm clothes and finding a sweater for Anna.

As they silently trudged to St. Jude's, every time Daniel looked over at Anna, he saw tears, her cheeks like windows trickling rain. But Daniel could not cry. He had wanted to when he knelt down in the street next to his father's blood. But somehow he could not.

He wondered if crying was something one did when there was time to stop and think about the loss. You don't stop and cry in the middle of an earthquake. Daniel's thoughts were thoroughly garbled. He tried to focus. He had to somehow find his mother and Jacob. He had to find a safe refuge for himself and Anna. Right now, there was neither a place nor time for grief.

4

Escape

Anna and Daniel arrived back at St. Jude's just after 8:00 the next morning. Daniel knocked on the locked front door of the school and Father Beneš himself let them in. Brother Tomas hovered nervously just behind him. The men looked haggard, as if they had slept little, and both the wrinkles in their black slacks and the smudges around the collars of their clerical shirts looked as though they had not been changed from the day before. Daniel learned that they had searched late into the night for him. They had tried especially hard to hide their efforts so as not to unduly upset the other students. They were now relieved to see he was safe, but surprised to see him with a girl. He quickly explained that Anna was his older sister, even though it was obvious Daniel and Anna were related from their identical high cheekbones and foreheads and somewhat square jaws that indicated Slavic blood might have slipped into their otherwise Jewish genealogy. Although Anna was a year older than Daniel, a recent spurt of growth had left the younger boy a couple inches taller.

They followed the two men into Father Beneš's office and sat down, hungry and exhausted. Daniel somberly reported the black news that had befallen his family. Anna stared at the floor, the occasional tear tracking down her face.

When Daniel finished speaking, Father Beneš was silent. He looked pale and sickened, and suddenly years older. Brother Tomas was similarly shaken.

When he finally spoke, Father Beneš was so outraged he could hardly control his anger. A vein throbbed on his forehead. "This is shocking. Monstrous. And Cardinal Masaryk has called for us to support the Nazis, that they're good Christians as opposed to the godless Communists. Seems to me neither one ever *has* or ever *will* know God."

Brother Tomas stared pensively out the window, then suddenly drew back in alarm. "Father—look!"

An SS car had pulled up in front of the school, and several soldiers were piling out.

Father Beneš turned to Anna and Daniel. "Quickly, up to the bunk room! Both of you!" he ordered. "I'll see what they want."

They hurried out and ran up a stairway to Daniel's dormitory on the third floor.

Meanwhile, Father Beneš and Brother Tomas conferred hastily. "We have no choice but to let them in," said Father Beneš grimly.

They walked together slowly to the main staircase. Father Beneš called out "I'm coming, stop your pounding!" He turned to Brother Tomas. "For how long could we hide them? All the boys know Daniel is a Jew. One of them will talk. In such a group there is always a Judas.

Besides, all the SS would have to do is pull down his trousers and there would be the evidence." Father Beneš thought a moment more and then decided what to do. "Send them out the back way. I'll deal with the Gestapo and we'll figure out the next move later."

Daniel and Anna crept down the third floor corridor that opened onto the courtyard below.   Before the two of them reached Daniel's dormitory room, Father Beneš opened the school's door and the Nazis stepped just inside the courtyard. Daniel peered down through the balustrades and strained to hear the words of the exchange. Anna silently slid in beside him. From this vantage point they could see clearly, but were themselves hidden in the deep shadows.

"How do you do? I'm Father Beneš," said the priest with forced cordiality, extending his hand.

The Nazi colonel ignored the gesture and saluted instead. "Heil Hitler! Colonel Strock of the Gestapo."

Father Beneš did not return the salute and responded coldly, "Yes, well. What can I do for you?"

Anna grabbed Daniel's arm, gripping it tightly in terror. "He's the one," she whispered.

At first Daniel didn't understand. He looked at Anna's petrified expression and then gazed back down upon Colonel Strock. Daniel stiffened. The hair on his neck prickled like a thousand needles sticking into his skin. This was the SS man who had killed their father. He stared at the face of Colonel Strock, forever etching it into his memory.

Strock had close-cropped light brown hair, a square jaw, and hard steel-blue eyes. He was a handsome man, yet somehow repellant, as though the evil in his heart could not be contained and radiated like a burning ember from his countenance.

Inside the dorm room behind them Daniel heard someone moving about. At this time of day normally all the boys were in class. His curiosity aroused, Daniel, followed by Anna, ducked into the dormitory.

The room was dark and deserted. Daniel quickly made his way to his own bed. Suddenly a voice startled him and Anna.

"Hey, Kip!" the voice spoke out enthusiastically. There, all alone, sat Josef on the floor next to his own bed, calmly reading one of Daniel's books, taken without permission from Daniel's trunk. It was still too early for Josef to head for the train depot, so he was killing time. Beside Josef's bed was a packed suitcase—rather a shabby piece of luggage with one leather strap broken, not what one would expect a young man of Josef's pedigree to carry. Daniel had seen Josef's luggage before and wondered how odd the rich must be, taking perverse pleasure in squeezing bargains out of strange things; they would think nothing of spending 100 koruna on themselves for a sumptuous meal that might sustain six people for a week, but were unwilling to spend 50 koruna on decent luggage that would last decades. Josef, not bothering to hide the fact that he was reading one of Daniel's treasured possessions, relished a good opportunity to tweak the boy. But Daniel was too preoccupied to notice. Josef quickly forgot about annoying Daniel when he caught a glimpse of Anna. She tried not to look at him, to hide her puffy bloodshot eyes. Josef took her behavior as flirtation. In the dim light, he couldn't discern how frightened she was but could see her fine features, and he was riveted.

"Where have you been?!" asked Josef, genuinely curious.

"Nowhere" muttered Daniel, suspicious of Josef's motives.

His eyes still appraising Anna, Josef cheerfully retorted, "Funny, that's where I'm going! They need me back in Zabreh, so I'm leaving today. But it'll be great to see everyone again. My family and all."

Anna looked up nervously and for a breathless moment caught Josef's eye. She looked away uncomfortably, for the mention of family threatened to unleash her grief. Ignorant of the events of the past two days, Josef again misread her actions as coquettishness. He smiled broadly.

"So who's this?" Josef asked Daniel with a tantalizing rise of his eyebrows.

"My sister," responded Daniel dourly.

Relieved that it had not been stolen during his absence, Daniel took his watch from the shelf above his bed and strapped it on his wrist. The watch had been his most treasured possession since receiving it for his bar mitzvah from his father. Now it had infinitely more value; it was all he had left of his father and of the business that had been in the family for over a hundred years.

"So, does she have a name?" inquired Josef, again smiling coyly, hoping to catch Anna's attention.

"Anna," replied Daniel coldly.

But Josef's next question was interrupted when Brother Tomas hurried in.

"You must leave quickly!" he said to Daniel in a hushed, urgent tone. "Gather what you can carry. Go down by the bend in the river. One of the brothers will meet you there in an hour."

Daniel had changed out of his old clothes into clean shorts, woolen knee socks, and a shirt, and now he pulled on a navy blue wool sweater. Reaching into his trunk, he pulled out his arithmetic book, withdrew some sheets of neatly folded papers, and stuffed them in his shirt pocket. He tossed a sweater and a jacket to Anna for her to wear. Then

Daniel and Anna scrambled out the rear door of the dorm. As they disappeared down the back stairs, Josef asked, "What happened?"

Brother Tomas hesitated to answer at all, and replied with purposeful vagueness, "I don't know." He then rushed out, leaving Josef alone again.

Meanwhile, in the courtyard, Father Beneš dealt with the Gestapo.

"I understand you harbor Jews here," the colonel stated smoothly.

"We accept boys of all faiths. Naturally we have had Jewish students," replied Father Beneš.

"A bad practice. I suggest you halt it immediately. It would be a shame to see this fine school shut down on account of a few filthy Jews."

"An excellent suggestion," said Father Beneš, barely concealing his contempt. "We'll take that under advisement. Is that the purpose of your visit?"

"I am looking for one boy in particular. Daniel Kippelstein."

"We're looking for him, too, Colonel. He disappeared after football yesterday. No one has seen him since."

"Hmmm. How inconvenient. It would be regrettable if a team of my men were to search the school. I imagine there are many valuable items here that could be broken or lost." The Father watched as Strock then turned and accidently-on-purpose knocked over a beautiful porcelain vase which shattered on the unforgiving stone floor. "Oh, so sorry. How clumsy of me."

Father Beneš momentarily forgot Jesus's teaching and savored the thought of choking the life out of Strock and sending his soul to the smoking abyss where it rightfully belonged. Fortunately, Father Miklas approached, distracting Beneš from his vengeful impulses.

"Father Miklas, these men are looking for Daniel. Would you please go and see if he's returned to the bunk room?"

"Surely, Father," he agreed.

As Miklas turned to go, Strock ordered a private to accompany him.

Father Miklas took a circuitous route to the dorm room, walking as slowly as he could without appearing to stall. He walked next to the private, a portly, somewhat disheveled oaf, who seemed content to proceed at the laggardly pace. Father Miklas thought the soldier was hardly an advertisement for Hitler's finest. When they finally reached the dorm room, only one boy was present.

Josef, who was again sitting on the floor next to his bed, immediately stood to attention.

"Who are you?" asked the private.

"Josef Czerny."

Father Miklas pointed. "Here is Kippelstein's bed. You can see he is not here."

"Hasn't been slept in," the private noted and opened the trunk. "His things are still here." The Private then turned to Josef. "Have you seen Kippelstein?"

Josef looked at Miklas and then at the SS private. There was no hint of what he should say. Miklas could give no facial indication without being observed by the private. Josef didn't know what to do. Should he lie in front of Father Miklas? But he sensed something was wrong. Very wrong. And while he didn't want any trouble with the SS, he certainly didn't want to help them either.

"No, sir," Josef answered cooly. "He disappeared last night."

The private took Josef's word for it and reported back to Strock, who smiled tightly. "We shall monitor the situation here at St. Jude's, Father," the colonel promised as he departed. "You will notify us if Daniel Kippelstein returns, will you not?"

"Of course," said Father, confident that the sin of bearing false witness would be forgiven in this instance.

5

Remembrance

After frantically sprinting across the football field, Daniel and Anna picked their way through the thicket to the river's edge, in a wooded area a quarter mile from St. Jude's.

The bend in the river was quiet and overgrown and flooded usually twice a decade. It had not been a wet winter, so this spring there was minimal flooding. Some large berms had been built over the years to constrain the river, but many of those had been partially eroded away. High brush and wild bushes as well as many poplar and cottonwood trees thrived on the wet sandy soil near the river. The Vltana had carried and deposited junk too: a torn shirt caught on a dead tree branch, empty beer bottles, a rusty coffee can. Across the river there were more woods and more flood plain, although Daniel could see rooftops and at least one of

Prague's spires some distance away.

They sat and waited. Daniel skipped stones across the water to pass time. Anna sat on a large rock and held her head in her hands. Still shaken by the close encounter with their father's murderer, she turned to her brother and asked, trying to suppress her own panic, "Where will we go? What will we do?"

Daniel tried to sound rational and under control. He was going to have to appear strong, not something at which he was particularly skilled, at least in his own mind. In truth, he felt as weak as a willow branch. But he put on his best face. "Let's wait for Brother Tomas. We'll see what he says."

Daniel thought about their options. Both their father's parents were dead. The grandparents on their mother's side had moved to America two years previously. They had an aunt in the Ukraine, but that was a great distance and furthermore in the communist Soviet Union. He knew Stalin was hardly a friend of the Jews.

Anna made a suggestion. "What about Mrs. Milenic and Mrs. Klokow?" They were the neighborhood gossips in their mid-sixties. After some consideration both Anna and Daniel agreed that the two women's slavish commitment to authority and their unending loquaciousness made them a very last resort.

Daniel and Anna also had an uncle in the Sudetenland from whom they had received no word for the past six months. After discovering firsthand how the Nazis dealt with Jews, they didn't want to even contemplate his possible fate.

They waited and waited. Daniel took the neatly folded sheets of paper out of his shirt pocket, the same papers he had removed from his arithmetic book. It was his journal begun at the suggestion of one of his teachers at Anshe Shalom, the school he attended before St. Jude's. The first entry was on July 11, 1938.

It was a hot, sticky summer night, and in his journal Daniel recalled slouching in the window seat of his family's parlor, to be near any breeze should it arise, and devouring Otto Kralka's *Redskin Revolt on the Rio Grande*, the latest from his favorite author. The book was a Czech portrayal of America's Indian wars on the Great Plains, in which the United States Army fought by driving Model T's and firing machine guns, à la Al Capone. Although Kralka's pulp tales were ludicrous by anyone's standards, even Daniel's, he, along with thousands of others, enjoyed the stories and bought them because the heroes were strong and handsome and their girlfriends beautiful with ample breasts. He liked that the bad guys were easily distinguished, usually by sinister mustaches, and were always vanquished either by bullet or jail. In short, he was fond of the books because they painted the world as he wanted it to be, not as it actually existed. Aware of the quality of the material, Daniel hid the contraband inside his physical science book, and thus appeared to be a dedicated student rather than a consumer of intellectual junk.

His little brother Jacob had thoroughly impressed even unbiased observers by tearing through the complete works of Jules Verne ("Show-off," was Daniel's only comment). His sister Anna was devoted to the works of Cervantes and Mark Twain. She similarly annoyed Daniel by sprinkling dinner conversations with allusions to *Don Quixote* and *The Prince and the Pauper*. It was hard to impress his parents with quotations from Otto Kralka's tumid prose.

Etched in the margin of his journal, Daniel saw his grades from the spring term. He felt they were perfectly respectable— B's, except for a C plus in German—but, compared to Anna and Jacob's predictable straight A's, B's might as well have been D minuses. Daniel wasn't dull-witted; in fact, he was quite bright. It was just that Anshe Shalom had a very smart, hard-working student body, and Daniel chafed under those circumstances, so he didn't apply himself nearly as much as A's would require there.

Until St. Jude's, Daniel's experience with music had also been seemingly unsuccessful. He knew everyone in Prague was music-crazy, both Jewish families and Gentiles alike, but into this sea of artistic ambition, Jacob, and especially Anna, conspicuously swam ahead of the pack.

Daniel had started piano lessons at age seven and discovered his hand-eye coordination required to read the music and strike the keys in a competent fashion was limited at best. His parents thought he would grow into it, but after five years of lessons that were largely punishing for their lack of progress, he was allowed to quit. Just a few months after beginning piano, his parents, detecting his frustration with the instrument, decided to get Daniel a violin and concurrently start him in lessons. The violin lessons and practice sessions were so excruciatingly painful to the auditory senses, the scratching noise of bow to string so stunningly unpleasant, that after four grueling months the lessons ceased and the violin put away until young Jacob picked it up to considerable success. No one at home ever thought of asking Daniel to open his mouth to sing.

That night, as Daniel had recorded in his journal, Anna took her seat at the family's Bosendorfer grand, and arranged sheet music for her evening practice. She did a few minutes of warm-up exercises, limbering her fingers for the more difficult pieces to follow. Their mother sat down on the sofa with her needlework basket, ready to enjoy the piano recital. Daniel slouched even more and made certain the true nature of his literary pursuit remained hidden from view.

Anna plunged into Bach's Prelude in C Major. As the notes flowed over him and filled the well-appointed parlor, Daniel found his attention drifting away from rebel Indians in a faraway land and instead following the strains of the familiar music.

His father came home and stood in the doorway, drinking in Anna's performance. His eyes burned brightly with pride in his daughter's musical skill. Solomon crossed the room to crank open the tall casement windows even further. "Let's get some more air in here!" Daniel knew the room would get no more fresh air; instead, this was his father's way of letting everyone on the street hear and envy the beauty of his daughter's playing without him having to immodestly say so out loud.

Before long, Daniel overheard some comments from the street a half story below. "That must be Anna playing." It was Mrs. Klokow and Mrs. Milenic from down the block as they returned from the market. As the neighborhood gossips, the plump maiden ladies were the first to judge and condemn any local misdeed. Anna's abilities, however, were anything but condemned. "Isn't she wonderful?" one of them marveled.

Try as he might to resent and envy Anna's talent, Daniel could not, for he knew how hard she worked to develop it. He often wondered what he might accomplish if only he put his mind to it. Unfortunately, he hadn't found anything he wanted to put his mind to. Except the collected oeuvre of Otto Kralka.

An hour later, Anna finished her practice. Daniel, the only listener left in the room, closed his book, and as Anna placed her music back in the piano bench, he stopped and turned to her. "That one thing ..."

"The Bach?"

"Yeah. You're finally getting it."

"Finally?" she asked wryly.

"No, I mean it. It sounds pretty ... okay."

Anna blinked and, as if recognizing this was the best compliment her younger brother could muster, she smiled. "Well, thanks, Daniel. About time you noticed."

Both their father and mother, subsequently busy at other things, had been listening to Anna play from elsewhere in the house. As they entered the dining room for dinner, they enthusiastically complimented their daughter.

"To think we are so lucky to have such a gifted musician," her mother gushed.

"Anna, you play like an angel," her father pronounced.

Then Daniel remembered them scrambling to be even-handed and praise Jacob and him as well. So Father launched into a panegyric on his children.

"I must be the luckiest father in the world. My youngest boy, who is brilliant, will be a great scientist. My Anna will be a world-renowned musician. And Daniel—" He fumbled for the right words and career. "—And Daniel, someday you will be great at something, we just don't know what!"

While it was intended as a compliment and confidence-booster, it had come out as anything but. Daniel had accepted the faint praise with a brief, uncomfortable smile and sat silently at the dinner table. He recalled what he had thought at the time; that he'd show his father; he'd do better than a dozen Jacobs or Annas. The memory of his mean-spiritedness left him choking back shame and remorse. A long pent-up tear finally made its way down Daniel's cheek.

6

A Fateful Decision

Father Beneš had mixed emotions after the SS left St. Jude's. He felt happy they had gone, foreboding that they had come at all. As he returned to his office, Brother Miklas approached.

"Where is Daniel?" Beneš asked.

"I don't know. Brother Tomas ..."

Just then, behind Beneš and Miklas, Brother Tomas emerged into the courtyard with Josef in back of him carrying his dilapidated bag. In shorts and knee socks with a warm gray sweater and a dark gray herringbone newsie cap, Josef looked ready for his excursion.

"Brother Tomas, where is Daniel?" Beneš asked again.

"I told him to meet us at the bend in the river in an hour."

"Good. Gather all of Daniel's things and bring them to him," Beneš ordered Father Miklas.

"And just leave them?!" Miklas protested. "They can't carry it all! They have nowhere to go!"

"Do you have any better ideas?" Beneš countered.

"Excuse me Father, but what did Daniel do?" asked Josef.

The priests looked at each other silently debating what, if anything, they should say. Finally Beneš offered this. "The SS killed Daniel's father and took his family away."

"Why?" Josef asked, genuinely horrified.

"No one knows. Probably for no reason at all, except that they're Jews," replied the priest. Changing the subject, he said, "Now let's see you to the station."

As they opened up the doors and began to say their good-byes, two SS cars and a truck with half a dozen SS troops rolled up in front of the school. The Nazis leave had been brief indeed, occupying the short time it took for Strock to round up additional men and trump up an excuse to search St. Jude's. Colonel Strock got out of one of the cars and strode arrogantly up to Father Beneš.

"Good day again, Herr Padre," he said with great insincerity.

Father Beneš's eyes narrowed and he didn't respond to this obviously disrespectful greeting.

Strock continued, "Now, there have been reports that the school may be hiding weapons and ammunition."

"What?! That's insane!" retorted Beneš, flabbergasted.

"Perhaps, but alas, it falls upon me to check out these reports. No one may come or go from here until I say so!" he ordered with a cruel smile.

"But, Colonel, Brother Tomas and this boy need to catch a train. Here are their tickets," Father Miklas pointed out.

Strock snared Josef's ticket and looked at it suspiciously. After a long and tense perusal of the simple train ticket, Strock said, "All right, he can go."

Brother Tomas and Josef turned to leave. As they did, Strock grabbed the brother's arm hard and said, "He goes, not you."

"But, Colonel, he's just a boy ..." Beneš protested.

"Fine. I'll take *both* of their tickets. Is that what you want?"

Father Beneš was silent.

"And this stays," Strock ordered, indicating Josef's clothes bag.

Jumping to Josef's defense again, Beneš argued, "But, Colonel, those are just the boy's clothes."

Josef stood there, helpless.

"Go! Before I change my mind!" the colonel shouted.

Without another word, Josef turned and hurried out the front gate, empty-handed and alone.

"Godspeed, Josef!" urged Father Beneš.

"May the Lord be with you!" said Father Miklas and Brother Tomas. But Josef did not as much as glance back in his haste to flee the presence of the SS.

"Let's have a good, thorough look around," Strock said to his men with a sliver of a smile. They spread out in all directions, scurrying like a swarm of cockroaches.

Father Beneš engaged Strock in some conversation.

"What did Kippelstein do?"

"We discovered his father was a Communist. And a Jew. A terrible combination."

In fact, three years before, Solomon had attended a meeting of the Workers Party because he worried his own workers might try to organize and he thought he had better get ahead of it all. But the meeting comprised such wild ranting and screaming, such vitriolic spewing of hate, that he ducked out after only twenty minutes. And his workers never showed the slightest interest in joining up with that bunch. However, someone at the meeting had recognized Solomon and recorded his name in attendance. When the Nazis invaded and raided the Workers Party headquarters, there on one of the multitudes of lists was the name Solomon Kippelstein. That and the fact he was Jewish was all the pretext the New Order needed to warrant his and his family's roundup.

"You'll find the Kippelstein boy is not here. I just don't want you to waste your precious time," Beneš offered.

"We'll see," Strock replied coldly.

At the river's edge, Daniel checked his watch. Only forty-five minutes had elapsed, but it seemed like hours. Brother Tomas would soon be here, he felt certain. To pass the time, he returned to his journal, which only served to stimulate his memory. On that July evening Vlasta had cooked another of her mouth-watering dinners. All that remained were a few scraps of sauerkraut and dumplings in the gold-leafed china serving dishes and the well-cleaned carcass of a roast goose on a silver platter. Vlasta had topped off the meal with a rich apple cake drizzled with powdered sugar, while Father pontificated on world affairs. On his, and nearly everyone's mind, was the Nazis' recent annexation of Austria.

"The Germans claim their people are being mistreated."

Daniel remembered that neither he nor Anna had been very interested. Anna had stared blankly out the window and he'd considered vacantly the physics of his fork.

As fathers sometimes do, Mr. Kippelstein continued his lecture despite an obvious lack of interest from his audience.

It fell to their mother to keep the conversation going. "So why are they saying they're being mistreated and need the 'protection' of the Nazi armies?" she asked, twisting her napkin, intent on her husband's answer. Despite Solomon's assurances that all would be well—that although this was worrisome, to be sure, it would pass—Daniel could sense his mother's growing anxiety. He also could sense that as the bad news came harder and faster, like the labor pains preceding some unnatural birth, it grew more difficult to share Solomon's rosy outlook on their future.

"They feel that since they are Germans, and therefore superior to all other forms of life, especially the lowly Jews, Czechs, and Slovaks, equal treatment is in reality unfair," Solomon proclaimed.

Daniel's boredom arose from the fact that he had heard all this a dozen times before. Like his mother, though, his disquiet had grown with each new turn of events. At his school, Anshe Shalom, many fellow students had already left Prague rather than face the possibility of a Nazi occupation.

In the fall of 1937, Daniel's class had begun with twenty-two students. By New Year's it had shrunk to fourteen and was combined with the year-older class to reach twenty-one. By July that new class had diminished to eight and so few teachers remained that talk of shuttering the school grew more concrete. Daniel's school was dying of attrition, as those who could leave did so, bound for the United States, Palestine, Scandinavia, any place of refuge.

There were some other portents of bad things to come. Daniel recalled that the preceding June, his younger brother Jacob, on the way home from his school, was set upon by six boys in the neighborhood and beaten with sticks. As the boys took turns thrashing Jacob, they chanted "Jew, Jew, Jew, Jew." Finally Jacob managed to escape them and sprint home. While not terribly injured, Jacob was bloodied and had several nasty welts on his arms and neck. Naturally Solomon and Esta were outraged. Solomon, bolstered by a Jewish elder and good friend named Shlomo, went to confront the parents of two of the boys. After telling the parents of the incident, Solomon boldly asked what they would do about it. The boys' father replied, "Your son should stay off the street my boys are on when he walks home." Solomon was so incensed he and Shlomo went directly to the police to report it. The policeman they spoke to didn't even write down any information: no names, no locations, nothing. He just nodded and said he would take care of things and then showed Solomon and Shlomo out of the station. Daniel remembered his father and Shlomo venting their anger and discouragement in the Kippelstein's living room. And he remembered thinking what else could they do? The answer was not much.

So Solomon Kippelstein did give some consideration to fleeing his homeland, but there were so many entanglements keeping him in Prague. He and his family lived a comfortable life; his watch company was profitable. How could he start all over in a new country and ever expect to achieve the same level of prosperity? True, there were some lunatic anti-Semites, but most of Czechoslovakia was still decent and humane, and there were lunatic anti-Semites anywhere you might go. Besides, Solomon had come to think of himself as being a Czech almost as much as he was a Jew. As a consequence, flight seemed cowardly. To leave meant conceding victory and his beloved Czechoslovakia to the narrow-minded, fascist Nazis, and this was a prospect Mr. Kippelstein could not tolerate.

Daniel's father thus chose to be one of those who would not be moved. Concerning the annexation of Austria, his father had said, "That was different. Most of Austria is German. This is Czechoslovakia. Hardly the German's cup of tea.

"Besides, the Nazis would not *dare* invade Czechoslovakia! We would fight and the British, French and Russians would fight alongside us!" Solomon declared defiantly.

Daniel put both hands to his head and covered his eyes at his father's astonishing myopia. He found little consolation in the fact that his father was far from being alone in his beliefs; in fact, Solomon Kippelstein was accompanied by multitudes of the best and the brightest from around the world. But few of those multitudes would pay such a steep and dear price for their nearsightedness as Solomon and his family.

7

Hindsight

As long as they didn't have to, the Kippelstein family would not leave Prague; they took comfort in Solomon's determination. Daniel's journal reflected his father's thoughts and a young man's brashness. "I dare them to invade our homeland. We and our neighbors will send them all home in wooden boxes!" he wrote. But others were less certain, and before long, Anshe Shalom closed for lack of pupils.

His parents' initial reaction to the news was alarm. "What will we do now?!" his mother had asked. "How will Daniel keep up with his studies until all this trouble is over?"

Not every Jewish school in Prague had closed. Anna and Jacob's schools, in fact, had remained open. However, at Daniel's age, a good number of boys began to leave school to start working in a trade or their father's businesses. Thus, when his school closed, there were no others remaining for boys in his age group.

Daniel had half-heartedly toyed with the idea of working for his father, but he wasn't particularly attracted to watchmaking. He despised the prospect of sitting at a workbench for hours on end, clasping the delicate tools, handling the minuscule parts. He had no idea what he wanted to do with his life, but he sensed that he was not destined to remain in a world circumscribed by the small pool of light emitted by the workbench lamps.

He dreamed of being a flyer like Charles Lindbergh, cruising low and solo across the Atlantic and landing safely to cheering crowds. Or a ship captain hauling vital goods across the globe. Those vocations seemed dashing and romantic and exciting, but he really didn't know anything about them. He dreamed big, but he kept his big dreams largely to himself. In the end, practical considerations always brought him back to reality.

Even if a place could have been found for him in the Watch Works office or on the sales staff, Daniel's father would have none of it: "You must get the best education you can. You'll have the rest of your life to spend working."

There was one alternative: send Daniel to St. Jude's, a Catholic boys' school that was reputedly one of the best in the city. Daniel's journal noted the immediate rift this option caused between his parents. In his mind he could still easily hear the argument.

"Solomon, are you crazy?! We're Jews! We may not be the most observant Jews in Prague, but we *are* Jews! And you want to send our boy to live among those heathen Catholics?!"

Father shook his head. "Esta, just because Daniel takes advantage of a Catholic education will not turn him into a Gentile.

Besides, what other choice do we have?"

Mother gave him a dark look. He noticed her concern but barreled onward. "Look, I'm not denying it will be difficult for Daniel to be in the extreme minority. But I've been told that the brothers at St. Jude's are good, decent men who live the principles of their religion. Daniel won't be mistreated there. Besides, the world isn't all made up of Jews and a boy had better learn to get along in such a world."

Under normal circumstances, Mother would have fought harder, even begged, if necessary. But the ever-present shadow that Hitler cast had weakened her resolve.

Soon after this discussion, Daniel's father left work early one August afternoon to take Daniel to his interview at St. Jude's. Despite his personal philosophy that school was a grind, an unpleasant fact of life dreamed up to cut into his playtime, Daniel missed having the friends school provided. He was sure St. Jude's would be a great improvement.

Father Beneš greeted them from behind the desk in his study, a room well lit by the afternoon sun slanting in from the west. They exchanged a warm, hearty handshake. Daniel remembered being impressed with the strength of the priest's grip as well as the fact that his arms were as hairy as an ape's. Beneš indicated chairs, and Daniel and his father sat down.

The two men engaged in small talk, carefully avoiding any mention of the growing German menace. At some subtle point, the introductory remarks phased into a brass-tacks discussion. Father Beneš asked if Mr. Kippelstein was aware of St. Jude's cost.

Daniel could tell this obviously hurt his father's pride. Apparently, Father Beneš was unaware of the Kippelstein Watch Works, and of their family's generous gifts to the synagogue and their alms to the poor. Mr. Kippelstein replied curtly, "Daniel is not a charity case. We can afford our share."

Then he asked a question that in turn offended Father Beneš. "With the growing hostility being shown toward Jews, can we be certain that St. Jude's will treat Daniel even-handedly and without prejudice?"

Father Beneš's intense brown eyes met Mr. Kippelstein's blue ones, as the priest assured him, "We are a school, Mr. Kippelstein, devoted to Christian principles. At St. Jude's we teach our boys courage and tolerance. How could we do so if we did not practice it ourselves?"

Both Daniel and his father sensed this came from the heart, and was not mere lip service. It was especially important to know, since Daniel would be the only Jew at the school. There had been two other Jewish boys at St. Jude's the previous year, but they, like so many others, had left Prague with their families.

Once they were home, Daniel received a stern lecture warning him of the dangers of Catholicism. "Daniel, don't listen to any of their pagan hocus-pocus! Now, Catholics are fine people, but that religion of theirs is the most heathenish pack of superstitions on earth." He got up to pace, warming to his subject. "They conveniently forget that Jesus himself was a Jew! King of the Jews, in fact! They'll tell you that the Jews killed Christ, which is a lie! The *Romans* killed Christ! Remember that! And remember that they call it the *Roman* Catholic Church! I think it's more than just a coincidence!"

Daniel had heard this all before on numerous occasions—so many, in fact, that he could do a fairly accurate impression to the considerable amusement of his sister and brother. He thought it best to let his father get it out of his system, so he just sat there, nodding in solemn agreement.

Three days passed before they received a letter from Father Beneš stating that he and the faculty would be proud to welcome Daniel Kippelstein into St. Jude's school. Daniel had felt joy and relief, tempered with some cynicism. He was sure it didn't hurt his cause that his father could pay the full tuition. Times were tough, and a full-paying student was always welcome, even if he was Jewish.

The excitement of packing and preparing to leave for St. Jude's obscured any qualms he might have had about being the only Jew in a Catholic boys' school.

On his first day he and his father marched up the great stone steps to the massive wooden door of St. Jude's. It was late in the afternoon on a warm September Sunday, when many of the boys were out enjoying their freedom or visits from their families. The school enrolled three-hundred boys aged eleven to seventeen years old. About half of them lived in the bunk rooms on the second and third floors. The other half were day students who resided close enough to go home at the end of each day. One of the younger brothers led them up to the dormitory. Daniel's father carried the two suitcases holding his son's belongings.

The air was heavy with the stink of urine, ill-washed feet, pungent cleaning solutions, and, overlaying it all, a persistent odor of cooked cabbage wafting up from the dining hall. Not at all like home, which was redolent of lavender sachets, fresh-baked challah, and his father's after-dinner cigars.

His father briskly took his leave. After all, the family would be back to visit the following weekend. Daniel carefully arranged his clothes in his chest, then laid down on the bed and read the junk novel he had smuggled in beneath his underwear.

The journal recorded the first day's shower fiasco, the memory of which was so vivid that Daniel hardly needed to be reminded of it. His classes were rigorous but the intense regime prevented the fertile minds of his fellow students from wandering and devising new ways to persecute him. It also kept Daniel from missing his family too much.

He lived for Sundays, when the family came to visit. If the weather was good, they would picnic along the river in the Lefensko Gardens. One Sunday in October remained fixed in his mind, like a film he could play at will, back and forth, freeze-framing particular tableaus he wanted to savor. It was a day of weather perfection—the autumn sky over the seven hills upon which Prague is built was a deep, crystalline blue, with fluffy bits of clouds floating high above on a warm, light breeze.

The Golden City was set before them, Prague of One Hundred Spires. It was one of the first times that Daniel appreciated the loveliness of his birthplace and suspected that it was unlike any other on earth.

All around them people enjoyed the afternoon in happy communion. Impromptu games of football erupted, all to the sound of music that came from every corner of the park. Although a dozen different violins, accordions, flutes, and guitars played disparate melodies, it all somehow blended together into one harmonious concert.

Vlasta had packed a huge picnic hamper for their alfresco outing. There was cold sliced goose breast, a covered dish containing *holubky*, or stuffed cabbage rolls, smoked beef tongue with mustard and thick slices of rye and pumpernickel, all to be washed down with cold bottles of Prague-bottled beer. For dessert, the Kippelsteins feasted on kolachys and *houska*, a sweet braided bread loaded with raisins and nuts and smelling richly of lemon and vanilla.

After gorging themselves, Mother and Father lay down together on the blanket, warning Jacob and Daniel not to venture too close to the river. The boys did so anyway, scattering white geese with smooth stones pried out from the muddy bank. Lovers drifted by in rowboats, and more energetic souls powered sculls down the Vltana River, which bisects Prague. Anna leaned against a tree and lost herself in *Jane Eyre*.

The memory of this one particularly gorgeous day sent a tear streaming down Daniel's cheek. Not wanting to appear weak and irresolute to his sister, he tried to halt the flow and, as discreetly as possible, wiped his eyes and sniffling nose.

His thoughts of the past were interrupted by Anna, who had been sitting quietly twenty feet away from Daniel, but facing another direction, absent-mindedly twiddling a braid, totally absorbed in her book. She now stood before him, looking not at him but downstream, as if the solution to their dire situation somehow beckoned from there. Suddenly she broke the silence, "Daniel, I can't cry anymore." She said this with such sadness and calm that it unnerved him. "I just can't."

He looked at her dry, reddened eyes, and tried to console her. "Maybe God is testing us. We'll be okay. Mother and Jacob are okay, too. I'd know it in my heart if they were dead."

"I'd know it, too," she agreed. Left unspoken was the fear that in prison they might suffer horrors worse than death.

Also left unspoken were Daniel's growing worries. By now they had been waiting over two hours. Brother Tomas was nothing if not punctual. Where was he? How would Daniel get the rest of his belongings? He hadn't eaten in a day and Anna hadn't eaten in two. His gut rumbled with anxiety and hunger; it felt like it had a lump in it, as if he had swallowed a dozen olives whole. But what could they do? Without conferring with Anna, he decided to wait another thirty minutes and then, if Brother Tomas had still not come, they would take action. What action exactly remained uncertain.

Anna was feeling even more intense hunger pangs. "I'm so hungry, if I don't get some food I don't know how much longer I can survive."

Daniel had no response for her, but the word "survive" triggered a memory of Father Pothan's lecture from the preceding morning. As part of science class the Father was addressing Darwin's theory of evolution. Father Pothan had no trouble reconciling his religious beliefs with Darwin. In his view, God created the earth and surely part of God's plan was that the strongest organisms would survive. Father Pothan found the Nazis' arrogant belief that they could "improve" man in their image an outrage. The father's words were still fresh in Daniel's head.

"Darwin says that survival is for the fittest. The popularity of this notion is understandable given the only ones around to repeat it are survivors, and it serves as a comforting pat on the back justifying their own existence. Truth be told, survival is often strange and improbable, as elusive and unpredictable as the wind. In fact, human survival is rarely comprehendible, but perhaps with the perspective of fifty years or so, and with the help of God, some reason might be culled from the scrambled fragments of survivors' lives." Daniel had taken scrupulous notes but didn't begin to understand what Father Pothan had said until this moment.

Daniel turned back to his journal. There were just a few recent entries in his diary, written in the late winter but before the invasion. The triviality of the entries, concerning test scores and holes in stockings, made Daniel sigh over how his life had changed. He and his peers at St. Jude's, immersed in schoolwork—their main complaints being cabin fever and boredom with the dining hall cuisine—gave little thought to the Nazi threat. As Daniel reflected on it now, he realized they were not alone. It seemed as though all of Czechoslovakia was slumbering, lost in a sleepy state of self-delusion that they would continue to stand unmolested by the Nazis, that the fascists would remain politely poised on their borders, like wolves eyeing a herd of sheep, and venture no further.   On March 15, 1939, Czechoslovakia was rudely awakened. From the steps of St. Jude's, Daniel and a dozen boys watched silently as Nazi tanks rolled slowly by, heard the deafening, sickening screech the tanks made against the Prague streets, and witnessed the occupation begin. To Daniel's utter disbelief, all of Czechoslovakia's allies, the British, French, Soviets and Americans, sat passively, like fatuous pigeons on a telephone wire, and watched it happen. Not a shot was fired as the Nazis swarmed across the Czech countryside.

Nazi tanks suddenly appeared on almost every corner, and swastikas befouled lampposts, store windows, public buildings. Daniel couldn't venture a halfblock from his school without seeing that crooked cross, the hateful symbol of Nazi dominance. Hitler's minions, in their brown shirts and Nazi armbands, were omnipresent. At St. Jude's, there wasn't much talk among the boys of the invasion. When the subject did arise, most of the boys nurtured the same hope that was current in Prague, that things would not get worse, that the Germans to a great extent could be trusted.

Suddenly Daniel and Anna heard a rustling in the woods nearby. Daniel grabbed his sister and pulled her behind a sandy berm as he quickly folded up his journal and stuffed it back in his shirt pocket. He desperately hoped the rustling meant Brother Tomas or Father Miklas had finally come. As he peered cautiously over the top of the berm and through some tall grass he saw, of all people, Josef Czerny.

Daniel sunk back down to the ground and rolled his eyes in disgust.

"Who is it?" Anna asked.

"The boy from the bunk room. He's a jackass."

Josef walked to the river's edge and looked up and down the flowing water. He crouched beside the fresh footprints and examined them with the professional intensity of a cavalry scout. He concluded Daniel and his sister either had been here not too long ago or were still around someplace near. "Kip! Kip! Hey, where are you?" he called out.

Anna and Daniel held their breath in their hiding place.

"Kip! It's me, Josef!"

They didn't reply, although Anna leaned forward slightly as if tempted. She glared at the hard-hearted and distrustful Daniel.

Josef looked around; he appeared vulnerable, an aspect of his personality Daniel had never witnessed. Josef sighed and turned to leave. Anna elbowed her brother. He looked at her as if to say, "You don't know what we're in for!" She gave back a look of equal ferocity that clearly retorted, "I don't care!" Daniel finally, reluctantly stood up.

"What do you want? Where is Brother Tomas?"

Josef trotted over to their hiding place.

"The SS came back. They're searching the whole school. No one can leave," he replied.

"How did you get out?" asked Daniel skeptically.

"I had a ticket to catch a train."

"Is Brother Tomas coming?"

"I don't know," Josef answered. "I stayed and watched. They're still there."

"I thought you had a train to catch?" Daniel asked, like a barrister catching a witness in the middle of a lie.

"I do. The train doesn't leave for another hour. I stayed and watched as long as I could."

"Where are the rest of my things?"

"The SS wouldn't let *anything* out."

Daniel kicked at a protruding rock planted firmly in the ground. His foot absorbed a good deal more pain than the rock suffered. In frustration, Daniel turned on Josef. "Hah! What rubbish! You probably hung everything out in the courtyard for everyone to laugh at!"

Josef set his jaw, genuinely angry. "I'm sorry I came," he said, and turned to go.

"Why *did* you come?" asked Daniel, sure his motivation could be nothing but treachery.

"Because I don't know if anyone else will," he replied evenly.

Daniel had had about enough of Josef's phony solicitude. "Oh, boo hoo hoo, we don't wanna be anyone's charity case."

Anna watched this exchange of hostilities with alarm. Here they had just listed their lack of prospects, and her younger brother was throwing away possible salvation. Salvation that, incidentally, came in a very handsome package.

"Hear him out, Daniel," she begged.

Josef pulled out a decent-sized bun he had pinched from the St. Jude's kitchen at breakfast that morning.

"Are you hungry? I ate this morning, so ..."

Anna's eyes grew large and she licked her lips. "I haven't eaten in two days."

Josef offered the bread to her.

"I'm hungry too," Daniel spoke up.

Josef looked at him contemptuously and then tore a tiny piece of the bread and gave it to Daniel. The much larger piece went to the grateful Anna, who devoured it with frightening speed. Daniel wolfed down his small bite but seemed gypped by the exchange.

Josef smiled at Anna sweetly, showing off his dimples. "Look, I don't know what kind of trouble you're in, but it's just that ... my father helps everyone. Maybe he can help you."

Anna's face brightened considerably. Was this a ray of hope? A lifeline? Daniel, however, knew Josef all too well.

"What? Is this a joke? Where does everyone pop out and start laughing? Big joke on Kip. Look, Anna, see this black eye?" By now his right eye was somewhat discolored and slightly puffy. In the light of succeeding events it seemed like a minor occurrence, until now. "Who do you think gave me this?! Oh, it was by accident, of course. A complete and total 'accident.'" He emphasized his displeasure by crossing his arms over his chest and petulantly thrusting out his lower lip.

Daniel's melodramatic pose struck Anna as funny and she laughed for the first time since the nightmare began. Daniel didn't take kindly to her response and she sensed his displeasure. She instantly stifled her mirth and asked, almost pleading, "Daniel, where else can we go?"

"All I know is he can't be trusted."

For some reason, Josef wasn't his usual cocky, combative self. Instead, he was quiet and appeared to be struggling with troubles of his own.

"Maybe it's not such a good idea," he agreed. "My parents don't like Jews anyway. They'd probably make you stay out in the barn."

"You see, Anna," Daniel said, his suspicions confirmed. "What did I tell you? We can do better than that."

"When you think of something, I'll consider it," replied his stubborn sister. It became apparent that Anna had her mind made up. She was casting her lot with Josef.

"Anna! You can't!" cried Daniel. "He wants us to sleep with the pigs and horses!"

"Do what you want," sighed Josef in resignation. "I have to go now or my train ticket will be worthless." He turned and started to walk away.

"Wait! I'm coming with you!" called Anna.

Daniel was stunned. The strange, inexplicable power Czerny had over others was doing its nefarious work on his own sister! "Anna, I forbid it! You will *not* go with him! Stop!"

It was futile. She continued to follow Josef. And even though Daniel knew it was stupid, knew Josef would either get them all killed, turn them over to the Gestapo, or abandon them at some inopportune moment with a jolly laugh at their expense, he followed too, albeit very reluctantly.

When he caught up with them, he asked, "Well, Mr. Big Shot, what happened to *your* suitcase?"

"Mr. Stupid! The Gestapo took it, along with all your stuff."

"At least when you get home you can buy new things," Daniel needled.

"Oh shut up, Kip ..."

"Where do you live, Josef?" asked Anna.

Inwardly Daniel steamed. It was so transparent that she was falling under Josef's spell. His own sister!

"Zabreh," Josef replied.

Anna asked, "How are *we* going to get to Zabreh with you?"

"Train," he replied cryptically.

"But you only have *one* ticket," Daniel pointed out.

Josef was prepared for this petty objection. "Right. So we sell it, get some money, buy some food, and hop a freight. We'll be tramps, just like Charlie Chaplin!"

Daniel was horrified. He looked at Anna. She merely shrugged and kept pace with Josef, as though it was a capital idea.

"Hop a freight?!" Daniel asked incredulously. "Hop a freight?!" he said more quietly, as if to himself. Again, more forcefully he questioned, "Hop a freight?!!", hoping the repetition would bring them to their senses.

But it did not. Josef and Anna just kept walking.

And so, despite the opposition, Daniel followed along, not willing to abandon his sister, yet convinced they were lemmings heading straight off a cliff.

8

A Train Ride

Josef had no trouble selling his train ticket for half its face value outside the Prague central train depot. Neither of the Kippelstein children had eaten much of anything since at least noon the previous day, so with some of the money Josef bought bread at a bakery nearby. While Daniel and Anna hadn't thought much about food, the tantalizing scent of fresh-baked bread had their stomachs turning somersaults of joy and instantly revived their appetites. The three of them tore into the warm, thick-crusted bread like feeding sharks, while a half dozen birds swept up the few crumbs that managed to fall to the ground.

When they were finished and the gymnastics in their bellies subsided, they felt better, but were still desperately hungry. They had to be careful, however, with the little money they had, for Zabreh was a journey of 110 miles and who could tell how long it would take by freight train.

A discarded newspaper lay in the gutter. Daniel picked up the dirty and crumpled paper and looked through it, hoping to find some report of their father's murder and the factory fire. He quickly learned how the news was being managed by the "New Order."

A small headline buried below the fold on the fifth page read:

Man Dies in Factory Blaze

A fire, which started in a storage area, took the life of businessman Solomon Kippelstein. The fire broke out late yesterday afternoon in the Kippelstein Watch Works, which employs 35 people. The factory was badly damaged in the blaze but it was contained and didn't threaten any neighboring structures. Firemen thought Kippelstein may have died trying to put the fire out by himself ...

"That's a lie!" cried Anna, outraged. "I was there!"

"It's like it didn't even happen," Daniel murmured.

"What does it say about Mother and Jacob?" Anna asked.

Daniel scanned the article. "Nothing. Like they never existed."

Although Anna thought she could no longer cry, tears sprang to her eyes, but tears of rage rather than grief. "Lies, it's all lies!"

All three of them read the story again to confirm that their eyes weren't deceiving them. Josef wadded the paper into a ball and tossed it with disgust into an ash can. "The Nazis run everything now. You can't expect them to report the Gestapo's murders."

"How will people ever know?" Daniel wondered.

They walked toward the nearby freight yard, their anger and pain stewing silently. After walking several long blocks, the trio's depressed spirits began to lift. Near the freight yard, Josef picked up a stick and wielded it like a sword.

"You know, we can't just take this. We can fight back. Like the Three Musketeers! I'll be D'Artagnan!"

Anna also picked up a stick and challenged Josef with an, "En garde!" She squared off with him in mock swordplay.

Daniel refused to be sucked into their foolishness. So he sulked. But out of the corner of his eyes he watched. It was hard not to.

Anna seemed to leap into the role-playing with gusto. She used her copy of *Huckleberry Finn* as a shield to block Josef's parries, and cried "Touché!" as she snaked her slender arm through his defense and jabbed his abdomen with her stick. First Josef and then Anna turned on Daniel, poking him lightly in the chest. He was not amused.

"You know, if you weren't such a sour apple," said Josef, "You wouldn't be so miserable all the time."

"I'm *not* miserable and I'm *not* a sour apple! I'm a realist! I just don't want to live in a dreamland, pretending life is a big bowl of cherries and all is well!" Left unspoken was Daniel's conclusion that his father's overly optimistic worldview had gotten him killed and his family scattered.

Anna stepped in. "Shut up, both of you. We're not getting any closer to Zabreh with all this arguing."

Now the mood swung to the surly side. The two boys walked on in stony silence, each narrowly eyeing the other with suspicion and resentment.

They approached the railroad tracks, which lay several feet above them on an embankment. An old, grizzled, mean-tempered railroad bull spotted them and kept a watchful eye on them. He sat near his guard shack a hundred yards away, sucking on a cigarette, waiting for them to set foot on his turf. Josef, Anna, and Daniel sat down on a pile of railroad ties.

Finally, after an eternity of twenty minutes, Daniel asked, "How long do we have to wait?"

"As long as it takes," replied Josef testily. "Do I look like a railroad timetable?"

More time passed. It crawled all the more slowly because Daniel kept looking at his watch and announcing the infinitesimal creep of minutes. It was worse than enduring geometry class knowing football was next. Anna dozed off. Daniel wished he could do the same, but he didn't trust Josef. He was sure Josef wouldn't wake them when the train began to move and would leave without them. Not that Daniel actually cared. Good riddance, he thought. But Anna would be massively upset and never forgive him, no doubt.

"It's been more than three hours," Daniel observed, rather pointedly.

"Listen, you whiny baby, it'll go when it goes!" Josef snapped.

Anna woke up and rubbed her eyes. "Stop it!" she commanded. "Isn't there enough fighting in the world already?" She demonstrated her commitment to pacifism by punching them both in the arm. Hard.

"Oww!" cried Daniel, wincing in agony.

Rubbing his arm, Josef said with a pained expression, "She's strong ..." He got no sympathy from Daniel, who had been at the receiving end of his big sister's fist on countless occasions.

A whistle blew.

"That's it!" Josef shouted.

A train lurched into motion. They scrambled up the

embankment.

A three-foot high barbed wire fence impeded their access to the tracks. Josef easily stepped over. Then he took Anna's books and, as she held her dress tightly around her legs, he lifted her clear.

At that moment, the railroad guard spotted their movements, threw down his cigarette, and hollered, "Hey! Where do you kids think you're going?!"

He was old, but wiry, and was headed their way, running in a gimpy fashion and brandishing a billy club. He didn't look like the type to ask questions before clubbing them to a pulp. They took off after the train, away from the charging old coot.

Being shorter than Josef, Daniel didn't have such an easy time stepping over the fence, and his pants got hopelessly hooked on the barbed wire. Unaware of Daniel's entanglement, Josef and Anna ran for the train. Josef called over his shoulder, "Hurry up!"

"My pants! They're stuck!"

"Get rid of them!" advised Josef, helping Anna into a boxcar. The train started to roll, very slowly at first.

Daniel pulled hard at the wire and felt his pants rip.

"Come on!" Josef shouted. The train picked up speed as the power of the locomotive overcame inertia and the great weight of its payload.

Hopelessly entangled, Daniel watched the boxcar slowly roll away. At the same time, the railroad guard was closing in on him. Only fifty yards away now, the guard, like the train, seemed to be picking up speed.

Daniel lunged forward and heard a loud RIIPP! But the barbed wire still held him fast.

The train rolled faster. The guard approached menacingly. Desperate, Daniel grabbed his pants and tried to wrest them free from the clutching talons of the barbed wire. There was only one alternative. He unbuttoned his fly in record time and dove out of his shorts, abandoning them to flap in the breeze like a flag. Without regard for his dignity, Daniel sprinted for the boxcar in his underwear.

"Stop right there, kid!" yelled the angry old man.

"Run, Daniel!" cried Anna.

As Daniel outpaced the guard, the train was outpacing him. Gasping for breath, the boy finally made it to the open car, where Josef and Anna leaned out and frantically urged him on. But the train picked up more speed and they slipped beyond his reach.

"Hop on the next car!" instructed Josef.

On the outside of the boxcar following Anna and Josef's, Daniel noticed a small platform just large enough for his feet and iron handles leading to the roof of the car. With one final lunge he grabbed at a handle and jumped. He was on! He clung to the side like a scared kitten. Anna and Josef cheered like fans at a soccer match. The guard, defeated in his valiant attempt to foil the freeloaders, gimped to a halt and cursed.

The moment of triumph, however, was fleeting, for Daniel hung immodestly clothed some distance from Anna and Josef. Josef shouted, "Can you get to the couplings that hold the cars together?"

He looked around the corner of the boxcar to the couplings joining his car with Josef and Anna's. There appeared to be enough room to stand—certainly more than in his present position. Also, the windchill would be less, no small factor in his semi-dressed state. Furthermore, there was a metal ladder that climbed to the top of Josef and Anna's car.

Daniel took a deep breath, and counted to three. He whirled

around the corner, switching handholds, and swung his feet to the ledge between the cars. Once accomplished, it seemed rather easy, and built up his confidence for the next maneuver—whatever that might be.

The cars were old, built of weathered wood, with sizeable cracks between planks in the walls. Josef found a gap near the coupling point and yelled to Daniel, "See? That was easy. Now we gotta think of a way to get you inside."

Daniel had assumed that surely the boxcar would have some sort of trap door on top. "Can't I climb inside through the roof?"

"Of course not, you fool," scoffed Josef.

Daniel blanched. The thought of spending the rest of the trip to Zabreh between cars in his underpants was unacceptable. "You mean there's no way into the car through the roof?!"

"Well, there's a way. Just not through the roof," conceded Josef weakly.

"Are you sure there's no roof hatch?" demanded Daniel, certain they were somehow conning him. He was *positive* there had been a roof hatch in a movie he had seen featuring trains and the glorious lives of footloose hoboes.

"No," Anna assured him. "Just a chimney pipe. Way too small for you to fit through."

The two debated Daniel's plight sotto voce. He couldn't make out a word they were saying, which was extremely irritating under the circumstances. He felt like a hospital patient who listens helplessly while doctors calmly discuss the removal of his bodily organs as if he were not there.

"What's going on?" he demanded. "You know, I'm freezing out here."

"Okay, here's the plan," Josef began. "You climb up on the roof ..."

Anna interrupted, "... we pass a rope through the chimney. You tie it around yourself ..."

Now Josef interrupted, "... while we hold onto the other end and you swing down through the side door."

Daniel had a few minor objections. "That's not a plan, that's suicide!"

"You got a better idea?" countered Josef.

He thought. He didn't. He sighed and tried to fire himself up for the ordeal.

"It'll be a cinch," Josef enthused, a bit jealous that he was not the one performing the maneuver. "You'll be just like a commando in the Great War!"

Sure, Daniel thought. On a train barreling along at forty miles per hour, in his underwear. No problem at all.

With Anna and Josef shouting advice and encouragement, Daniel reluctantly started the climb to the roof, as much to escape their contradictory instructions as to get into the boxcar.

Suddenly, another train streaked by going the opposite direction. Because the tracks were so close together, it was like a bomb exploding; the noise was deafening and the shock of the unseen approach nearly shook Daniel loose from the ladder. It emphasized the vulnerability of his position, and he decided that regardless of the risk, he had to somehow reach the relative safety of the boxcar's interior.

Daniel waited until the train passed, then continued his climb. He overheard Anna say excitedly to Josef, "He's doing it!"

He glanced down at the ground rushing past and realized that one slip might mean death. Everything his mother had ever warned him about the danger of hanging around the freight yard came racing through his mind. "Daniel Kippelstein, if I ever hear about you setting foot near those trains, your father will whip you within an inch of your life!" she'd threatened when he had expressed rail-riding ambitions.

When he had nearly reached the top, the train rounded a tight curve. He held on precariously as centrifugal forces tried to fling him off onto the rock-strewn right-of-way. It seemed like an eternity before the train completed the curve, and his muscles ached from the strain. When the rails straightened out, he gingerly began to pull himself over the top.

Not good timing. As he stuck his head up, he had barely enough time to duck it back down to avoid decapitation as the train roared into a tunnel! He was enveloped in utter darkness and unbearable noise as the sound waves reverberated in the claustrophobically narrow space.

When they emerged a short time later, he yelled to Josef, "What happens if I get on top and we come to another tunnel?"

"Hope that you don't," Josef offered ineffectually.

Daniel looked cautiously over the top. No tunnels or low-hanging overpasses were in sight. The roof of the boxcar sloped gently in two directions from the center. There was a narrow plank on top of the car, which served as a walkway. He climbed up and crawled on his belly toward the small chimney pipe in the middle of the car. Up ahead he saw the front of the train start around another curve. He got an ominous, sick feeling deep in his gut that he ought to flee his precarious position. Yet there was nowhere to go. It was like watching dominoes fall as each successive car reached the curve. Inevitably, the force of the turn hit him.

He lay flat and clung to the narrow plank as the unseen hand of gravity pulled at him, trying to tear him loose and throw him aside. Before his strength gave out, thankfully the train straightened, and he began to inch forward again.

"Daniel! I can't hear you! Are you still up there?" Anna called.

He answered, "Yes, I'm almost to the chimney! Where's the rope?" By now he expected to see Josef's hand protruding from the chimney, offering the end of a rope they had found coiled in the boxcar; an integral part of their plan.

He heard them scrambling about below, then his heart momentarily stopped and felt like a large rock in his chest when Josef said, "I can't reach it!"

The bright, sunny morning had turned into a gray, damp afternoon, with low-hanging clouds threatening rain. By now, the threat had turned to promise, and a light drizzle commenced. Besides chilling him to the bone, Daniel had yet more trouble keeping a grip on the rain-slickened wood. He clung perilously while Josef and Anna continued their dithering in the car below.

"I still can't reach it!" Josef reported.

Up ahead, the locomotive and leading cars began to snake around yet another curve. "Please, God, no," whispered Daniel. He managed to hang on again, unsure how. He heard a loud thump and commotion inside the car. Apparently, the sudden turn had caused Josef to lose his balance.

"Boy, this is dangerous," observed Josef.

No kidding!! Daniel thought.

As the train came out of the curve, Anna's hand emerged from the chimney, holding the end of the rope. Josef had made a stirrup of his hands and boosted her up. Daniel grabbed the rope and pulled several feet through the chimney pipe. He wrapped it around his waist twice. He was so intent on his preparations that he failed to notice another tunnel looming, a mere half mile in the distance.

He glanced up and his heart sank into the pit of his stomach. "Hurry up with that rope!" he cried in utter panic.

Anna pushed it through.

"Let out some more!" he shouted.

The tunnel was now less than a quarter mile away. He sat on ten feet of loose rope. It would have to be enough; he had no more time.

Down below, Josef held onto the other end. Daniel was to slowly slide down the roof and then swing over the side and into the car. By now, he should have done so, but the move required complete trust in Josef, trust that the Catholic boy would and could hold on until he was safely inside the car; trust Daniel entirely lacked. Yet if he stayed on top of the boxcar, they'd be scraping his body up with a spatula. And if he stalled much longer, he would be making his leap as they entered the tunnel, with similar gory results. It was now or never. He didn't trust Josef, but he was less willing to gamble that there would be sufficient clearance to survive the tunnel.

With no time left to agonize, Daniel leaped out over the side like a rappelling rock climber. Josef was alarmed by the sudden tautness of the rope. But he anchored the rope firmly as Daniel arched out, then swung into the boxcar. As Daniel flew through the boxcar's open door, he smashed feet first into a pale, sweating Josef.

A split second later, they were engulfed in the tunnel's blackness and deafening noise.

Anna shouted to Daniel above the roar inside the tunnel. "Are you okay? Did you break anything?"

Josef answered presumptuously, "Yeah, I think he broke *my* ribs!"

Shortly they emerged into the light. Daniel saw the rope dangling out the door of the boxcar and assumed Josef had let go.

"See!" he reported to Anna. "He let go of the rope! I told you I couldn't trust him!"

"I let go because your feet were coming through my rib cage!" Josef shot back.

"What difference does it make?" asked Anna. "You're safe and sound ... sort of," she added uncertainly. She immediately moved on to the next item on the agenda. "We need to get you some pants before you freeze."

Daniel *was* freezing and damp. And rather than feeling joyful at being safe inside the boxcar, he was still simmering over the fact that they were there in the first place. He slumped down against the wall of the car and stared blankly out at the passing countryside. Since the roof and walls had ample leaks, cold rain droplets occasionally seeped through, hitting the back of his neck and his bare legs, exacerbating his condition.

Anna, however, was not deterred by Daniel's ill humor or a lack of haberdashers along their route. She discovered some empty burlap bags in the corner of the car where they had found the length of rope. With her teeth, she broke a thread at the bag's corner and pulled it out.

Josef, who always had to be the center of attention, was milking the plight of his injured ribs for all it was worth. He rubbed them and moaned, "You didn't have to kill me! It was *my* plan that got you here."

Anna quickly corrected him, "It was *my* plan."

"Oh, yeah," replied Josef sheepishly. "But if I hadn't hoisted you up there, he would have never reached the rope!"

Daniel agreed sharply, "It's true. If it wasn't for Josef, we wouldn't be here at all!"

Josef, who could be rather slow to perceive irony, merely took the comment in a positive manner and grinned contentedly. Daniel glanced at him, shook his head, and sighed to himself, "Hopeless."

Anna finally presented the burlap bag to him. "Here, try this on."

He looked quizzically at the bag, which she had opened up to form a sort of skirt. He shrugged and wriggled into it. "How do I keep it from falling down?" he asked.

"Use the rope," she suggested.

Unfortunately they had nothing with which to cut the rope. Even after he wound it around his waist a number of times, several excess feet trailed behind him. Josef found the fitting session most amusing.

"That's the prettiest little frock I've ever seen," he simpered, imitating an effeminate dress designer.

"Oh, shut up," growled Daniel, who wished he could think up a far more stinging retort. He was warmer now, but the "skirt" itched terrifically. Before long, he found himself groping and scratching places no polite person should. He tried to be discreet, but it seemed that every time his hand reached down to minister to his irritated groin, Josef spotted him at work and snickered pitilessly. While Daniel was no longer on the roof of the train, exposed to the wind and drizzle and possible decapitation, the torments he suffered within seemed every bit as noisome. And, as was often the case, there was Josef Czerny, front row center, witness and appreciative audience to his distress.

Anna began to chat with Josef. Her mood had lightened somewhat. Perhaps it was due to the hope Josef's wealthy family held out, or perhaps it was Josef's disarming charm. Regardless of the reason, the result, in Daniel's view, was disgraceful; for there was Anna, taking in every stupid thing Josef said and flipping her hair away from her face in the most flirtatious way.

Daniel was certain that before this was all over, Josef Czerny would give them ample opportunity to regret the impulse to travel with him. They'd entrusted their lives to an utter nitwit.

Sick of listening to their jabbering, Daniel decided to occupy himself by updating his journal. He had two problems, though; down to his last quarter page and already writing so minutely only a flea could read it, he needed fresh paper and something with which to write. He discreetly asked Anna, "Do you have a pencil and some paper in your notebook?"

"Sure, somewhere," she replied.

Anna opened the notebook containing her music. She handed him a few pieces of loose-leaf paper, and a pencil. "Oh, use this to write on," she added, giving him the notebook itself.

Bracing the notebook on his knees, Daniel began to write. He didn't start with the previous day, when their flight began, but tried to put events into context by going back a couple weeks to his last entry. In that entry, Daniel's big concern was not Nazi tanks on the streets of Prague, but someone's smelly socks that had been left on his bed in the bunkroom. The train grew colder and damper and Daniel's miserable itching continued, but he barely noticed as he filled the page with the tumult of the past two weeks.

9

The Estate

The train stopped in two towns before arriving in the Zabreh railroad yard. Josef's easy familiarity with the freight yard and the ways of boxcar travel in general made Daniel suspect that perhaps he had done this before. With his family's wealth he could certainly afford to ride first-class; thus the fact that he was gutsy enough to travel via rail for free raised his stock in Daniel's critical eyes.

Daniel had some trouble keeping pace with Josef and Anna as they wove their way between dozens of railroad cars and the maze of track. He had to somehow keep from scratching his irritated groin, maintain modesty in his burlap skirt, and hold onto the tail end of twenty feet of rope that held up said skirt. The other two chatted on, quite oblivious to Daniel's difficulties and growing rancor.

By the time they emerged from the freight yard and reached the residential streets of Zabreh, night was falling. Anna asked, "How much farther is it, Josef?"

"A ways," he replied vaguely. "We should find a place to sleep and continue on first thing in the morning."

"Why not push on and get it over with?" complained Daniel.

"It's not really safe," insisted Josef. "Bandits. They'll size up your charming gown and assume we're rich." He leapt on top of a waist-high brick wall and pranced down its length as though he were a circus tightrope walker. Mimicking the voice of a circus master, he intoned, "High above the crowd is Prague Circus's greatest performer - Czerny the Magnificent!" He was showing off egregiously, playing strictly to Anna. Then he pretended to lose his balance, wobbling and frantically waving his arms. "Whoa!" he exclaimed.

Anna was quite shocked that he would thus endanger his life. "Don't be stupid! Get off that thing!" she firmly demanded.

Josef almost "fell" again. Daniel rolled his eyes heavenward, unsure with whom he was more annoyed: Josef, for being such a show-off, or his sister for believing the moronic act.

"Please get down!" she pleaded, genuinely concerned.

Apparently so taken with the tone of her voice, Josef wavered, truly lost his balance, and fell, disappearing into the yard on the other side of the fence.

Anna and Daniel rushed to the wall and peered over the top. Josef was nowhere to be seen.

He slowly emerged from behind a forsythia bush, holding a freshly picked yellow daffodil, grinning from ear to ear.

"Cheap trick," judged Daniel.

"You scared us half to death," Anna chastised Josef. He put one hand on top of the wall and presented the flower to her with a graceful bow. When he straightened up something in the yard caught his eye.

Without a word he ran to a clothesline where laundry was hanging to dry. He grabbed a pair of trousers and whispered urgently, "Let's get out of here!" as he vaulted over the fence back to Anna and Daniel's side.

He threw the trousers at Daniel and dashed up the street. Anna and Daniel followed him, Daniel now encumbered by pants in one hand, the unruly coil of rope in the other.

A safe distance from the yard, they slowed to a walk.

"Thank you for the flower," said a grateful Anna, pausing to admire its delicate beauty.

"You're welcome," replied Josef, oozing smarmy sweetness.

Daniel made no comment, but shuffled along sullenly. His poor attitude was more than apparent, so Anna attempted to force some civility out of him.

"Daniel," she chided, "don't you have something to say?"

"What?" he replied, knowing full well what she meant. Whenever they failed to say "thank you" at home, Mother used those very same words.

"Thank him for the britches," said Anna coldly.

He certainly hadn't asked Josef to steal the pants for him, and thanking him would be galling, to say the least. Daniel also sensed they were ganging up on him. "He stole them," he countered.

"He stole them for *you*," Anna charged right back.

"No, he stole them for *you*," he clarified, not giving an inch of ground. "To impress you! So you wouldn't think he was such a Donkey Boy!" He had never called Josef "Donkey Boy"; not to his face, at any rate.

Josef turned and kicked him squarely in the butt.

The force of the blow virtually lifted Daniel a few inches off the ground. "Oww!" he howled in undignified pain.

"Say 'thank you,' put the stupid pants on, and you'll have one less thing to complain about," Josef said forcefully.

The disloyal Anna gave Daniel a very smug couldn't-have-said-it-better-myself look, prompting Daniel to mentally compose a stern lecture for her benefit. But for now, overmatched and outnumbered, he kept silent. He unwound his rope belt, wriggled out of the burlap, and kicked it into the street. He quickly pulled on the pants, to the scandalized stares of two old peasant women passing by. The pants fit around the waist but seemed to have been tailored to fit a man with a buttocks the size of two massed footballs. The excess of fabric, coupled with the loud, predominantly burnt orange plaid pattern, gave Daniel a clownish appearance. His voice laden with sarcasm, he said, "Thanks."

Josef smirked and Anna appeared satisfied that her recalcitrant younger brother had been whipped into line, but they were wrong. Daniel was biding his time. Payback would come, and it would be sweet. Of that, he was certain.

With Daniel's body decently, if unfashionably, clothed (although the itch remained despite his shedding the burlap), hunger was now the main concern. The bakery on the town square was already closed. Anna and Josef pressed their noses against the glass and ravenously studied the few remaining unsold items—several loaves of golden brown bread, doughy fruit-filled kolachys, and one houska, so tantalizingly near, yet so far. The air outside the store was still heavy with the yeasty scent of fresh-baked bread, candied fruits, and buttery kuchen.

Not one to endure suffering with stoicism, Josef ran to the back of the bakery to attempt a break-in. At first, Daniel balked at the idea of houska larceny, but his stomach overcame his objections and he followed

Josef. Josef hoisted him up to a window, which proved to be locked and too small to squeeze through anyway.

Bitterly frustrated and nearly nauseous with hunger, the three moved on. On the outskirts of town Josef found an empty barn. "We can sleep here tonight," he explained. "Then start for my family's place as soon as it's light."

They unlatched the barn door. It was so black inside, they were unable to see their hands in front of their faces. They felt their way along gingerly, lest they stumble on unseen objects or bang their heads on low beams.

"There must be a lamp in here somewhere," asserted Josef, who apparently knew his way around barns. He groped along the wall near the door, and located a kerosene lantern hanging on a nail. "Now for some matches," he asserted. Their eyes were only slightly more used to the blackness by now. He ran his hand over the filthy windowsill and discovered a box of matches.

Before he could light one, Anna moved a few more inches and encountered a large, snuffling object with a wet spot on its end. It snorted with surprise as she made contact. She suppressed a scream and jumped backwards.

"Th-there's something in here!" she whispered, terrified. "It's huge, it's — it's — "

Josef struck a match and lit the lamp. As the glow of the lamp illuminated the barn, Anna discovered that she had been eye to eye with a horse.

"It's a horse," reported Daniel matter-of-factly, although he had momentarily stopped breathing in fear as well. Anna and Daniel had little experience with barnyard animals. Their family's former stable had housed automobiles since the mid-1920s.

Josef was far less astonished to discover a horse in a barn than were the city kids, and ordered, "Quick, cover the window. They'll see our light from the house."

Daniel found a ratty horse blanket and with Josef's help, covered the window. He asked Josef, "We have to sleep with a horse? In hay? Let's take this lamp and keep on walking to your family's estate."

Josef looked at Daniel with extreme annoyance. "I told you before, it's too far. Take my word for it. Besides, sleeping with a horse is no worse than sleeping with you—King of the Snorers!" He did an exaggerated imitation, which sounded more like the honk of a dying goose. Daniel knew he didn't snore; even if he did, it was nothing like that racket.

Anna broke into giddy laughter, causing the horse to pull back his head in skittish dismay.

"Stop it," chided Daniel. "You only encourage him."

"Well, he's right," she giggled. "You *do* snore!"

He crossed his arms and fired back, "At least my feet don't stink to high heaven, like some gypsy who wears the same pair of socks for six months!"

"Aah, my feet don't stink," said Josef dismissively. "You have an over-sensitive nose. A bug farts halfway across the room, and you fall over and faint!"

Anna giggled all the more, blushing at the off-color reference. Daniel ignored Josef and assured her, "My bed was next to his! Believe me, we'll be better off sleeping in that stall with a horse than anywhere in range of his feet!"

By now the banter had crossed the line into irritable hostility.

Josef made a fist and got into Daniel's face. "If I hear you snore, you'll be sleeping on the moon," he promised.

Anna suddenly felt very tired. "Okay, shut up now," she ordered listlessly.

The three sat down on the floor, at an impasse, the lamp flickering between them. Anna regarded the sulking faces of the two boys in the shadows and decided that whatever they were going to do, whether argue like overtired toddlers or stare each other down, she wasn't having any part of it.

"You two," she sighed. "What big babies! I'm too hungry and too tired to put up with this. Good night!"

She put down her books and arranged the hay in the unoccupied stall into a bed for herself. Josef and Daniel eyed each other warily, then without another word followed her example, and went to sleep.

10

Brutal Truth

The following morning Daniel awoke to the faint cooing of pigeons. He arose, stiff and cold, having slept soundly due more to extreme exhaustion rather than any comfort in his surroundings. While the stable was still as dark as the inside of a barrel, he could discern a sliver of gray at the edge of the blanket-covered window. He pulled off the blanket, illuminating the interior with the first light of dawn.

He peered out the window. Nothing stirred in the barnyard; no chickens, geese, or goats. The only living thing on the farmstead appeared to be the horse. And the itchy little creatures that were making a feast of his flesh. They seemed to have multiplied over night.

He looked back at their accommodations. Anna still slept, curled into a fetal position for warmth. And Josef—where was Josef?!

He glanced into the other corners of the dusty, cobwebbed barn, but Josef was gone. He looked outside the window again. No Josef. He ran to Anna and shook her.

"Anna! Wake up!"

Anna slowly awoke, rubbing her eyes. Disoriented, she had momentarily imagined she was home in her own bed, and was disappointed to awaken and find that despite her dreams, the daylight brought no change in her circumstances.

"He's gone. I told you he couldn't be trusted," raved Daniel bitterly.

"Maybe there's an explanation," said Anna, trying to be generous. Josef had been so nice to her, so considerate. "We'll ask around town and find out where his family lives."

They brushed off the straw that had clung to their clothes. Anna gathered up her books and she and Daniel slipped stealthily out of the barn, leaving the only evidence of their stay, a daffodil, lonely and wilting on the hay where Anna had slept.

Outside Daniel continued his indictment, "Why didn't he just leave us in Prague instead of dragging us to this godforsaken town? It's obvious he planned to lose us all along."

Compared to Prague, Zabreh was not much. In fact, compared to almost anywhere, Zabreh was not much. If not for the very few motorcars (mostly belonging to German invasionary troops), one could have as easily been in the medieval Bohemia of 1339 as in 1939.

The heady scent of the bakery drew them irresistibly to the display window. It was filled with all manner of fresh items the baker had been creating since well before sunrise. Anna and Daniel stared at the mouth-watering display, their noses greedily inhaling the heavenly odors.

Unfortunately, they had no money. Their stomachs contracting in pain, they entered the bakery and asked how they might get to the Czernys. The baker vigorously shook his head no, that he did not know of the Czernys' home. The children must have radiated hunger, though, for without a word, he handed them each a poppy seed kolachy.

Out on the street, they gobbled up the pastries. As kolachys went, they were not quite on a par with Vlasta's, but to Anna and Daniel they were ambrosia. It barely took the edge off their hunger, yet gave them a small surge of energy. They asked four more townspeople, who all indicated no knowledge of the Czernys. The fifth person, however, was the lucky charm and gave them directions. As they began their hike to the Czerny estate, Anna and Daniel both wondered how in a town so small it would be so difficult to find someone who knew Josef's family.

Once outside Zabreh they walked several miles along a quiet country road. The road consisted of three dirt ruts, two on the outside for wagon wheels and one down the middle for horses. On both sides of the road, the fields, still a week or two away from the planting of hops, cabbage, or sugar beets, appeared exhausted and untended. Oddly, they passed no one. At that time of day they should be seeing any number of carts driven by peasant farmers, bringing their early spring produce and livestock into Zabreh for sale or barter.

Daniel had a growing feeling that something was amiss. Josef's letters spoke of vast holdings. These were only small, run-down subsistence farms, with few signs of life about them. With each crest of a hill or bend in the road, he expected the landscape to change from hovels to castles, but it did not. It was like a ghost town, only there wasn't even a town; a ghost countryside. There was a stillness and silence like that which precedes a colossal thunderstorm. Yet the clouds, while as thick and opaque as a down blanket, were not the least bit threatening.

At last, they came to a small farmhouse, which, according to the directions, should have been the Czerny estate. Estate? Even by local standards, this farmstead was small, decrepit, and seriously neglected. The townsperson's directions had been quite brief, though, and perhaps they had missed some critical turn.

Daniel stared, uncomprehending. "This can't be right," he said.

"We must have taken the wrong road at the edge of town. I'll knock and ask for directions," suggested Anna.

He shrugged and followed her up the walk. There was an unearthly quiet all about. It gave Daniel a creepy feeling, as if there were spiders crawling on his neck. The most impoverished of farms usually have some life about them—at the very least, feral cats to feast on the burgeoning rodent population. Even the birds seemed to avoid this desolate place.

As they drew closer, they noticed that some of the windows were smashed. Obviously, the house had been abandoned, but Anna knocked anyway. There was no answer. Since the door was ajar, she hesitantly pushed it open. They peered inside, and then silently entered.

It looked as though a tornado had passed through. Every piece of furniture was upturned and broken, dishes smashed, cushions strewn. Whoever had ransacked the house had been as willfully destructive as possible. Little was worth salvaging.

Anna walked over to a shelf under a window that had been knocked down, leaving its contents in a pile on the floor. She found a framed photograph, the glass broken in ragged shards. Handling it carefully so as not to cut herself, she held it up to the light. It was a family photograph.

When Daniel heard Anna gasp, he rushed to her side and looked over her shoulder at the photograph. There was Josef, a few years younger, smiling mischievously, his arms around the neck of a lolly-tongued, adoring dog of indeterminate ancestry. With him were an older brother, three sisters, and his parents. Everyone looked very stern and serious except Josef, the dog, and the youngest sister.

Anna set the picture down on a table, the only unbroken object in the house. They said nothing. A cold wind swept through the front door and out the back, which was also open. Anna followed the wind out. Daniel trailed behind. Outside they saw a figure, sitting on the ground, his back to the house. Anna and Daniel proceeded a few more steps. It was Josef. He didn't acknowledge their presence, or utter a word.

There was something on the ground in front of him. He was staring at it as if gripped in a hypnotic state. As they moved closer, they realized what he couldn't take his eyes off of; the badly decomposed remains of a dog.

"This was Misha," Josef began slowly. "She was mine. Probably starved or froze."

Anna and Daniel noticed with horror the chain attached to the dog's collar. "They didn't even have time to let her loose," said Josef, as if in a trance.

It was evident that the same juggernaut that had shattered their lives had wreaked havoc on Josef's. Daniel felt a stirring of compassion for Josef. The smaller boy reached out and offered his hand to Josef in a gesture of solidarity. Inexplicably, Josef turned his head away and angrily blurted out, "Leave me alone!"

Stung, Daniel stalked away. Anna knew what Josef was feeling. He needed to be left alone. As an injured animal often snaps at a human attempting to help it, Josef had instinctively responded in the same way to Daniel. Rather than try to placate either boy with words, she turned and walked back into the house.

She picked up the photo again. Tears slowly welled in her eyes, then overflowed down her cheeks. The adventure of hopping the freight and sleeping in a stable had almost made her forget why they were on the run. They were hunted. Josef had held out hope of a safe haven, a happy ending. Now it was apparent that he was among the hunted, too. She at least had Daniel; for Josef, not even his dog had been spared.

Daniel's spirit rebelled at the imposition of yet more pain. He had enough of his own; his sympathy turned to anger for Josef's charade of a life, for bringing them to this miserable dunghill of a farm.

He followed Anna into the house and vented his spleen. "Now we're really in trouble! It's even worse than I ever imagined! His whole life is a lie. And he's dragged us down with him."

Anna's eyes betrayed her anger and shame that her brother could be so callous. "Don't you have an ounce of compassion?" she erupted.

"He doesn't deserve compassion! You saw it. I offered to help and he turned on me like a cobra!"

"Who knows what happened to his family?! Don't you see? Now he needs our help."

"We can't help ourselves, Anna. We've come here to the edge of nowhere and now we're supposed to help him?"

"I'm sure he expected that we'd all find help. Not an empty house and a dead dog."

"Oh sure, he meant well, so that makes everything all right," retorted Daniel.

She didn't reply. Instead, she whirled about and started back outside. Daniel grabbed her arm.

"Fine. You go ahead and help him. But first he's going to do some explaining. I want to know why he lied."

Anna angrily flung off his hand and marched outside. Josef remained where they had left him, seated on the ground, not moving, staring blankly, like a zombie. Cautiously Anna went to his side.

"We'll help you ..." she began.

Josef slowly raised his head and looked into her eyes. "Help me what?" he asked, confused.

"We want to help you find out what happened to your family."

"I know what happened. They're all dead," he replied dully.

"How do you know that?" insisted Anna.

Josef just sat, staring yet unseeing. "I know."

"We'll go into town and find out," said Anna resolutely. Daniel glared at her, as if to remind her they first had some questions that needed answers. She sighed, and began very gently.

"Before we do, can you please tell us one thing? We came a long way with you. Didn't you know something was wrong?"

Josef remained silent.

Daniel stepped in as diplomatically as possible, considering his anger and wounded pride. "No one's been here for months. How could you not know?"

A good minute passed. Finally Josef responded, his voice barely audible. "I didn't know for sure. I had a bad feeling... that's why I wanted you to come with me. I guess, I didn't want to face it alone."

"What about all those letters?! The hundreds of servants? Prince of Bohemia?! Nothing like this was ever mentioned!"

The emotional outburst finally elicited a response. Josef turned and looked up at them defiantly. "*I* wrote them."

"*You* wrote them?" repeated Daniel, perplexed.

Josef sadly shook his head, then spoke in a voice so full of emotion and bitterness, he could barely control it. "How would you like to be the poorest kid at a rich kid's school?! The only one whose parents never wrote, never visited?! The only one whose dog starved to death?!"

Now Daniel realized that Josef's hectoring and harassment was all part of the disguise, the role Josef felt he had to play to make it at St. Jude's. It all made sense. All the suspicion and anger he had borne toward Josef slowly began to wash away like a sand castle beneath the incoming tide.

Daniel himself had been an outsider, the only Jew at St. Jude's. Yet he had a family who visited him weekly, wrote numerous letters, sent presents, and cared about him. In short, his family loved him. Without that, Daniel felt certain he never would have survived.

But Josef had nothing. To come from such a grindingly poor life as this, from a family who apparently didn't care enough to write—Daniel had trouble even imagining what a burden that would be to bear. No wonder Josef had created such an extravagant fantasy life for himself. Reality had been more cruel than a Siberian winter.

Anna knelt down and spoke softly, "Come on, Josef. Let's go."

Together, Anna and Daniel helped him to his feet and started him walking on the long trek back to town.

11

New Resolve

They did not speak a word on the walk back into Zabreh. No words would have been adequate, nor were they really necessary. One thing became evident, however; the closer they got to town, the more determined Josef became to discover what had befallen his family.

When they reached the center of Zabreh, they spotted a grocer outside his store on a ladder. He was painting over a sign that had said "Rosenbaum's Market."

Josef called, "Have you heard of the Czerny family, sir?"

The grocer shook his head in the negative far more violently than the innocuous inquiry warranted. "Never heard of them. I have no idea who you mean. Czerny, you say? No idea."

The shifting of his eyes, emphatic denials, and eagerness to dismiss the whole subject led the three to believe that he knew something about the Czernys. Nonetheless, they nodded their heads, thanked him, and moved along as quickly as possible.

Anna and Daniel remarked on their difficulties finding someone who knew the Czerny family and could give them directions.

Josef was thoroughly perplexed. "That's unbelievable. Everyone in town knew my parents ..."

They passed a boarded-up café. Josef remarked that the last time he had been home the café was open and thriving, a gathering place for all the locals. They peeked inside, hoping against hope to see some morsel of food that the rats might have overlooked. Of course, there was nothing but filth and disarray.

A few doors down from the café was a beauty parlor. It did a respectable business lacquering fingernails, permanent-waving hair, helping the local ladies do whatever was necessary to turn them into Greta Garbos or Marlene Dietrichs. A lost cause, but a reasonably lucrative one for the salon. Anna observed that the beauty parlor was always the best place for news, rumors, and gossip, and thus they might learn something inside.

The establishment was small, occupying the front portion of a one-story building. They stepped into a tiny waiting area not much larger than a closet; it was furnished with two threadbare pieces of overstuffed furniture, and a coffee table scattered with movie magazines. Clark Gable's face appeared life-size on one, Rita Hayworth's sultry gaze beckoned from another. The ashtrays were filled to overflowing, and the potted plants on the windowsill were dingy with dust.

The poor housekeeping did not extend to the business end of the salon. They passed through an arched doorway into a small room lined with mirrors on one wall where two young ladies waved hair and a third did manicures. Whether it was highly competitive prices (and correspondingly low wages for the help) or the Zabreh women's egos, or both, this establishment appeared to be thriving. Beauticians and customers alike all chattered at once, creating a happy din.

On the wall above the counter containing stocks of lipsticks and night creams were certificates from a Munich beauty school for Olma von Shutzbar, apparently the owner. There were a number of photographs bearing only a passing resemblance to the woman who stood before them in a pink smock embroidered with the name "Olma." She was much plumper than she was in her earlier photographs. Her skin was as white as veal, her naturally rosy cheeks further heightened by cherry red rouge and punctuated by unnaturally kohl-ringed eyes. A cigarette dangled from her lips, smoke encircling her face like some hideous vapor treatment meant to enhance youthfulness or some such nonsense. Her appearance was almost cartoon-like, a grotesque exaggeration of Hollywood starlets, as if she were a living, breathing, overweight Betty Boop. Despite the somewhat frightening first impression, she had a friendly, gap-toothed smile, and greeted the three warmly.

"Hello, children. What can I do for you?"

Josef removed his family's photo from his shirt and showed it to her. "Do you know Marie Czerny?" he asked, indicating his mother.

She looked at the picture intently. "Hmm. Marie Czerny. Yes, I've heard of her ..."

"I'm her son," said Josef hopefully.

A serious look crossed Olma's face like a dark cloud on a sunny day. "Last fall when the Germans invaded the Sudetenland, there was some trouble," she said in a low voice. "A railroad bridge just outside of town was blown up. I'm just repeating what most of the townspeople think; a day later a pro-Nazi group from nearby, went on a rampage, rounding up the people along with their families that they suspected were

involved or else that they just didn't like. We don't know what happened
... they may have been shipped to labor camps in Germany or ..."

The unsaid implications of the "or" weighed like lead.

"Do you think my family might be one of them?" pressed Josef
with quiet determination.

Olma avoided the issue entirely. Referring to Anna and Daniel,
she asked, "These your friends?"

He nodded yes. She looked the three of them up and down; by
now their flight had left them somewhat worse for wear. She asked, "You
hungry? Maybe you'd like some bread and cheese?"

This offer seemed almost too good to be true, and it so surprised
them they were speechless. Their eyes, however, lit up like stars on a clear
night, prompting Olma to clap her hands together. "Well, that answers that
question! Go in the back and I'll be right with you."

Olma's living quarters were located in the rear of the building,
separated from the salon by a beaded curtain in the doorway. The three
walked into Olma's small, old-fashioned kitchen and sat down at her table.
Josef noticed Daniel's itching, which had not abated one bit.

"What's wrong with you?" he demanded. "You're scratching
yourself like some monkey at the zoo!"

Striving to maintain some semblance of dignity, Daniel staunchly
refused to answer.

"I bet you've got lice," stated Josef matter-of-factly.

"Sounds like you've had experience with such disgusting things,"
Daniel volleyed.

"Enough to know I wouldn't want to be you if you've got them,"
he countered.

Daniel tried to ignore Josef's dire diagnosis, but the need to scratch was so extreme he couldn't stop himself. Josef gave him a supercilious, I-told-you-so look.

Since Josef seemed to be an expert, Daniel asked in a roundabout way, "Let's say someone thought they might have lice or something, but didn't know for sure. How could you tell?"

"You look," Josef said with disdain.

Self-conscious, giving Josef a sidelong glance, Daniel got up and walked over to a corner. With his back to Anna and Josef, he peered into his pants. "What do you look for?" he asked.

"Here, let me. I'll tell you," said Josef impatiently, starting toward him.

"Forget it!"

"Okay. It's no skin off my nose. We'll let Anna look."

"No!" Daniel responded in vehement dismay.

"Oh, come on," said Josef incredulously. "She's only your sister. It's not like she's a *real* girl."

Anna scowled, and Josef realized his faux pas. He smiled weakly and backpedaled. "I mean, to *you*, anyway."

Anna was not appeased. "If it's all the same to you, I want no part of it," she said firmly.

"Well, I guess that leaves me," said Josef.

"Look, I'll be fine," insisted Daniel.

"Oh, grow up. I've seen you a hundred times in the shower anyway—I won't laugh. I promise."

Begrudgingly, Daniel opened his pants. Josef peered inside— and burst out laughing. At that moment Olma walked in. Daniel was sure she thought they were a couple of perverts.

"What's going on?" she asked.

"He's swarming with lice or crabs or some disgusting bug!" Josef laughed mercilessly.

"Here, let me see," said Olma authoritatively.

"Sure, let's have the whole town come look at my crotch!" Daniel cried, outraged.

"That could be arranged," needled Josef.

"Come on," ordered Olma. "Let me see."

Much aggrieved, Daniel opened his pants again and this time Olma took a good look. "Yes, we got a problem," she said. "Out of those clothes. We need to give you a bath and wash those clothes in lye soap."

Daniel gave Josef a poisonous glare. This louse infestation was all Josef's fault. No decent person in Prague ever got lice. Oh, he had heard of such things, usually in horrified, whispered reports between Vlasta and his mother, concerning some acquaintance who had contracted them while staying in unsanitary hotels in barbaric places like France or Italy.

"Don't look at me like that!" objected Josef. "I don't have 'em and I didn't give 'em to you!"

Olma set a metal bathtub in the middle of the kitchen floor and filled it with hot water heated on her stove, a process that took over an hour. As they waited, she stuffed them full of canned peaches and cream, fresh bread and thick slices of local cheese. At last, when he stripped and immersed himself, Daniel told himself it could have been worse. The tub could have been out in the beauty salon. Or better yet, out in the street, for all the citizens of Zabreh to witness his delousing!

While Daniel scrubbed himself in the bath, Olma washed out his clothes in the sink. They described to her the events that had brought them to her doorstep. Olma expressed disgust, dismay, and sympathy for their plight, but not shock. In the short tenure of the Nazis, she said, it had already happened repeatedly to friends and acquaintances.

Once Daniel was clean, he wrapped himself in a blanket. Well fed, warm in the cozy kitchen, he felt comfortable for the first time in days.

Olma noticed Anna's books. "Why'd you bring those along?"

"They're all I've got left," Anna replied.

Olma revealed, "I lost everything once. In 1934 I left Munich and came here. I'm German. I'm one of the nationals Hitler is supposedly protecting here in Czechoslovakia. Do I look like I need protection?"

Olma definitely struck the young refugees as one lady who could take care of herself.

"Why did you come here?" Anna asked.

"To escape Hitler. My husband was a Communist." She gazed out her window at the alley. "It was a warm spring night. May twelfth. We owned a tiny house, but we had lilacs, at least a dozen bushes. We didn't have a lot of money, and froze every winter, but the lilacs in May made it worthwhile.

"It was after dark. Karl was late. Dinner was already cold. I was getting worried. Then I heard a knock on our front door. I opened it and found my husband lying on our steps. His body looked like a sack of potatoes. The Nazis had beaten him to death ..." She began to choke back tears.

Her three guests could not respond. While they felt less alone knowing that they were far from being the Nazis' only victims, it also made them feel all the more hopeless.

She continued after some success in fighting back her emotions. "First the Nazis went after the Communists. Now it's the Jews. The Catholics are next, just you watch. By the time they're done there'll be no one left but them. It's sad to think that a great country like Germany could sink to making him their leader."

She regained her composure and changed the subject. "Your clothes should be dry by morning." She held out some folded papers and a spent bullet casing. "I found this in your shirt pocket."

Daniel said nothing, but Olma's eyes wouldn't let go of him. Of the bullet he finally admitted, "It reminds me of my father."

She shook her head in disagreement. "It reminds you of your father's killers. Don't let hate rule you. You can fight them and overcome them, but if you let hatred infect you, they've already won." Aware that her words probably had little effect, she handed the shell back to Daniel. "You should try to move on as soon as you can. Jews aren't safe here. And as for you," she said, turning to Josef, "if word gets out you're back in Zabreh, the Nazis will probably round you up, too."

"Where can we go?" Daniel asked.

"I don't know," she replied. "Bratislava isn't safe either, but it's a much bigger city, so it's easier to hide. You might find help there."

"I have an uncle in Bratislava," offered Josef. "And he's rich!"

Daniel rolled his eyes in disbelief. "Yeah, and you had a wealthy family in Zabreh, too," he said skeptically.

"No, I really do," Josef insisted. "He's pretty well off, anyway."

Daniel nodded dubiously.

Olma placed a stack of bedding on the table. "You kids sleep on it," she advised. "You can decide in the morning."

"Thanks, Olma," said Anna. "Thanks for everything."

Josef and Daniel added their thanks to hers, and bid Olma goodnight. As soon as they heard her shut the door to her bedroom, Daniel began mimicking Josef in a most dramatic fashion. "I have a rich uncle in Bratislava!"

"I do! Cross my heart!" Josef insisted.

"I do!" Daniel parroted, "Cross my heart!"

"Stop it, you two!" cried Anna, sick of their petty bickering in light of their tenuous situation.

Daniel had to have the last word, so he summoned as much disgust as he could muster and uttered, "Donkey Boy."

"Shut up ..." was Josef's dismissive response.

"Shut up, both of you!" Anna demanded. "What is this 'Donkey Boy' business, anyway?"

Daniel looked at Josef and they both burst out laughing.

"Well, what is it?" she insisted. "Tell me!"

Ignoring her demand, Josef started to make up his bed on the floor. Then he reconsidered. "You tell. She's your sister."

"You're the Donkey Boy, you tell!" Daniel sputtered before tucking himself under his blanket. Josef turned away, pretending to be asleep.

Anna was fed up with their game. "All right. I don't care. I don't want to know. It's probably too childish and trivial for words."

She closed her eyes and feigned sleep.

Daniel goaded Josef in a loud whisper. "Go on, Donkey Boy. Tell."

"I said I don't want to know," insisted Anna firmly, by now dying to know, regardless of how childish and trivial it might be.

Josef lay there silently, refusing to budge an inch, knowing full well Daniel was bursting to reveal the great secret. At last Daniel said teasingly, "Okay. It means he has something big, like a donkey's, and it's not his ears."

"Oh, his nose!" Anna laughed.

"My nose?!" cried Josef, offended. "I don't have a big nose!"

"No, it's not his nose," countered Daniel. It slowly dawned on Anna exactly what part of a donkey's anatomy they referred to. Josef began to shake with suppressed giggles, and Daniel joined in the merriment.

"I should have known!" she cried. "Boys are so disgusting!"

This only increased their prurient chortling. Anna vehemently fluffed her pillow and closed her eyes tightly, determined to go to sleep. But after a while Daniel noticed her eyes open slightly, studying the back of Josef's head. When suddenly Josef turned toward her, she quickly closed them but not before, for the briefest moment, they caught each other's glance.

None of this made any sense to Daniel, or maybe it did, but he decided it wasn't worth contemplating.

In the morning Olma baked them fresh bread. It was hot and delicious, their enjoyment tempered only by the fear it would be the last good meal they would have for some time.

Over breakfast they argued about the best course of action. As Daniel talked with his mouth full, Josef imitated him in the most offensive manner, spraying crumbs.

But whom did Anna chastise? "Daniel, don't talk with· your mouth full!"

He finished chewing and set forth his proposition in a more mannerly fashion. "I say we go to our aunt's in the Ukraine."

"The Ukraine?" said Josef incredulously. "That's in the Soviet Union! Even if we could get past the borders, it would take a week. Besides, have you heard the stories about life there under Stalin? Mass executions, starvation. You'd have to be crazy to go there."

"It does seem awfully far," added Anna.

This business of Anna siding with Josef at every opportunity was now more than annoying; it was thoroughly out of control, Daniel thought morosely. "No one said this would be easy!" he argued. "Anyway, I don't hear any better ideas."

"Sure you do," Josef reminded him. "My uncle in Bratislava."

"We've already learned not to rely on your relatives," said Daniel dismissively.

Rebuffed, Josef's voice grew cold and distant. "Fine. Do what you want; go wherever."

"How about this?" suggested Olma. "If you're going to go to the Ukraine, the only way is by rail. And the best place to catch a train heading east is in Bratislava."

"So we stick together until Bratislava," concluded Anna, relieved.

It seemed logical enough, although Daniel's mistrust of Josef was resurfacing with a vengeance. However, he agreed, and looked forward to telling Anna, "See, I told you so," when the uncle proved either to be nonexistent or a toothless beggar.

They decided that the best way to Bratislava would be upon the Morava River, which flowed southwest into the Danube just above Bratislava. The roads were too heavily patrolled by the Germans, who would be highly suspicious of three teenagers traveling on foot.

The only objection to this plan was, no boat. But Olma solved that shortcoming with her usual breezy efficiency. She led them down to the river's edge. There in the weeds was a flat-bottomed punt, about twelve feet long. Daniel and Josef flipped it over and placed it in the water, testing for leaks. It was riverworthy.

"Who does it belong to?" Anna asked.

"Who knows?" replied Olma carelessly. "Probably a fisherman in town. We're just 'borrowing' it."

"We've been borrowing a lot of things lately—train rides, trousers, now this," Anna pointed out.

Olma's Communist leanings became evident. "Think of it as socialism in action," she reasoned. "To each according to his needs. And you need this."

They thanked Olma, who had done so much for them in such a brief time. Even in their youth and inexperience, they felt that their brush with Olma was an encounter that had saved them.

As they pushed off into the river, she offered this advice. "You'll be safest traveling at night. Sleep during the day." Again, they thanked her.

"Good luck!" she cried as they pushed out into the current. "God be with you! And remember, Daniel—bugs are only attracted to the sweetest boys!"

Daniel blushed a deep rose red and once out of her earshot he grumbled, "Sweet. I hate being sweet!"

12

Helpless

Following Olma's advice, they beached the boat for the day in a reedy shore area overhung with willow trees just outside Zabreh. She had supplied them with blankets, but they were unnecessary as the three dozed in the warm, spring sunshine. After a time, however, Anna unfolded one and wrapped herself in it, only to throw it off a short time later as she fitfully slept.

When night fell, they began their journey in earnest. There was a slight chill in the air, so Anna and Daniel huddled under the blankets, but Josef appeared to be unaffected. He took off his shoes, rolled up his pant legs, and dangled his feet in the water as they drifted along.

"It's not that cold," he observed.

"I'm shivering," reported Anna. "You'll catch your death."

"Let him freeze his feet," advised Daniel. "If he keeps them in the river, we can't smell them."

Dark and silent the river flowed on carrying them downstream through the moonless night. "How long did Olma say it would take to reach Bratislava?" asked Josef.

"Three nights, at least," Daniel recalled.

"It doesn't seem like time exists here," observed Anna dreamily.

They found that the night wasn't so quiet after all, echoing with its own peculiar variety of sounds. Water lapped up against the boat and the shore, the wind blew softly through the trees, and occasionally they heard nocturnal wildlife crashing through underbrush along the shoreline or cattle lowing in the fields on the flood plain. They had to keep alert for the horns of larger boats, although night traffic on the upper Morava was sparse.

As the night wore on, the three grew bored. Even if there had been anything of interest along the river, it was too dark to see it.

While darkness surrounded them, inside the boat this night there was light. Despite all they had lost, these three refugees from the shadow of war still had too much hope to give up their fight. Josef asked, "Know any good jokes?"

Daniel shrugged. He could never think of a joke when he needed one, although he knew hundreds. Anna seemed uninterested, but Josef persisted.

"How do you leave Monte Carlo with a small fortune?" he asked.

Daniel had heard this one, but couldn't remember the punch line.

"Go in with a *large* fortune!" answered Josef, honking with laughter.

"Oh, that one's as old as the hills," said Daniel, unimpressed. However, it toppled the first domino. "What does every girl want?" he riddled.

"Please!" cried Anna, scandalized.

Egged on by her reaction, Daniel answered, "A rich man with a strong will—made out to *her*!"

While Josef roared, Anna didn't even crack a smile, determined to remain proper despite the low company.

"Okay, now for a sanity test," Josef proposed. "How do you save a drowning Nazi?"

Daniel had heard this one because it had circulated about the bunk room at St. Jude's, so he waited to see if Anna could figure it out. She eventually gave up and shook her head. "I have no idea."

"Good," replied Josef. "You're sane. If you know how to save a drowning Nazi, then you're nuts!"

Josef gave Daniel a top-that look, and the competition was on. Daniel's mind began to retrieve Nazi jokes. "Why do Nazis wear one-inch heels on their boots?" he asked, then answered their befuddled looks. "So their knuckles don't drag on the ground!"

"I thought I said *good* jokes," said Josef disparagingly.

Anna entered the fray. "What's the definition of 'mixed emotions?'" she challenged.

Josef and Daniel were stumped.

"Watching your brand-new Mercedes drive off a cliff and burst into flames—with Adolf Hitler inside!"

They all laughed so hard the boat wobbled, threatening to take on water. Josef asked, "What's the difference between a German woman and an elephant?"

"I don't know," said Daniel, playing the straight man.

"Fifty pounds and a gray dress!" he delivered.

Finding this hilarious, Daniel and Josef pounded the sides of the boat. Anna, however, was not amused.

"Come on, you guys," she chided. "Not all Germans are bad."

"Uh-oh, here comes a lecture," predicted Daniel.

"What do you mean, they're not all bad?!" Josef protested. "They invaded our country! They killed your father ... probably killed mine, too. For no good reason."

"Their government invaded," corrected Anna. "And the Nazis are doing the killing. That doesn't mean the average German supports them."

"But they voted for that government," Daniel pointed out.

"When Hitler got elected, only a third of Germany supported him. That leaves two-thirds who did not," Anna reminded them.

In an aside to Josef, Daniel whispered, "She likes being the smartest one around." Then he said in a louder voice, "Well, they're all stuck with him now."

"And we're stuck, too," Josef added ruefully.

"Still, you shouldn't blame a whole country for the faults of its leader and the minority who support him," she contested.

Daniel didn't like hearing this. Naturally, his hatred blazed hottest against the Nazi commander who had killed his father, but all Germans, by association, were also to blame. He wasn't about to temper his rage by making exceptions to his blanket recriminations. He could have argued with Anna; that by standing by and letting Hitler bulldoze the surrounding nations, by remaining silent when they should have been alerting the world to Hitler's crimes, by not doing whatever was necessary to subvert the Nazi's well-oiled machine, the German populace was just as guilty. But he didn't care to argue about it. Or think about it. It brought too many painful feelings roiling to the surface.

Josef seemed to feel the same way and pleaded, "Okay, okay, no more arguing. We won't solve anything with our opinions anyway."

By now the sun was rising and they looked for a place to hide the boat and sleep the day away. They found refuge under a rock bridge blackened with one hundred and thirty years of soot. They pulled the boat onto the dark gray silt at the river's edge beneath the bridge, with the Morava still licking the lower portion of the vessel. They stayed in the boat rather than stretch out on the ground and risk getting wet and even dirtier. Mid-afternoon they were awakened by a downpour, which they watched silently from the relative dryness of their cover under the bridge.

After the rain let up, the three travelers discovered that unused to their night-shift schedule and nearly frantic with hunger, they were unable to sleep. To pass the time, Anna offered to read from *Huckleberry Finn*. She turned to where she had left off, a lifetime ago (so it seemed) in Prague. Odd how she had dreamed of doing this very thing, although it was now proving to be a different river, and they faced different dangers from Huck and Jim's. Despite everything, she felt a strange inner peace that everything was going to work out, that hungry and uncomfortable as they were, as long as they remained on the river the Nazis could do them no harm. "'Chapter Six. Pap got to hanging around the widow's too much and so she told him ...'"

Josef objected, "Skip that part! I hate Pap Finn. He's just not believable, always drunk and beating Huck."

"What's so unbelievable about that?" Anna retorted. She knew for a fact that Vlasta had come to work for them in order to flee from a father who beat her regularly.

"Nobody acts like that," insisted Josef. "Besides, stories about slavery are so dated. That doesn't happen anymore."

Anna regarded him with wonder. "And what are the Nazis doing to us?"

Josef ignored her point and persisted in testy tones, choosing to alter his argument. "All right. But those Americans don't know how to talk! All that slang—who knows what they're saying."

Anna gave up on selling Huck Finn to this philistine. "Okay, I'll just read to myself," she said decisively.

"No, I want to hear," Daniel interjected. "Read the part where Jim can't trust Huck for turning him in," he said archly, giving Josef a self-satisfied look.

Josef didn't seem to care that Daniel still distrusted him, and the biting comment ran off him like water off a duck. Instead he shot back, "Read the part where Jim gets lice!"

Somehow Daniel missed that section when they read the book at St. Jude's. "Jim? Get lice?! Wait ... that never happens!" he realized indignantly.

"Sorry! Must've just made it up!" said Josef cavalierly. However, his remark elicited the desired response from Daniel, who quietly steamed.

"How about if I skip past the Pap Finn part," offered Anna. She paged forward and began reading. "'We judged that three nights more would fetch us to Cairo ...'"

Josef continued to critique. "Nobody talks like that! I can't understand half of this nonsense."

Anna turned and gave Josef a good punch in the arm, the same arm she had punched a few days before. Daniel suspected he might develop a permanent black and blue mark as a result.

"Oww!" Josef cried. "What'd you do that for?"

"Because I felt like it," she replied sadistically, and hauled off and punched him again, harder.

"Oww!" cried Josef. "Knock that off!"

"Then be polite and shut your mouth," she answered coolly.

Josef opened his mouth to protest, but Anna quickly made a fist whereupon, to his credit, only silence passed his lips. She resumed reading. "... at the bottom of Illinois, where the Ohio River comes in ..."

Now Daniel disturbed the reading by giggling helplessly at the plight of Josef, cowed by a girl as (supposedly) meek and sweet-tempered as his sister.

Through clenched teeth Josef responded, "*You* shut up," and waved a fist, but drew back when Anna looked at him reprovingly. She continued.

"'We would sell the raft and get on a steamboat and go way up the Ohio to the free states, and then be out of trouble.'"

It eased Daniel's mind to hear Huck speak of freedom, escape, a safe refuge. If Anna had her dreams, so had he. There was a time he had considered a career as a cowboy. His bicycle then became his horse and the Vltana the Rio Grande with thousands of imaginary cattle needing to be driven across it. But like his junk novel buried inside his science book, the seemingly practical and realistic boy kept these wild ideas safely to himself.

He also kept to himself how much it bothered him that despite their money, his family never traveled. Except for occasional weekend trips to the country, their entire world was circumscribed by the city limits of Prague.

Daniel had been born, however, with a wanderlust unknown to his father and mother, and he hoped one day to go to America and see the Mississippi himself. The largest river he had ever set eyes on was the

Danube, but he understood that the mighty Mississippi dwarfed it many times over. That was hard to imagine. He wanted to see cowboys and Buffalo Bill and the Statue of Liberty. But first they had to get to Bratislava.

Josef began yawning profusely and Anna stopped reading. Finally, all three dozed off again, but none slept well. Every time a cart or automobile rolled overhead, the bridge seemed to groan and rattle. Then the rain rallied with new fury, and although they were protected from the worst of it, occasionally gusts of wind reached them and the rain dampened the blankets.

Daniel awoke late in the afternoon and discovered that Josef and Anna were already up. He heard Josef urging her, "Please take my blanket. I'm not cold."

"You're sure you don't mind?" Anna asked wanly. "For some reason I have such a chill."

Even in the gloomy half-light beneath the bridge, Daniel could see that Anna didn't look well. Her eyes were glassy and ringed with dark shadows, and her skin had an unhealthy flush. He tried to chalk it up to exhaustion and hunger, yet could not quell his anxiety.

Noting their concern, she assured them, "I'm just tired. Hungry and tired. Once we get some sleep and a good meal, I'll be fine." She wrapped herself in Josef's blanket and leaned against the embankment.

"Do you want some water?" he asked.

She nodded yes. Josef picked up a coffee can they had found in the bottom of the boat, undoubtedly used by the former owner for bailing purposes. He rolled up his pant legs and waded out up to his knees, past the stagnant backwash to where the current ran clean, and scooped it full of water. Thus far they had drunk the river water with no ill effects, undoubtedly because it was swollen with fresh snow melt from the mountains and less polluted than at other times of the year.

She smiled, watching Josef as he brought the water to her. As she sipped, she cast her eyes down at his exposed legs and said with a shy grin, "You have nice legs."

Nice?! What a stupid thing to say, she thought. She immediately began to think of kicking herself. Muscular. That's what she should have said. You have muscular legs. But she'd already blown it.

On the other hand, Josef was astonished to receive such a compliment, even though it was a common occurrence in his daydreams and in the letters he wrote to himself. He looked down at his legs and his chest puffed out with pride. He didn't think she'd blown it. Obviously, Anna had made his day... possibly, his year.

"Thanks," he replied modestly. The three lay down again to catch a little more rest before darkness fell. Anna immediately went to sleep. But Josef continued to watch her, his eyes filled with concern and wonder.

13

Disaster

They had only been asleep for an hour when Daniel awoke to the sound of Anna muttering incoherently. He bolted upright and leaned over his sister. She had cast off her blankets. Her skin was ghostly pale and as clammy as uncooked meat.

He frantically shook Josef awake. Then Daniel put his wrist to her forehead. "She's burning up!" he whispered, his voice quaking.

"Put all the blankets on her," advised Josef. They tucked them tightly around her as she rambled in delirium. Josef gently tried to rouse her. Slowly, she regained consciousness.

"Anna, Anna," Josef soothed. "How do you feel?"

"My side hurts ... my throat ... dizzy," she replied, weak as a newborn calf.

"Where are we going to find a doctor?" asked Daniel in despair.

"We're in the middle of nowhere, we can't travel during the daylight."

"As soon as it's dark, we'll continue down river. We'll look for a doctor at the first town we come to," said Josef. For once, Daniel agreed wholeheartedly with his course of action.

As soon as the sun began to set, they carried Anna to the boat and made her as comfortable as possible, wrapping her firmly in the blankets. She continued to alternate between deep sleep and delirium, shivering and heavy perspiration. During the brief periods she was lucid, they tried to keep her hydrated with river water.

As they floated along, each bend in the river produced an agony of suspense and hope, followed by numbing disappointment when all they found in the shadowy darkness was more farmland or forest. By Daniel's watch it was 9:30, three hours later, before they saw the dim lights of a town.

The town was Kromeriz, a farming community much like Zabreh. They beached the boat on the outskirts and lay Anna down on some soft grass near the riverbank. Josef went into town and asked about for a doctor. He was told that the doctor was out of town but would be returning in the morning. There was nothing to do but sit and wait, and watch Anna grow steadily worse.

"I think we could use a prayer," Josef suggested, trying to be positive, and began, "Hail Mary, full of grace ..." but trailed off. "I wish I had more practice. I don't know what to say except Dear Lord, please make her better."

"I'm not so good at prayers either," sighed Daniel. "We never were very religious. We celebrated the holy days, but most other times we sort of took God for granted. Now that we need Him, I'm not sure how to get through. Or if He'd even listen."

Josef nodded. "With everything that's happened... I sometimes wonder if God remembers we exist."

Daniel replied vehemently, "Even if He's forgotten all of Europe, He knows Anna. He won't forget her."

Josef sighed bleakly, and brushed some sweat-soaked hair off the shivering girl's forehead. They could only hope.

The following morning Josef took Anna in his arms and they set out on the short trek into town. She was limp as a used rag, too weak to even ask where they were going and why.

They walked down the town's main street. A large Nazi flag hung from the town hall, which happened to be across from the doctor's office. This made them uneasy but no less determined to get help for Anna. When they entered the doctor's office a young nurse jumped to her feet, obviously alarmed by the intrusion of three strangers. She was nervous and wound as tight as a piano string.

"Who are you?" she snapped. "What do you want?"

Daniel stepped forward. "She's sick. She has a fever."

Staring down her sharp pointy little nose at these three vagrants, the nurse hesitated then said imperiously, "I'll get the doctor." As she left the room she glanced back, eyeing them suspiciously.

She soon returned with the doctor, a balding man in his mid-fifties. His skin was as white as flour and he was almost lifeless in his lack of animation; his only emotion appeared to be annoyance.

"What seems to be the problem here?" he asked.

"She's very sick, a fever," Daniel repeated.

"First of all," the doctor began, "who are you and where are you from?"

Daniel replied calmly, "I'm Daniel. This is my sister Anna." He purposely omitted their last names.

Josef added, "I'm Josef. We're from Zabreh. Can you help her?"

The doctor seemed more interested in interrogating them than healing. "Zabreh?" he inquired. "What are you doing here? So far away? Where are your parents?"

"What difference does it make?" answered Josef impatiently. "She's sick!"

Concentrating on Daniel and Anna, the doctor simply looked them over. Finally he said in a contemptuous voice, "You're Jewish. I'm prohibited by the new government from treating Jews. They're supposed to be treated by special doctors. You see, all the Jews in this area have been relocated to a camp outside Prague. For their own protection."

"She's not Jewish," insisted Josef. "She's my sister. He's Jewish. But she's not."

"But he said ..." contradicted the nurse.

Josef cut her off. "He was mistaken!"

The doctor looked them over disdainfully, and it was obvious he wasn't believing any of their story. "I'm sorry," he added coldly. "If it is discovered that I treated her, the Germans will arrest me and then this whole district will be without a doctor, and that would help no one. Surely you can understand my situation."

Their fierce, accusative glares indicated that they did not.

"Please help her," insisted Daniel, ignoring the man's cowardly rationalizations.

"I'm sorry," he said, seemingly at peace with his own heartlessness. "I have the entire community to consider."

Daniel's fury mounted, and he was determined not to let the good doctor off so easily. "What will the community think if you let her die?!"

"If I treat her and the Nazis find out, they may very well kill me and my entire family!" shouted the doctor. "And they won't give a damn about the community. I'm sorry," he concluded brusquely. "I can't help you."

They turned to leave, but in anger and frustration, Daniel struck out at a tray containing a variety of instruments and a jar of alcohol. The tray flipped over, and the nurse shrieked as the jar smashed on the floor, filling the room with astringent fumes. The instruments flew in all directions. A thermometer shattered and spilled beads of mercury across the grimy floor; a hypodermic needle broke off rendering it useless. As the children dashed out, they heard the doctor order, "Summon the authorities!"

Once out on the street they fled as fast as they could with Anna, as inert as a lump of clay, cradled in Josef's arms. He panted, "What did you do that for?"

"Because the coward deserved it!"

"Now they'll call the SS and have them down on us!"

"We'll push on to Bratislava," Daniel countered, ignoring the possibility raised by Josef. "We'll surely find a doctor there."

Troubled, Josef reminded his usually practical companion, "That means traveling in daylight."

"We have no choice," said Daniel. "She may die if we don't."

"But we'll be seen! The SS is probably already on the lookout for us."

"All the more reason to get away from here!"

They arrived back at their landing site completely out of breath but safely, and they lay Anna down on the floor of the boat. She was still unconscious when they hurriedly pushed off into the river's current.

Daniel steered the boat while Josef attended to Anna. As she moaned in delirium, he tried to cool her forehead with a cloth dipped in river water. He kept assuring her, "We'll make it. Don't worry. We'll get help soon." While he seemed to be addressing her, it was clear he was trying to bolster his own spirits and, in some unexplainable way, notify God of their plight.

They felt naked and exposed out on the river in the bright sunshine. They imagined Nazis behind every bush that trembled in the breeze, suspected snipers in every tall tree. They were sure that each passing peasant was a Gestapo informer (although they saw few such people — the countryside seemed to have been depopulated).

Near midday they approached a bridge. Even at night they were suspicious of bridges because sometimes a Nazi soldier or two would be posted near the structure to prevent sabotage. They had no wish to test these soldiers' unpredictable moods and reactions. If they happened to be in a trigger-happy frame of mind, what was it to them if they practiced a little sharpshooting on couple of hapless boys in a boat?

This bridge in particular caused their chests to tighten with anxiety. As they approached, Daniel saw a German soldier hunkered down alongside one of the abutments. The Nazi spotted them about the same time. He immediately stood up and took aim with his rifle.

Since the river was wide and slow at this point, the soldier had ample time to line up his targets. Even a poor marksman could easily pick off both Daniel and Josef. The soldier had them in his gun sight.

Then Josef did the most astonishing thing. He stood up in the boat, saluted the Nazi, and shouted with fervor, "Heil Hitler!" He then quietly but forcefully urged Daniel, "Do it!"

Daniel was afraid if he stood up he would capsize the boat, and he could not bring himself to say those words. He would rather have taken a bullet. He did, however, manage a passable Nazi salute.

Agonizing seconds ticked by as they waited for the soldier's response. Finally, after what seemed like an eternity, the soldier lowered his rifle and lackadaisically returned their salute with a mild, bored "Heil Hitler!"

They passed under the bridge and floated out of range. Daniel felt befouled, and he was consumed with guilt for having given the salute. Apparently, Josef felt no better. He said grimly, "I only did it for Anna."

They had little time to brood upon the bridge incident, for Anna's moans became louder and more desperate by mid-afternoon. Then the moans became shrieks, carrying across the water like cries they had heard in the night of rabbits being torn apart by foxes.

"She's getting worse!" said Daniel frantically. "We have to stop at the next town and find another doctor."

"I'll go alone this time, so they won't think she's a Jew," Josef said.

"What will you say when they ask where your parents are?"

"I'll think of something," replied Josef, although he had no idea. Daniel was sure he would, however. Perhaps his questionable knack for prevarication could be put to good use in their situation.

As Daniel watched the careful way Josef ministered to his sister—giving her small sips of water between bouts of moaning, keeping the wet cloth on her head—his feelings toward Josef began to be altered. He had been so certain before that Josef had no redeeming character traits whatsoever. Hard as it was to admit, perhaps Daniel had misjudged his nemesis. Perhaps he wasn't a nemesis at all.

Now that they urgently needed to get to a town, none appeared.

Only farms and woodlands for another three agonizing hours. Around 6:00 p.m. they saw the buildings of the small town of Hodonín.

The sun was setting when they beached the boat. Josef again gathered Anna in his arms and struggled up the riverbank. Daniel waited anxiously behind. His arms and hands clasped white-knuckled around his knees, he was too wrung out with tension and worry to do anything more than just sit and stare at the brown water.

Panting from the exertion of carrying Anna's eighty-five pounds, Josef returned only fifteen minutes later. "Get back in the boat," he gasped.

"What happened? Are they after you?" asked Daniel, as they once again shoved off.

Josef shook his head. "I asked one of the men in town where the doctor was. He said the doctor was Jewish and the Nazis sent him to Germany to do special work for them there. Now, if someone gets sick in Hodonín, they have two choices—a veterinarian in Breclav, or if they're really sick, a human doctor in Bratislava."

"Where's Breclav?" asked Daniel.

"Sixteen miles west. We'd have to walk and the roads are probably patrolled by the SS. Bratislava is forty-five miles downstream. At the rate we're going, we could be there before dawn."

By now the sun had set, and Anna's frenzied moans diminished, then stopped. This appeared to be a good sign, and it allowed Daniel to get some sleep while Josef took over the chore of navigation. A few hours later he awoke to the sound of Anna speaking coherently.

"Josef, where are we?" she asked.

"We just joined up with the Danube so we're not far from Bratislava," he said softly. "We're taking you to a doctor."

Anna managed a slight smile, unseen in the darkness. "Why?

This fever?" she said dismissively. "Don't worry. I'll be fine."

Daniel felt such relief he nearly wept with joy. "How do you feel?" he asked.

"Fine. Really. A little tired but I'll be fine. It's the two of you I'm worried about."

Josef, who had placed his hand on her forehead, felt no such relief. Clearly, the fever had not abated. He gripped her hand tightly. With great effort she addressed them.

"Take care—both of you. You need each other more than you know. And never give up. Your freedom is too important. Promise me?"

Daniel had no idea what she was talking about and feared she was lapsing back into delirium. He tried to reassure her, "Anna, we're almost to Bratislava. We're going to find a doctor for you and you'll get better."

"Promise!" she repeated, ignoring her brother's entreaties.

"I promise," said Josef quietly.

"She's out of her head again!" panicked Daniel. "Where's the wet cloth?!"

Anna closed her eyes and was quiet. Josef knew she had left them, but he leaned down and placed his cheek close to her nostrils to be sure. The fevered exhalations had ceased. Her journey had ended.

"Where's the stupid wet cloth?!" demanded Daniel, denying the truth.

Josef just stared sadly at Anna's pale, lifeless body.

Frantically, Daniel held up her limp wrist and tried to get a pulse. Finding none, he checked the carotid artery on her neck. Still, he refused to believe it.

"She's not dead! She can't be! She was just talking to us! We're almost to Bratislava!"

Josef ignored him and gazed across the water. Indeed, the lights of the city lay before them a few miles down river. Against the gradually lightening sky was the silhouette of the Austrian royal family's enormous castle; the unmistakable sentinel to all travelers on the Danube that Bratislava lay ahead.

Both Josef and Daniel had forgotten the original reason they had traveled to the city—to somehow find a passage to freedom. It had instead become a race against death to find a doctor for Anna. Yet she remembered; in her dying moments she had kept her perspective.

Freedom now meant nothing to Daniel with the realization that his sister was dead. A crushing weight of grief dropped like an anvil upon his shoulders, a debilitating sadness unlike any he had ever known.

He was able to detach himself from his father's murder. All he had seen were some bloodstains on the cobblestones, a spent bullet casing, and Anna's report. Perhaps at some level he believed she had made a horrible mistake, that the man she had seen shot only resembled their father from afar. But this was no mistake. Anna had died practically in his arms, while he leaned over to hear her last words. As heavy as the grief was, his sense of helplessness seemed to weigh even more. There had been nothing he could do to save her. As they drew nearer to Bratislava, the city lights seemed to reproach him. So close ... so close ...

By now the rising sun was driving out the night. Neither boy spoke, yet each seemed to know his role in doing what little they could for Anna. A decent burial was in order. They pulled the boat ashore near a grove of burr oak trees. Josef left to find (or more likely, steal) shovels to dig the grave.

Now alone with Anna, Daniel carefully combed her hair with his fingers and wrapped the blankets around her as a shroud. Then a dam broke inside him and he began to cry. Tears flowed and harsh sobs racked his body—for Anna, for his father, for the unknown fates of Jacob and his mother. And for himself. He cried out to God, "Why? Why?" What horrible deed had he committed to bring God's wrath down on him so completely? He felt as though he had been personally singled out for persecution and wondered what possibly could be next. Maybe God would kill *him* next. Perhaps death was preferable.

This thought particularly frightened him and made the tears gush forth even harder. How could Anna accept her death with such equanimity? He wasn't ready to die. He wanted to live, to be free.

By now, his sleeves were damp to the elbows with his tears. As the strength of his will to survive became self-evident, he realized how ridiculous and hysterical his thinking had become.

He glanced up. Almost appearing out of nowhere, Josef was standing next to him holding two shovels. Daniel was somewhat embarrassed by his tears until he looked at Josef and saw his puffy, reddened eyes. Neither one mentioned the other's state.

Somehow Josef had "found" some bread and they split it between them. Under normal circumstances they would have thought it delicious, but that morning it was like sawdust in their mouths. They chewed mechanically, more out of duty to their bodies' need for fuel than any desire for sustenance.

After finishing their meal, they rose wordlessly and began to dig. They selected a spot sheltered by tall oaks on a knoll above the river. The surrounding grass was cropped close to the ground; evidence of sheep. Daniel reflected that Anna would have been pleased with this spot, with its pleasant view of the Danube and gamboling spring lambs for company.

The ground was hard and they encountered roots, so the task took nearly the entire day. Neither spoke a word. Although the weather was pleasantly cool, they worked up a heavy sweat and needed frequent rests, for one loaf of bread after their long fast was not nearly enough to fill two growing fourteen year-olds.

At one point Daniel stopped digging and felt an extraordinary rage building inside of him. It was God's fault. He realized he hated God. In anger he took a shovelful of dirt and heaved it. He hated Him for taking Anna. He took another shovelful. He hated Him for taking his father. And another shovelful. Hated Him for Hitler. He took a savage shovelful. Hated Him for the Germans. Hated Him for this whole damn disaster. But he caught himself and leaned on his shovel. It wasn't God who had done these things; these were acts of *men*. Even Anna's death, despite his best rationalizations, could have been prevented had the right person done the right thing. Daniel realized it was hard to hate humanity, though, especially when you're part of it. It's much easier and more convenient to hate God. Yet despite such ease and convenience, Daniel's heart wasn't in it. His rage dissipated like a balloon whose end is untied. For even if a bolt from heaven had killed his father, not some twisted men, it would have been impossible for Daniel to blame God, at least not for very long. The truth, while hard, was too real, too palpable. Like the sun in the sky, the truth was impossible to ignore.

Daniel's thoughts turned to possible causes for Anna's death. Pneumonia? Scarlet fever? Something in the river water? Why she caught it—why he and Josef didn't? Deep down he knew that even if they had found a doctor, it was doubtful he could have done anything to save her life.

Nonetheless, Daniel's conscience haunted him and he heaped

blame upon himself. It didn't help her to be lying in the bottom of a boat floating down the Morava River on cold spring nights. Or going hungry. But what else could they have done? He looked at his watch. A week ago at this time she would have been having some cookies and tea with Mother, Jacob and Vlasta in the warm, tidy kitchen of their home. He would have been on the football field, playing on Josef's team and despising him as an arrogant boor. He couldn't help thinking his former life was irretrievably lost, henceforth to exist only in his memory.

By the time they finished digging, little daylight remained. They decided to wait until morning to inter Anna in her makeshift grave, for they were utterly exhausted and wanted to give her proper honor. Yet they were unable to sleep. Their bodies were sore, their muscles trembled from exertion, but their eyes remained wide open.

They lay on the ground and stared up at the millions of stars in the heavens. Daniel was still haunted by the question "Why Anna?" She had all the talent, at music, in school, and people liked her. She had so much more to offer the world than me, he thought. Large tears welled up in Daniel's eyes as he thumbed through Anna's piano books.

"From now on, every time I hear a piano I'll think of Anna. She was always practicing. Always memorizing some piece. Trying to get it perfect." He had been going over Anna's life, first in his mind and now out loud to Josef. Her piano playing, her dolls, how she used to punch his arm with her fist clenched but the knuckle of her middle finger protruding and what a nasty bruise this produced. Her smile, her dancing eyes, her tears when she was eleven and Father refused to get her a puppy.

He went over and over his stockpile of memories until there was simply no point anymore. He swore he would never forget; never. But she had already drifted away and there was nothing he could do about it.

Perhaps that is what hurt most; the powerlessness, the utter powerlessness that he felt at this moment, in the face of death and a cruel, arbitrary world.

"What is to become of me?" he silently asked the equally silent river.

Then, interrupting this quiet, Josef began.

"I liked her from the first time I saw her. That morning in the bunk room at St. Jude's. How long ago was it? I don't even know what day it is... I know she was scared, but she tried not to show it. She was so brave."

In the moonlight he stood up and went to the riverside to look for rocks. He found a good skipping stone and hurled it across the placid river's surface. With awe and envy at his graceful skill, Daniel watched it skip.

"And I'll never forget the way she punched me," Josef added. "My arm will never forget it too."

"Why?" asked Daniel. It seemed like such a silly thing for them both to remember.

"It showed me she wasn't afraid."

Daniel nodded. She was not a rebel, nor was she foolhardy, but neither was there a cowardly bone in her body. She drew back at nothing, from hopping a freight to punching a much larger boy in the arm. Hard.

After a long time, Josef added, "And she liked my legs ..."

Daniel gaped at him in disbelief that he could display such self-absorption at a time like this. "You are so conceited!"

"No girl ever liked anything about me. But she did."

"You're kidding!" said Daniel in even greater incredulity. Even though he knew the girlfriends in Josef's letters were imaginary, he still found this revelation surprising.

Josef shrugged. "At least they never said so. If it wasn't for her, I'd still be sitting on the ground back at our farm."

A shooting star blazed across the night sky, burning itself out below the western horizon. Daniel closed his eyes and made a wish; that Anna was in a better place, one of safety and tolerance, a world quite the opposite of the one he inhabited.

"What's to become of us?" he wondered in despair.

Josef winged another stone across the water. "I don't know."

"Anna was all that kept us from killing each other."

"I know," said Josef quietly.

"Do you think people were just made to fight with each other? I mean you and me, we really didn't have anything to fight about ..."

"So we made things up."

After a pensive silence, Daniel asked, "Is there anything about me you think is, you know, good? Don't answer if you can't think of something."

"That's easy," Josef replied quickly. "You're smart. I wish I was as smart as you." He tossed another stone, effortlessly making it skip several times. "What about me?"

Daniel admitted, "Well, I wish I was athletic like you."

Josef seemed to have found a mother lode of smooth, flat stones and rapidly fired them over the water. He skipped a beauty, at least eight hops.

"And do you want the truth?" Daniel asked.

"Sure."

"I'm glad my feet don't stink like yours."

There was a long pause when neither boy said anything; then they broke into heartfelt laughter, which started small and grew, like a snowball rolling downhill, and cut through the pain at least for a moment. After a while, they calmed down and watched the river quietly flow. The stillness of the night and the enormity of the world reminded them of their plight.

"I miss her so much," Daniel said sadly.

"Me too," seconded Josef in a near whisper. "Me too."

They finally drifted off to sleep well after midnight, and woke with the first weak light that heralded the dawn. It was time to say their final good-byes to Anna.

After shaking off the thin veil of slumber from the most fitful and unhappy night of his short life, Daniel stopped and, one last time, looked at his sister's face. Her pale skin, her eyes locked shut, her unmoving chest, she seemed two-dimensional. Her now cold hands were crossed over her chest, as if in some vain attempt to keep herself warm. Her lips and the skin under her fingernails were the same deathly shade of gray. The sight made him weak and slightly dizzy until a thought hit him. She had suffered enough; her suffering was over. In fact this wasn't even her. Like a cello without strings, all that was left was a shell, hollow and empty. The real Anna, the true essence of Anna, the music of Anna, was far away from here, safe and unsoiled by the horrors of this world. Somehow these thoughts brought him enough comfort to continue.

They placed her blanket-wrapped body gently into the hole they had dug, along with her piano books. Earlier Daniel had removed a page of music from one of those piano books. It was the first page of Prelude in C Major. Although he wasn't certain, he thought this was one of Anna's favorite pieces. At least she seemed to play it often enough. And actually he had grown to like it quite a bit. He folded up the page and placed it inside Anna's copy of *Huckleberry Finn*. Daniel had considered burying all her belongings, but thought better of it. Just as the watch was a tangible token of his father, the novel and the sheet of music were the only things he had left to remind him of her.

Josef asked if he could keep Anna's necklace with the Star of David. Since Daniel already had one, he was only too happy to grant Josef's wish and thoroughly touched by the Catholic boy's sentiments.

As they shoveled the dirt upon her, an occasional tear silently flowed from both boys' eyes. When her grave was filled, Josef placed a cross he had made out of tree branches in the ground to mark the spot. At first Daniel thought it was inappropriate, but realized any symbol of the Jewish faith would invite desecration. He shuddered at the thought of her being terrorized even while in the grave.

They stood, their heads bowed, and prayed silently. Then Daniel said in Hebrew, "Shema Yisrael Adonai Eloheinu, Adonai Echad!" He translated for Josef: "Hear O Israel: The Lord is our God, the Lord is One!" After this he began to recite the Mourning Kadish. These were two of the few Hebrew prayers he knew pretty much by heart, and it seemed right. He also secretly prayed that he didn't mangle the Hebrew and leave out too much. Josef certainly wouldn't know the difference, but Daniel thought maybe, just maybe, God might be listening in and he didn't want to reflect badly on himself or Anna.

Josef recited the Prayer of St. Francis. Daniel could not help but learn it at St. Jude's, and joined him.

> Lord, make me a vessel of thy will,
>
> Where there is darkness, let me bring light,
>
> Where there is doubt, let me offer faith,
>
> Where there is sadness, let me bring joy,
>
> Where there is despair, let me offer hope,

And where there is hatred, let me sow love.

Josef paused, and could not go on after this line. His mouth would not move; his voice would not speak. Daniel waited for him to gather himself, to continue; finally, haltingly, he did.

> For it is in giving, that we receive.
>
> It is pardoning, that we are pardoned.
>
> And it is in dying,
>
> That we are born to eternal life.
>
> Amen.

Josef crossed himself and the two boys stared silently at the cold still earth. Daniel then began to sing "Ave Maria," his voice clear and pure in the cool morning air. The tune, so sweet and beautiful, brought tears rushing to Josef's eyes. But Daniel continued, his voice faltering only twice from emotion. When he held the last two achingly gorgeous notes, Josef went down to his knees and laid his head on Anna's grave. When Daniel finished, the tears he held inside could not be contained any longer. Finally Josef barely managed to bring himself to speak.

"Daniel, what's to become of us?"

After a few moments Daniel also went down to his knees and replied with quiet desperation, "I don't know. I really don't know."

14

Bratislava

They sat there without speaking for what seemed like the longest time, but it was perhaps fifteen minutes. Finally, leaving behind the boat, they gathered up their few belongings and moved on, taking to the road on foot. Josef broke the long silence. "You know, you sing good."

Daniel didn't respond but turned around to take one last look at the waters of the Danube as they rolled by Anna's grave.

They walked on and after a bit Daniel spoke up, "Last night I dreamed we died and went to heaven and saw Anna and our parents, and Misha was even there."

"I don't think we'll be so lucky," Josef said darkly.

"What? To go to heaven?"

"No. To die."

Daniel left Josef alone with his thoughts until the road widened and they approached the Bratislava city limits. Changing the subject, he asked, "Are you hungry?"

Instead of answering the question, Josef spoke his mind. "You know what our problem is?"

"What?"

"We're cursed."

"Cursed? What do you mean?"

"We have a bad luck hex on us."

Under normal circumstances, before their world had caved in, Daniel would have snorted in derision and made a pointed comment as to the illogic of such a statement. However, that morning it made perfect sense. How else could so many bad breaks happen to two people in such a short period of time?

"So, what do we do about it?"

Josef knew as much about curses as he did about the algebra they had started to study a few weeks before; enough to cause damage but not enough to exorcise whatever demons harassed them.

"Simple. We don't step on any cracks."

Daniel didn't follow. "Huh?"

"You know, step on a crack, break your back. Not that you actually break your back; it's another way of saying you'll have bad luck."

Daniel experienced fleeting anxiety as he recalled the countless number of cracks he had violated in a heedless lifetime. "Like don't touch wood," he offered as a further example, "unless you knock on it good."

"Exactly. And we need something to chase the hex away, like a snake's tooth, or fur from a goat's tail."

Daniel nodded decisively. "Or milk from a titmouse. So, where are we going?"

"To Bratislava. What I wouldn't give for a loaf of Olma's bread," he sighed. With a threefold goal of bread, Bratislava, and good luck charms in mind, they picked up their pace.

After an hour's walk they reached the center of the bustling city of Bratislava. Neither had ever visited there, and both found it far different from Prague. It seemed older and dirtier, with a distinctly Oriental character. Even the people appeared foreign. Unlike the fine-boned Bohemians, the residents bore the wider, flatter cheekbones of Slavic ancestry.

They encountered few cars (except those belonging to German military personnel, whose presence made them feel like wanted felons), for horse-drawn wagons and bicycles were the primary modes of transport. The somewhat disorganized center of commerce teemed with street vendors selling everything from sugar-garlic pastries to questionable rutabagas that had been root-cellared since the previous fall.

The tantalizing smells of baked goods and cooking sausages filled their nostrils, and foraging for food became their first priority. They had no money, so it would have to be begged or stolen.

Stealing was highly risky, because if they were caught, a Nazi prison was likely to be the next stop. Thus fear, rather than moral scruples, was guiding their actions. It surprised Daniel how quickly a stomach screaming with hunger can overcome a lifetime of proper upbringing. It didn't make him proud but survival was now the only point of the game, and he resigned himself to that harsh reality.

Josef suggested they try to find jobs at a cafe or bakery, where they could either filch food or earn enough to live on. In the meantime, he intended to find his rich uncle.

While they were on the river, Daniel had grown somewhat

tolerant of Josef, and he'd tried to be accommodating since Anna seemed to be fond of him. Now that they had reached the goal of Bratislava, and Anna was gone, many of the old irritations started to resurface, and Daniel began to think it was time for him to head east to the Ukraine and leave Josef alone with his pipe dreams of rich relatives who existed only in his fertile imagination.

However, Daniel did believe Josef's theory that they were cursed and doomed to suffer bad luck unless they avoided cracks and knocked on wood. It was harmless and alleviated their fears by making them feel like they could do something substantive to ward off yet more vicious twists of fate. Thus, so as not to step on cracks, they found themselves jumping and leaping about the cobblestone streets of Bratislava looking rather foolish, like victims of some unexplained spastic.

This activity became increasingly bizarre as they reached the busiest thoroughfare in the city. The sidewalks were crowded with people whom they had to skip and dance around in their quest to avoid cracks; so intent were they that they passed by two bakeries and a sausage shop without noticing them.

Their concentration was broken when a man in his mid-thirties abruptly stopped, grabbed Josef's arm, and called his name.

Josef's face lit up in recognition. "Tomas!"

They hugged and slapped each other on the back in happy reunion, and Josef explained, "This is my brother Tomas! Tomas, meet Daniel, one of my school friends."

They shook hands. He had enormous hands, like Josef, and there was some family resemblance, particularly in the warm brown eyes, the color of fresh-shucked chestnuts. But Tomas had dark hair, in contrast to Josef's light, and Tomas was thinner and smaller, not nearly as physically imposing as Josef. Daniel remembered the photo of Josef's family and vaguely recalled an older brother who looked like Tomas.

"Where have you been?" Josef asked his brother. "What happened to Mama and Papa?"

Tomas looked about furtively and quietly suggested, "Let's go someplace where we can talk."

They followed him to a pub a few blocks away. They sat down at a rough-hewn wooden table, but before doing so, Josef and Daniel both knocked on the wood.

"What's that all about?" asked Tomas.

"Good luck," they both mumbled, slightly embarrassed as they became aware of how silly they must appear to more rational minds.

"Of course," agreed Tomas, humoring them. He ordered beers for all three as Josef loosed a barrage of questions.

"Now tell me. What happened?"

"I don't exactly know," replied Tomas in a low voice. "After the Nazis invaded the Sudetenland, I went up to Zabreh for a day on business. When I went home I didn't even go inside. It was apparent what had happened, so I left immediately, in case the farm was being watched. I asked around town and learned about the rail bridge on the river that had been blown up. I guess some local Nazi group blamed Father. They took him and number of others, presumably Mama and everyone else who was at home. I have no idea if they were killed or are in a prison camp."

Josef blanked out the darker possibilities. "Did you hear that, Daniel? My papa was caught blowing up bridges to stop the Nazi bastards!"

That was not precisely what Tomas had said. Some Nazi group had blamed Josef's father, but it was common for them to blame a hundred people for something only a few had done. Daniel wasn't about to point this out and bring Josef back down to earth, especially since the chances were good his father was dead.

"I suggest you keep your mouths shut about this," commanded Tomas in a stern whisper. "The 'Nazi bastards' would just as soon exterminate Czechs like cockroaches, and they'll use any excuse to do it."

Josef, duly chastened, quietly reported on the journey that had brought them to Bratislava—the flight from Prague via railroad, the discovery of the abandoned farm, the journey downriver, and the death of Anna. In conclusion he said, "We're looking for Uncle Eduard."

"I don't think he's here," said Tomas. "I haven't seen or heard of him if he is."

Daniel was surprised that the phantom uncle wasn't a complete fabrication.

"Do you know where he went?" he asked.

"Budapest, maybe," ventured Tomas.

"What are you doing here now?" asked Josef.

"I have a job with an accounting office," reported Tomas.

"Can we stay with you? We have nowhere to go."

Tomas looked torn between filial duty and wisdom, given the dicey circumstances. He shook his head. "It's extremely dangerous here. Let me think." He turned to Daniel. "What about your family?"

"He's Jewish," Josef interjected, and told of how Daniel's father had been shot and his business burned.

"The only people the Nazis hate worse than the Slovaks or Catholics are the Jews," Tomas remarked. "Even more than the Poles or Austrians. Or the French or the British. Or the gypsies or the Russians."

The truth of the Nazis' all-encompassing hatred made them

wonder if there was any safe asylum to be found on the continent.

Tomas asked Daniel, "What about the rest of your family?"

"They were taken away ... I don't know where they are," said Daniel.

"Labor camps, probably," concluded Tomas. "I'm sorry. Well, you won't be safe here, either. But I'll see if we can't come up with something for you in the meantime."

He walked to the bar, Josef and Daniel tagging close behind. He asked the bartender, "Jan, will you do me a favor? These two need something to eat, so put them to work earning their lunch. Now, don't coddle them any."

Jan, a tall man with hair the color of iron and hawk-like features, possessed the unblinking stare of a mannequin. He merely nodded, his facial expression as malleable as a rock. Coddling from this man would be the least of their worries.

Tomas turned to Josef. "I'll be back. I have some business to take care of, and I'll see what I can arrange for you."

From some people, Daniel thought, such a statement would leave one uneasy for fear they might never return. Not Tomas. He had an energy and focus like an ant, which can easily carry twenty times his weight without thinking twice. He would be back.

Jan, or Mr. Stoneface as they came to call him out of his earshot, handed the boys a bucket with two brushes and set them to work scrubbing out the garbage barrels. The job apparently hadn't been done since 1922, and it took them a couple of hours to cut through the greasy, slimy, maggoty mess to the rotting wood underneath. Even then, it wasn't good enough for Jan and he made them apply additional elbow grease until every last bit of crud was eliminated. "You'd think he could leave something behind for the flies," griped Josef.

Next on his work list for the boys was washing the tables and mopping the floors, and then swabbing down the cobblestone walk outside with mops and soapy water.

Famished and exhausted, Daniel and Josef thought that surely their labors were complete, but Jan had yet more adventures in sanitation in store for them. The ultimate challenge: The lavatory.

Poor aim was endemic among the boys at St. Jude's, but at least the charwoman came in weekly to clean. No brush had passed over this toilet in many moons, but they somehow brought it up to what they thought was an acceptable level of hygiene. But not Jan's level. In he walked, looked and sniffed, and commanded them to try again.

By now the boys suspected they were being punished for having been foisted on the unwilling bartender. Even though neither one had any previous janitorial experience, they felt they had done a more than adequate job. But they sighed and gave the floor and walls another coat of soapy water.

At last, Jan allowed them to sit down and placed a loaf of bread and a wedge of cheese on the table in front of them.

"A good day's wages," he said, implying they should be grateful.

"Thank you," they chimed in, excessive in their appreciation, but as he walked away out of hearing range, the truth emerged.

"This is it?!" Josef complained.

"Slave driver," added Daniel under his breath.

Daniel then called out to Jan, "Hey, when is Tomas coming back?" It had been over six hours by then.

Mr. Stoneface replied without blinking, "If he said he's coming back, then he'll be back."

Quietly, so only Josef could hear, Daniel fired back, "I didn't ask *if* he was coming back, I asked *when*." However, he was smart enough to realize that silence was the better part of valor in the situation. They both concentrated on stuffing their faces with the bread and cheese. After they had eaten their fill, they would consider voicing their complaints more strongly.

Having devoured every last crumb of their dinner, however, their grievances had lost considerable steam. Jan's glowering stone face, regarding them pitilessly from on high as he removed the empty plate, might also have been an inhibiting factor.

Their first day in Bratislava set the pattern for the following two weeks. Each night Tomas arrived at varying times, often not until after the boys had fallen sound asleep on a bench. He would take them to different sites scattered about the city: an empty office one night, the home of a Lutheran minister another. When they asked why they simply couldn't go home with Tomas, he refused to give any reason or excuse, only a warning glare that effectively shut them up.

Mr. Stoneface continued to work their fingers to the bone, but after several days Daniel and Josef had the place so spotless that patrons began to claim it was losing its comfortable, dingy ambience. As a result, the boys had more free time to play and mingle with the customers. Growing complacent, both entertained notions of settling down in Bratislava permanently.

One evening while they waited for Tomas, Josef played darts. Daniel gave it a try but was so hopelessly inept he soon quit and sat down to read a day-old newspaper abandoned by a patron.

Josef, who took to physical things like a dog takes to fetching or a cat takes to laziness, consistently hit bull's-eyes after only a few warm-up shots. He concentrated on his new pastime, and Daniel tried to find the truth behind the lies in the Nazi-controlled press. Thus engaged, neither witnessed a beautiful green-eyed blond girl walk in. Jan seemed to know her, and leaned down and whispered in her ear. She glanced over at Josef, and a few minutes later sauntered to his side and began to flirt blatantly with him.

Daniel noticed this activity and his eyes fairly popped, for she was absolutely gorgeous. Not to mention, an older woman, at least nineteen. Why would she be interested in a kid like Josef? Especially given the fact he had been wearing the same clothes for three weeks, had dirt under his nails from cleaning the pub all day, and his overgrown, uncombed hair hung in a lank mop around his ears.

Daniel surreptitiously ogled, peering over the top of the newspaper at the blonde. Hair a pale ash shade, breasts that were, well ... he sought a non-pornographic adjective—ripe? Full lips, eminently kissable. And she was coming on to Josef! Was there no justice in the world?

He sat close enough to overhear the blonde girl admire, "Oh, you're so good at this. Me, I'm terrible. Maybe you can teach me."

Josef, flustered but covering it well, merely nodded and smiled and kept throwing darts.

She introduced herself. "I'm Caryn."

"Oh, yeah," he managed, coming to his senses. "I'm Josef."

He threw another bull's-eye.

"So ... are you from around here?" she asked, standing so close he could smell the fragrance of her hair.

At that moment Tomas hurried in and sat down across from Daniel. Josef handed the darts to Caryn and very politely excused himself, relieved to be rescued from a situation that was quite over his head.

Tomas motioned to Jan for beers and reported, "I finally learned some news about Uncle Eduard. He apparently left Bratislava for Budapest five months ago. Except I couldn't locate him through my contacts there, either. He may have left already or been taken prisoner. I might have more information this evening. You two can stay with me tonight, but I think it's about time you left Bratislava."

"But I could stay here with you," said Josef enticingly.

"Josef, it may be more dangerous for Daniel, but that doesn't mean it's safe for you. The Nazis hate Catholics and Slovaks, too."

"How come it's too dangerous for us but it's fine for you?" Josef inquired.

"Because I know this place and have friends here. You don't."

Tomas noticed Josef's crestfallen look and said firmly and convincingly, "Little brother, I'm telling you—both of you—your best bet is stick together and go to Budapest."

"Budapest!" cried Daniel. "But I have an aunt in the Ukraine!"

Tomas repeated the flaw in that scheme that Daniel had heard before, and had chosen to ignore. "Daniel, the problem with the Ukraine is it's in the Soviet Union. Once you're in, you can't get out. And Stalin doesn't like Jews much better than Hitler does. At least the Hungarian border is open. I have contacts in Budapest. Maybe they can get you to Palestine, or South America. Just trust me on this."

He reluctantly agreed.

"In the meantime," continued Tomas, "we have one last night to enjoy ourselves!" He hoisted his beer to his mouth and chugged a good portion of it, while Daniel and Josef followed suit.

The beer gave Josef's confidence a boost, so it was back into the fray; he rejoined Caryn before the dartboard. Both Tomas and Daniel admired Caryn's good looks.

"He gets all the luck," sighed Daniel enviously.

"Not all of it, but he gets his share," agreed Tomas.

As Daniel observed Tomas, he could see a definite family resemblance but, at the same time, pronounced differences between the two brothers. Besides their different hair and build, Tomas had angular features and a more prominent nose. Josef, however, had more rounded features and dimples.

Tomas asked, "Tell me, what do you know about Josef?"

"We were at St. Jude's school together. He had the bed next to mine. He's basically a good guy." Daniel congratulated himself on his tact in glossing over so many of Josef's deficiencies. "Okay student. Athletic. His feet smell."

Tomas laughed heartily, even though Daniel hadn't intended it to be funny. "Does he ever talk about his father?" he asked.

Daniel shrugged. "Sure. But all it was was a bunch of stories about him being a wealthy landowner and stuff."

"My father never could afford to send Josef to St. Jude's."

"Then how?" asked Daniel. He knew there were a few scholarship students, but they were either highly intelligent or had church connections.

"I'll tell you on one condition. You must never tell Josef."

"I don't understand."

"You will. But you must never tell him. Do you promise?"

Daniel feared he was about to become party to a secret that he didn't want to know. Yet he agreed.

"Okay, I promise. But why tell me at all?"

"Because you're his friend and someone should know, besides me. In case ... in case something happens. You see, Josef's father really wasn't his father. We have the same mother, but I don't know who Josef's father was. Someone in town, I guess. Anyway, over time Father figured out that Josef wasn't his son. So he took to beating him, especially when he was drunk. He made life hell for him. Our Uncle Eduard was quite well off, and he arranged for Josef to go to boarding school. That's how he ended up at St. Jude's. Father didn't treat me much better, but I was older and ran away as soon as I could."

This explained the disparity in their looks. But Daniel still wasn't clear on one point. "You mean Josef doesn't know his father *isn't* his father?"

Tomas shook his head. "And it's important that you know because Josef has a way of building his father up into some kind of hero."

"Why would he make a hero out of someone who ... beat him?"

"The human mind is a funny thing. The only father he's ever known doesn't love him, doesn't want him around, and he doesn't know why. Josef copes with that by making things up. I'm telling you so that you don't go off looking for someone who doesn't exist because Josef talks you into it."

"Don't you think you should tell him the truth?"

"Someday I will. But not now. Not under these circumstances. I just can't."

Watching Josef play darts with the stunning Caryn, Daniel now had an altogether different perspective on the life his friend had led. Tomas was right; Josef had gotten his share of luck but nowhere near a lot of it.

Moments later, a woman in her mid-twenties with flowing light brown hair and sparkling, playful eyes sneaked up behind Tomas and blindfolded him with her hands. "Guess who?"

"Herman Goering?" responded Tomas. He turned and pulled her face down to his and gave her a long, juicy kiss. This was Ivana. Tomas had shown the boys a picture of her, which he kept with him. In person she was much better-looking and more charismatic. She and Tomas hadn't seen each other since before Josef and Daniel had arrived in Bratislava; Ivana had spent two weeks in Banská Stiavnica, a town about 100 miles east of Bratislava, tending to her mother who had taken ill. They missed each other greatly and this kiss demonstrated that. As they clinched, Daniel noticed the butt of a gun under Tomas's coat. He was startled, but said nothing. Josef, evidently finished with his dart game, walked up as Tomas and the woman unlocked lips.

"Guys, meet Ivana. This is Daniel and my younger brother Josef," said Tomas by way of introduction. "Shall we get out of here and go home?" he asked, and without waiting for a reply, put his arm around Ivana's waist and headed for the door. Daniel and Josef eagerly scrambled after them.

15

Tomas And Ivana

Tomas's apartment was six blocks away. They traveled down a poorly lit street patrolled by several German soldiers who staggered noticeably and talked loudly, as if drunk. While intoxicated, the soldiers were more casual in the performance of their duties, yet they could also be more unpredictable. Any confrontations with them were avoided by slipping into alleys and doorways whenever soldiers came stumbling into view.

Tomas's building was on a quiet narrow street with four and five story structures that shared common walls. Some buildings, and Tomas's was one, had dormer windows on the top floor. Since Tomas's apartment was on the top floor, on summer days or evenings, Tomas and Ivana would climb out their window and catch sunshine or enjoy a glass of wine on the roof. The rooftop retreat made the daily march up and down the four story stairwell worthwhile. His apartment comprised two rooms. The living room served triple duty as it was a kitchen and dining room too. Cramped into it were a small sofa, a table for dining, and along one wall, a two-burner stove and an ancient-looking oven. The other room was Tomas's bedroom. The bathroom, shared with other tenants, was down the hall. The residence was, however, considered deluxe by Bratislava standards.

Tomas gave them bedding and two pillows. "Hope you're comfortable. If you have to get up to piss, don't lock yourselves out. See you in the morning," he said tersely.

Standing behind Tomas as he spoke, Ivana was unbuttoning his shirt and at the same time massaging his chest. They obviously had more pressing matters on their minds. They turned and went into Tomas's bedroom, discreetly closing the door behind them.

The two weeks in Bratislava had been a healing time for Daniel and Josef. The hard work had kept their minds occupied and their nervous energy under control. They had eaten sufficiently (if not well) at the pub and at the safe houses where they had slept. Their grief gradually receded, but there were moments, like flashes from a camera bulb, when a woman who reminded Daniel of his mother would pass by the pub windows, or Josef would see a dog in the street that looked like Misha, and the hurt and loss resurfaced as piercingly sharp as ever.

During their stay in Bratislava, they had visited Tomas's apartment just once. This would be the first night they had slept there; Tomas always insisted the place was too dangerous. The sofa was too short to sleep on comfortably, so Josef and Daniel made their beds on the living room rug and began to undress. "You were getting along nicely with that girl tonight," commented Daniel, hoping to provoke a response.

"Who, Caryn?" Josef responded nonchalantly. "She's okay."

"Okay? Just okay? She looked more than okay to me."

"Well, yeah, she did look pretty good."

"She seemed very interested. Why didn't you show more interest back?"

Josef said nothing at first and seemed to be struggling with his emotions.

Daniel goaded him. "Come on, she couldn't take her eyes off you!"

Josef then blurted out, "You know why? Because she punched me. We were playing darts and she punched me. Right in the arm ..."

Daniel knew the sting. Familiar things would instantly bring Anna to mind. He hated the way he was thinking of her too, in such a sad and pathetic way, as a tragic figure. He wanted to remember her as she really was—dreamy, confident, happy. But the pain was still too raw to bring the real Anna back to mind.

They got into their makeshift beds, sighing with relief as their tired bodies settled comfortably on the thick rug. Daniel asked, "Josef, why would an accountant carry a gun?"

"What do you mean?"

"Tomas. I saw it, under his coat."

Josef had no idea, but suddenly, coming from the bedroom, came the sounds of groans, muffled squeals, and murmurs. The two boys looked at each other. There was something going on in there. Neither had ever been a party to the audio portion of the act, much less the visual, but quickly figured out what was in progress.

Josef leaped up and tiptoed to the bedroom door, Daniel right on his heels. Josef peered through the keyhole and hogged the view, shoving Daniel aside whenever the smaller boy made an attempt to grab a look.

After a few minutes, he allowed Daniel a peek, since there was little to see anyway: just the bed sheets moving in a large white hump over two bodies and four feet sticking out from the sheets, wiggling as if they had a life all of their own. The delicious sounds, however, they could certainly hear.

"Geez! I've never seen it done before!" whispered Daniel.

"You still haven't. You can't see a thing," Josef pointed out.

"Yeah, but you can use your imagination."

"'Use your imagination'?" repeated Josef incredulously. "I don't know how I could have thought someone as dumb as you are was smart."

Daniel ignored the comment, took one more look, and then somewhat reluctantly followed Josef back to bed.

As the boys settled back into their beds on the floor, the sounds continued to rise in pitch; but the novelty had worn off, and the noise became more frustrating than exciting. They quickly learned that when one is not part of the action, there are few things more annoying.

"I'd rather listen to you snore," said Josef in disgust.

"I'd rather smell your feet."

"That can be arranged."

Her moans increased, and Tomas's enthusiastic praise for her abilities grew in volume.

Josef wrapped the pillow around his ears to blot out the noise. Somehow, he was able to drop off.

But even after the histrionics in the bedroom had ceased, Daniel could not sleep. He lay there and looked out the window at the moon as it rose above the spires of a nearby church. Thoughts of Anna occupied his mind as well as worries about the fate of his family. Tomas thought they should leave Bratislava, but what then? Should he try and find Mother and Jacob? And if he found them, what could he do? Would he be safer across the border in Hungary, or should he push on to the Ukraine?

Too many choices, and none of them was particularly promising. It was crushing, to suddenly have thrust in his lap life-and-death decisions, when a few short weeks ago the biggest quandaries he faced were which trash novels to buy with his allowance or what kind of chocolate to get at the newsstand near St. Jude's. Most other decisions were made for him by his mother and father or by the brothers and Father Beneš at St. Jude's. He fervently wished to return to life before the invasion.

Daniel turned over on his side and scrunched his pillow around his head. He noticed Josef facing him, eyes closed in slumber, in exactly the same position as himself; on his side, with knees bent about halfway into the fetal position, his arms cradling the pillow around his head. Daniel purposefully rolled over onto his back. It was creepy, like looking in the mirror for the very first time in your life.

Unable to fall asleep, after a few minutes Daniel got up and opened the window to drink in the cool air of the spring night. One fortuitously placed streetlamp provided just enough light to read and write. Daniel quietly rummaged about in Tomas's desk until he found a pencil, and proceeded to update his journal. He had faithfully reported the day-to-day events in Bratislava, largely a peevish recital of complaints about how hard Jan was working them.

A car pulled up on the street below. There were several people inside, perhaps revelers returning from a night out on the town. Tomas's voice surprised him from behind.

"You're still awake?"

"Couldn't sleep." Daniel admitted.

Tomas was in his underwear. He explained, "I have to, you know," and went to the water closet down the hall.

When he returned he looked over Daniel's shoulder. "What are you writing?" he asked.

"A journal. It's so I can remember all that happened when I get old and senile. *If* I get old and senile."

Tomas appeared troubled. "May I see it?"

Daniel was about to object that it was personal, but after Tomas had shared the secret of Josef's paternity with him, he could hardly refuse. He handed the sheaf of papers to him, by now a dozen pages.

Tomas ignored the beginning and read the last two pages that dealt with their stay in Bratislava. After scanning them, he strode purposefully to his desk and returned with fresh sheets of white bond paper.

"Here. Recopy everything you've written while in Bratislava, changing all the names. *All* of them. Then we'll destroy the originals."

"But why?"

"What if the Nazis capture you, and find what you've written? You've given a virtual death sentence to me, Jan, everyone who's sheltered you over the past two weeks!"

Daniel lowered his head. The thought had never occurred to him.

Tomas softened. "In time you'll learn. Unfortunately it will probably be things a boy your age should not have to know."

Daniel noticed that the auto parked below hadn't moved. "That car's been there quite awhile."

"Which one?" asked Tomas urgently. Daniel pointed.

"Get dressed, quickly!" ordered Tomas. He ran to his bedroom, giving Josef a good wake-up kick in the butt en route.

"Hey, what was that for?!" Josef protested, groggy with sleep.

"Get dressed NOW!" commanded Tomas with a frantic edge to his voice. He disappeared into his bedroom.

As Daniel wriggled into his pants, a second car pulled up behind the first. He reported, "There's another car!"

Now fully dressed, Tomas dashed back in and tossed Josef and Daniel each a Luger P 08 pistol. "You may need these."

He might as well have handed them a newborn infant. The boys' eyes grew big as saucers as they gingerly handled the pistols.

"But I never ..." began Daniel.

"Don't worry," said Tomas calmly. "It's already loaded. Aim and squeeze, like in the cowboy movies."

Daniel looked with trepidation at the gun, sure the only thing he would blow away was his own foot. He whispered to Josef, "Don't worry?"

Tomas returned to the window and peered out carefully from the side. On the street below, an SS officer emerged from the second car and approached the first. He spoke briefly to the driver, then gave a signal. Five SS troopers spilled rapidly from each car and ran toward the entrance to Tomas's building.

"Let's go!" Tomas shouted. Ivana, dressed and armed with her own Luger pistol, raced in from the bedroom and began climbing out the window. The boys followed, with Tomas taking up the rear.

As she balanced on an uncomfortably narrow ledge, Ivana grabbed the gutter overhead, hoisted herself onto the roof and scrambled upwards. Tomas urged, "Go!"

Taking a deep breath, Daniel stuck the gun in his waistband and

followed, a fear-powered adrenaline rush giving him the extra strength
necessary to accomplish this gymnastic feat. Josef, however, hesitated and
admitted lamely, "I can't. I'm afraid of heights."

"What?!" cried Tomas in irritation.

"We have to go down!" he pleaded.

Daniel seemed to agree. "Yeah, I mean we'll be trapped up
here."

"You shut up and listen!" Tomas ordered, brooking no dissension
in the ranks. "The roof is the high ground. It's a trap only if there's a taller
building close by, but there isn't. It's a trap for the krauts because they're
sitting ducks. We pick them off. We go down in our own good time. Got
that?" He addressed Josef directly. "You decide what you're more afraid
of—heights or a Nazi bullet."

He directed Ivana, "Wait by the fire escape."

Daniel followed her, and Josef, pale and clammy-handed,
likewise pulled himself onto the roof, avoiding all downward glances.

They clambered across the ancient red roof tiles, crossed over the
peak, and dropped low behind a chimney. They panted hard as they
waited, Daniel and Josef both holding their guns as if they had vipers by
the tails. Ivana, however, was cool as an alpine stream; they got the
impression she had done this before.

Glancing about, Daniel took in the lay of the rooftop. All the
buildings on the block were connected and varied in height just a few feet;
thus only the street limited their movement. Across the expanse, chimneys
were arrayed like a forest of tree stumps, creating ample hiding places and
cover.

They watched Tomas remove his sweater and wrap it around his
gun hand. Below him an SS trooper was taking the same route to the

rooftop as they had. As he scaled the incline, Tomas fired. POOM! came a muffled sound, the sweater serving as a makeshift silencer. The Nazi fell backwards off the roof to the ground four stories below.

Moments later, unaware of the fate of his comrade, another storm trooper poked his head out of the apartment window and called, "Hans?" He climbed out the window of the apartment and up to the roof.

Observing all this, Josef turned to Ivana and asked, "Tomas isn't just an accountant, is he?"

Ivana simply looked at him without saying a word.

Tomas again aimed and fired. The second Nazi tumbled with a heavy thud to the cobblestones below. The firing of the gun, however, ignited Tomas's sweater, leaving him with a burning torch at the end of his arm. He threw down the sweater and furiously stamped out the flames.

Ivana finally responded to Josef. "He's in the underground."

"What's the underground?" Daniel asked. At this early stage of the war, he had no idea what she was talking about.

"The Resistance to the fascists," she explained.

Josef's eyes lit up with pride. "My brother works for the underground!" he swelled. That certainly beat being an accountant.

Ivana grabbed Josef's shoulder and commanded in a harsh and deadly serious voice. "Never say those words out loud again. You understand?"

Cowed by her sternness, Josef responded weakly, "Yes."

"Both of you. Or we could all end up dead. Clear?" It was clear.

Just then, Daniel's peripheral vision caught sight of a third SS trooper stealthily climbing over the gutter to the roof. Tomas, busy extinguishing the fire, hadn't noticed him. Afraid of compromising their own position, Daniel had to remain silent. Tomas quickly dispatched the fire, and unaware of danger's proximity, he trotted casually toward their hiding place. Meanwhile, the storm trooper got to his feet, struggled to maintain his balance and took aim directly at Tomas's back.

"HALT!" he shouted.

The awareness of his mistake was written all over Tomas's face, but he did not halt. Instead, he accelerated.

The trooper aimed and—BANG! A shot rang out. Tomas dove toward them, and the Nazi fell backward off the roof to the ground. Daniel saw Ivana lower her smoking Luger. She had aimed dangerously close to Tomas, but had hit her target instead of her lover.

The noise, however, alerted the Nazi's comrades that their quarry was overhead. "Abandon high ground!" ordered Tomas. They scrambled down a series of ladders, the makeshift fire escapes that linked their building to others on the block.

As Ivana led the way, Tomas needled her. "Nice shot. Who exactly were you aiming for?" She only smiled enigmatically.

He turned to Josef and Daniel, who were puffing from exertion and obviously experiencing a gamut of emotions, including terror, exhilaration, and satisfaction that there were three less Nazis in the world. "Now do you understand when I tell you how dangerous it is here?"

Ivana knew her way over the maze of rooftops and ladders, and before long they reached street level without encountering further SS interference. They fled through dark, tangled medieval streets and alleys until they reached some woods along the Danube south of the city. Taking turns at sentry duty, the four of them spent the rest of the night there.

Ivana took back the boys' guns. These arms had come from her father, who had fought for the German army in World War I and had gathered three additional Lugers (on top of his own) upon the Armistice. As a child growing up in rural Czechoslovakia, her father had taught Ivana to shoot and she had become quite excellent. So good, she had taught Tomas how to shoot. After a recent visit to her parents' house, she had brought these weapons back to Bratislava with her, guessing they would be needed.

By now the boys felt as though they had been running forever. Their hope that Bratislava would signal an end to their troubles had been a chimera. Tomas was right; they had to move on.

Ivana and Tomas left the boys in the morning but each of them returned separately during the day. Tomas brought them a boat; a long, sturdy wooden vessel that looked like a gondola. Ivana supplied them with blankets, food, soap, even some toilet tissue.

"Trust a girl to think of this," commended Josef as he held up the roll of coarse paper.

"Just the essentials!" she laughed, and slipped off into the woods, back towards town.

Tomas returned once more after sunset. He returned Daniel's copy of *Huckleberry Finn* with the journal tucked inside—minus the pages dealing with Bratislava, which he had burned. He instructed, "Now once you get going, if you ever get in trouble or need some help from the Resistance, find a beer hall, like Jan's place, one with no Nazis around. In a roundabout way ask the bartender. He may not be in the underground, but he'll probably know where to find them. I'm telling you as strongly as I know how: Be discreet. Hopefully, since you're so young, they won't suspect you of being Nazi sympathizers. It would be a hell of a thing for you to be shot by our own people."

Daniel didn't need to hear this; that not only did they have to dodge Nazis but friendly fire as well.

"Remember to travel only at night," Tomas further instructed. "You've got the directions for the contact in Budapest?"

The boys nodded.

Tomas's train of thought then shifted. "Uh, you guys didn't hear anything last night in the apartment before the SS arrived, did you?"

"No, I slept like a baby," said Josef. "Until I got kicked in the ass by some stupid gorilla."

"Good. Sometimes I forget how thin those walls are."

Now they knew what he was talking about. They looked at each other and smirked. Josef moaned, "Ooooh Tomas! Ooooh, yes, you big, strong, *big* man!" he enthused in falsetto.

Daniel pitched in with heavy breathing and additional groanings.

Regarding the boys ruefully, shaking his head until their performance was complete, Tomas then said, "Well, I'm certainly glad you didn't hear anything."

"Next time we visit, don't go under the sheets," advised Josef.

"I'll keep that in mind," said Tomas facetiously.

They spent the remaining few minutes making sure the provisions were properly stowed in the boat, and repeating the instructions for making contact in Budapest.

Daniel and Josef embraced Tomas and thanked him, aware that they might never see him again. They now knew the dangerous game Tomas and Ivana were playing. Even if the two lovers survived the occupation, the question remained, would Josef and Daniel? Tomas pushed the boat out into the current and shouted to the boys, "Good luck!"

As Tomas receded from view on the darkened shoreline, Daniel had a sinking feeling. For a few short weeks he had felt safe under

Tomas's protection. Tomas was so competent and quick-thinking, and what's more, effectively kept his thumb on the impulsive Josef. He knew his turf and he knew the Nazis and how to fight them. Comparatively speaking, Daniel and Josef knew nothing, and were once again adrift on the water, seemingly no closer to safety than ever.

About fifty yards offshore and out of Tomas's hearing, Josef said, "As soon as he can't see us, you're letting me off."

Daniel turned to him, aghast. "What?!"

"I'm not going to Budapest with you. I have to return to Zabreh and find my father and family."

"Josef, you're crazy! Tomas said our best hope is to reach Budapest!"

"You go on. You'll make it fine alone."

"No, I won't," Daniel argued. "Josef, be reasonable. Think. Let's say you find your family and they're imprisoned by the Nazis. How will you free them?"

"I don't know! I'll find a way!" he countered irritably, sure that he would.

Daniel felt desperate, not merely for his own sake but for Josef's. He was certain that a return to Zabreh, if Josef made it that far, would be a death sentence. "Are you going to knock on the gates of the detention camp and say, 'Excuse me, Mr. Nazi Commandant, my family needs to go now'!?"

Josef remained sullenly silent.

"At the very least you'll need the help of the underground. Wouldn't it be better to go to Budapest and meet some of the Resistance fighters? Maybe learn how they operate?"

"Tomas is already in the Resistance. He can teach me. And then

I'll be that much closer to Zabreh!"

Daniel shook his head. "Sure, but don't you remember Tomas saying the Resistance in Budapest will be able to supply you with counterfeit passports, papers, even fake train tickets? Tomas can't do any of that. With them helping you it won't be as hard as you think."

"You're making this up."

"Am not. Besides, how do you plan to get back to Zabreh alone? Walk? That'll take weeks, and you'll probably be picked up by the Nazis. Why not give the underground a chance to help you out?"

Daniel could tell Josef was weakening. He pressed, "If it's so easy to rescue your family, don't you think Tomas would have done it by now?"

Daniel had overplayed his hand, and Josef turned on him furiously. "Oh, I get it. Tomas couldn't do it, so I shouldn't even try."

"I didn't say that! But I think it takes a lot of planning and resources you don't have." He sought a parallel. "You can't just ride in on a big white horse, six-shooters blazing, like Randolph Scott, and single-handedly hold off hundreds of Nazi soldiers."

Josef knew Daniel had a point. He had no horse. No six-shooters. No plan.

"You know that going to Budapest is the smart thing to do."

Josef snarled in frustration, "Yeah, and how come *you* always know the smart thing?"

Daniel backed off. "I don't. But I think you're smart enough to recognize what the smart thing is."

Josef finally agreed, to Daniel's immense relief. "Okay, I guess three more days to Budapest won't set me back that far." He admitted in a more subdued voice, "If they're in prison, they'll still be in prison. And if they're dead ... it won't matter."

Josef took his place in the front of the boat as a lookout, while Daniel sat in back and held the rudder. Now that he had won his case, he wasn't sure he should have bothered. If Josef was so dense that he wanted to rescue a father who had regularly beaten him, well, let him go. He really was more trouble than he was worth.

Yet, they had been through a lot together, and Daniel felt a grudging admiration for him, despite his all too frequent lapses into pure bone-headedness. Besides, Daniel didn't want to travel to Budapest alone. By now he knew he was competent enough to handle it, although he felt safer and less lonely with Josef around. But once they reached Budapest and found the local Resistance, Daniel vowed that Josef could run off to join the cavalry and fight Indians in America for all he cared.

16

A Stranger

The night passed slowly and quietly, like the moon hiking across the heavens. They encountered little traffic except a barge headed upstream around sunrise. In the morning, as the light fog gently lifted, the spectacular beauty of their surroundings overwhelmed the two boys. The river was nestled in a valley between rolling wooded hills of spruce, oak, and birch trees that were bursting forth in a riot of greenery. Great shafts of sunlight cut through the mist and tree branches. Ephemeral pearls of dew gathered on a spider's web constructed in the boat's corner. The perfect serenity of this day's dawn banished all preoccupation with the difficulties confronting the boys.

They found a sheltered cove with a sandy beach, and pulled the boat ashore for the day. Although each had managed a catnap or two during the night, they were bone-tired and fell asleep on some grass just above the sandy shore.

When Daniel awoke they had been asleep for just over three hours. The noise he made while rooting around the boat for some scraps of food awakened Josef. In one bag Daniel discovered the soap Ivana had thoughtfully packed, and remarked, "It's been awhile since we had a bath — "

Josef, still a little edgy from the lack of rest, took it personally. "Oh, shut up! I've been keeping my feet in the river so much it's a wonder the carp haven't eaten my toes!"

"For once your feet aren't the problem. Even *I'm* beginning to smell like a skunk."

"Things must be bad," agreed Josef, unconvinced, but he reluctantly followed Daniel's lead.

Modesty demanded they undress in the underbrush framing the clearing, although there appeared to be no human inhabitants for miles. At the water's edge they discovered the Arctic temperature of the river water. Josef impulsively decided it would be best to take the plunge quickly rather than attempt a gradual immersion.

Mentally Josef counted to three, and dashed in. It was even worse than he had imagined. After all, it was only early May. The water's chill seemed to suck all the air from his lungs, and he was surprised at how rapidly he was losing feeling in his feet and lower legs. The cold felt like ten thousand needles pricking his skin.

Not that he would warn Daniel of impending hypothermia. Let him find out for himself. "It's great!" he baldly lied. "A little cool, but it feels fine!"

Ankle-deep in the water now, Daniel wasn't quite so enthusiastic about his own idea. But he couldn't very well back out. Wading in up to his knees, he decided on the slow-acclimation approach Josef had rejected.

In an effort to show Daniel what fun he was missing, Josef swam and splashed about like an otter. The hyperactivity also seemed to keep his blood from turning to ice. "It's great!" he repeated, more truthfully this time. After the initial shock, it did feel refreshing.

"It's freezing!" insisted Daniel.

Ignoring him, Josef discovered a large tree branch that hung out over the cove and offered an excellent diving platform. He shimmied up the tree and onto the branch. By now, the air felt colder than the water. He took his stance and dove in cleanly.

When Josef emerged, Daniel had ventured out a few more steps to a thigh-high depth; he seemed content not to venture further. Pansy, Josef thought, and returned to the tree branch. This time, instead of a neat, graceful, water-cleaving dive, he did a huge, dirty, butt-first cannonball. The splash was monumental, and when he came up for air, Daniel was completely drenched.

"Sorry ..." Josef said insincerely.

"You know this means WAR!" Daniel shouted, and dove after him.

Josef easily escaped his pursuer and climbed up the tree again. He did a back flip. Daniel followed suit with a cannonball. They exuberantly competed to see who could do the most spectacular dives, flips, cartwheels, can-openers, and cannonballs, with a few belly whoppers thrown in, inadvertently or not, just for the fun of it.

After nearly ten minutes of frolic, Daniel noticed something or someone watching them from the edge of the clearing. He informed Josef in a low voice, "We've got company."

Their observer realized she had been spotted, and took a few steps forward. She was a beautiful woman wearing gleaming black riding boots. In full habit complete with fawn-colored breeches that flared at the hips and a hunter green jacket, she led a perfectly trained Arabian stallion. A few wisps of hair the color of cinnamon peeked out from under her hat as she stood with steel-rod posture, her commanding presence requiring their attention.

"What are you doing on my property?" she demanded in German, with an upper crust Austrian accent. There was a husky, thrilling quality to her voice.

Both boys were semi-fluent in the language, especially at reading, having studied it all through grammar school. They also spoke it adequately. The problem was in understanding rapid fire, conversational German, since few people spoke with the clear diction and deliberate slowness of a typical foreign-language teacher. After a long moment of uncertainty, her question was deciphered.

"Nothing," Josef answered. They crouched low in the water to hide their immodest state.

"We didn't know it was your property," added Daniel.

"Of course you didn't, because like common louts, you never asked!" she retorted sharply.

"We're sorry, madam," said Daniel.

"You will call me 'Countess.' And stand up straight when you speak! You are, after all, addressing royalty."

Josef and Daniel glanced at each other despairingly, unsure if it was less respectful to stand at attention and expose all or remain hunkered down lest she see something she'd rather not.

"Countess ..." Daniel stammered.

"We're not decent," finished Josef.

She smiled archly and replied, "Let me be the judge of that."

"But ... but ..." protested Josef.

"My dear boy, I've seen many a man's shortcomings. I believe I will survive seeing yours. Now *out* of my river or I shall have you flogged!"

Still the boys did not move. The Countess shook her head in disgust, and with her hands disdainfully on her hips, turned her back to the boys.

They slunk from the water reluctantly and stood, their hands over their privates. "Go on! Get your clothes on!" she ordered with a wave, her back still turned.

They scrambled off to do so, and then stood frozen in place, unsure of what was next from this strange, intriguing woman. She faced them again.

"You slouch like weasels!" she bellowed. "Stand up straight! Act like you *are* somebody!"

They snapped to attention. Softening somewhat, she said, "You both are as skinny as rails! Come, it's almost dinnertime."

She seemed to be offering them food, a prospect the boys could not have been happier to consider. She mounted her horse in one smooth athletic motion and they followed behind her on foot. After an uphill climb of about a half mile, they emerged upon a clearing that offered a panoramic view of an enormous house, in their eyes, a castle.

Obviously, this was a woman of high rank; maybe she really was royalty and not some eccentric crazy. One thing was certain; she possessed an extraordinary vitality, as if life itself, in its purest, rawest form, seemed to glow from within her. Daniel cleared his throat and cautiously asked, "Ma'am, uh, I mean, Your Highness, who are you?"

"Very good," she replied from high in the saddle. "Introductions. I am Countess Maria von Hapsburg."

Daniel felt a rush of recognition. "Of the Hapsburgs who ruled Austro-Hungary?"

"The same," she answered. "We ruled over the golden age of Europe, until the damn fascists came along."

"What about the golden age of democracy in Czechoslovakia until the Nazis came along?" questioned Daniel somewhat recklessly. Sure he was endangering their free meal, Josef shot Daniel a look of aggravation.

"Democracy! Hah! The rabble is incapable of ruling! Why, look at the United States. Perhaps the largest, most backward country on earth. A disaster. It's no Hungary, to be sure. Now, who are you?"

They gave only their names.

"What brings you to my country cottage?" she asked.

Daniel hesitated. He wasn't sure if they should trust her, but she seemed open and straightforward enough, for a patrician countess. "We're on our way to Budapest."

"Why Budapest, pray tell?" she asked scornfully.

"We're trying to get as far from the Nazis as possible," said Josef.

"Let me save you some trouble," she offered. By now the three of them had arrived at the front door of her immense home. She tethered her horse just outside. They entered the structure into a huge hall, its ceilings supported by rough-hewn beams darkened from the smoke of thousands of expensive cigars. A chandelier fashioned from the antlers of numerous deer illuminated the space. The heads of similarly hapless elk, mountain rams, and bucks decorated the walls.

"I lived in Vienna until last year, when the Nazis annexed the country," she explained. "So I went to Budapest. But last fall the Hungarian government allied with the Nazis so Hungary could steal parts of Czechoslovakia when the Nazis invaded. I've stayed here the past three months, but I suppose it's only a matter of time before they come after me."

"Why would the Nazis want you?" Josef asked.

"I am royalty, my dear boy. They want my wealth. But it's all safely locked away in Swiss bank accounts, and they'd have to kill me before I'd give them access to it."

"Why don't you leave the country?" wondered Daniel.

Removing her hat, she shook her curls loose. She was an indeterminate age: somewhere between thirty and perhaps forty, maybe even older—it was difficult to hazard a guess. She had piercing azure eyes and milk-white skin unmarred by a single freckle. "You forget that this is my country. Besides, I refuse to allow the Nazis to dictate my departure. I will do so in my own way and in my own good time."

Obviously, she was a woman used to having her own way. The boys suspected that if the Gestapo ever did directly confront her, it would be a case of an irresistible force crashing headlong into an immovable object, like a car traveling at sixty miles per hour meeting a brick wall. If life and death were not at stake, it would be pure fun to watch.

A tall man in his late thirties entered the foyer and seemed momentarily taken aback at the sight of the two visitors.

"Pardon me, Countess, but I was cooking and didn't hear you enter."

She nodded. "I'll be having two guests for dinner. Viktor, I would like you to meet Daniel and Josef."

"How do you do?" asked Viktor most graciously, bowing to the boys. Ill at ease with all this pomp, the boys self-consciously bowed back. Josef's wild stories about dinners with the Prince of Bohemia had hardly prepared him to rub shoulders with actual royalty. And it was a far cry from life among the Jewish bourgeoisie of Prague. The boys tried to keep their mouths from gaping and their popping eyeballs implanted in their heads.

"Dinner will be served shortly, Your Highness," Viktor reported, and briskly exited.

They walked up a broad, ornately carved mahogany staircase into an immense dining room. The ceilings were twenty feet high, with trompe l'oeil paintings of clouds and blue skies accentuating the feeling of loftiness. The walls were wainscoted to a level of four feet, and the remainder was wallpapered with precious silk damask fabric in a faded rose shade. The walls held numerous portraits of long-dead Hapsburgs and landscapes in heavy gilt frames.

The dinner table, in the massive Louis XIV style of furniture, seated seventy. Huge candelabras, epergnes filled with marzipan candies, and fresh flowers were tastefully placed on an intricately embroidered table runner. Even two such unsophisticated boys as Josef and Daniel knew all this signified wealth, and lots of it. Where had it all come from? they wondered.

With no visitors for weeks, Maria was happy to explain to the newcomers. It turns out there were thousands of Hapsburgs sprinkled across Europe and most were comfortable but not rich like this. The dynasty's wealth had been largely dissipated by generation after generation of inheritance, and the not always astute investments of the inheritors. Maria, however, came from one of the more prosperous limbs of the family tree. And she married well, to a distant cousin, Claus, which more than doubled her already respectable dowry. Just two years into their marriage, Claus drowned in a shipwreck off the coast of Croatia near Dubrovnik. She inherited all of his holdings, and an able investor, she had grown the fortune substantially since his death.

By now the boys had also noticed that every enormous room they entered, the countess's presence alone seemed to fill it. The lights seemed to burn brighter; the chandeliers sparkled with more iridescence. No interior could contain her. She seemed larger than life, like a movie star, like Garbo. Yet this place was suffocating from the melancholy beauty of some lost era. The walls should have reverberated with the talk and laughter of dozens, if not hundreds of people. But only the footsteps of two boys and this elegant woman echoed long and loud through these lonely rooms and byways.

So vast was the dining room that both Daniel and Josef imagined the fun they could have playing indoor football there. Maria sat down gracefully at the head of the table and indicated that the boys should take the two chairs on either side of her.

Viktor emerged shortly thereafter with a platter heaped with several game hens, cooked to golden brown perfection and served with a cherry sauce on the side. Next he carried in a priceless Sevres serving bowl loaded with mashed potatoes and a boat of steaming, silken gravy. He rounded out the hearty lunch with baby carrots, grown in the estate's own greenhouse and sautéed in butter and honey. A plate of cherry and apple tarts, the fruit bursting through the flaky pastry, already graced the table.

Neither boy had ever eaten a game hen before. They surreptitiously watched Maria tackle hers, and followed her example. Although here and there they encountered bits of shot, it was delicious.

Neither could see how it was much different from a chicken, except smaller, but after their steady diet of Jan's bread and moldy cheese, it was sublime.

Maria explained, "I used to have over sixty servants running this house. Viktor's the only one left. Now, do you have more definite reasons for reaching Budapest than simply escaping the Nazis?"

Josef swallowed his mashed potatoes and, helping himself to more, responded, "I have an uncle there ... well, I did ..."

"And then what?" asked Maria. "The Hungarians have sided with the Nazis. You think they'll welcome a Slovak refugee and an orphan Jew?"

Doubt clouded over Josef's face. But he plunged ahead anyway and revealed his plans beyond Budapest. "I'm going to get some help and return to Zabreh to find my family."

With a look of utter disdain, Maria made him feel about four inches tall. "In other words you want to join them in a Nazi labor camp?"

Her blunt certainty made it difficult for Josef to respond. "Well, I-I don't know that for sure," he stammered.

"Don't fool yourself," she warned him. "From what you've told me, they're either in a labor camp or dead."

Her brutal honesty stunned Josef. As she patted her mouth with a snowy linen napkin bearing the royal crest of the Hapsburgs, she noticed his shattered look. "I'm sorry. I don't mean to be harsh ... but better to face reality ..."

"They're not dead!" said Josef with steely determination.

"All right, they're not dead," she agreed, as if pacifying an unreasonable toddler.

"What am I supposed to do, forget about them?" he demanded.

"Josef, face facts," Maria responded calmly. "What can a thirteen, fourteen-year-old..."

"Fifteen. Almost fifteen."

"... almost fifteen-year-old do? Grown men experienced with weapons and warfare are failing to turn back the Germans. The best thing for you to do is stay safe and sound until all this madness ends. It's what your family would want, I can assure you."

She said this with a finality that left no room for debate. Besides, they knew she was right. They finished their game hens and devoured several tarts in silence. At last she offered, "I have a proposal for you. There's plenty of room here, and as you can see, I have more than enough food. Stay for a few days. You can help me; I'm going to make my way to Switzerland."

"How?" asked Daniel, his interest piqued.

"That's for me to know. I have some petrol but not enough, what with rationing and shortages. Even the black market has been unable to provide me with sufficient quantities. I need your help to borrow some."

"'Borrow' some?" asked Daniel dubiously. That would be a good trick. Practically the only motor vehicles he had seen anywhere belonged to the Germans; apparently they were the only ones who could obtain fuel.

"We're getting pretty good at 'borrowing,'" bragged Josef.

"Fine! So what do you think? In exchange for food and a comfortable bed?"

The food was demonstrably first rate; even if they hadn't been half starved, they would have made utter pigs of themselves. The sleeping facilities were uninspected, but it wasn't much of a stretch to assume they would be more than comfortable.

"You don't have to make up your mind this second. Think about it. Take your time." She rose, and they jumped to their feet as she excused herself. She glanced back at them and said, "Give me your answer in, say, five minutes."

Alone in the cavernous room, they conferred frantically. "What do you think?" asked Daniel.

"I think she's strange. All the 'Countess' and 'Your Highness' this and that."

"I meant, what do you think of the offer? She needs petrol; so she probably plans to drive across Austria to Switzerland and doesn't want to stop for anything. Maybe if we help her, she'll take us too."

"I don't want to go to Switzerland. I didn't even want to go to Budapest!"

"Look, she's right about Budapest," Daniel reasoned. "They're with the Nazis now and it'll be no better there than in Prague or Bratislava."

"But we have my brother's contact with the Resistance."

"Well, we can at least stay for a few days and help her. Maybe she'll even pay us. We'll have some good food and decent beds. That won't hurt any."

Josef was far from convinced. "I knew this would happen. I should have gone straight to Zabreh."

Maria glided back into the room. "Well?" she asked.

Josef avoided Maria and Daniel's eyes. It was his way of conceding without appearing to have given in.

"Josef?" Daniel inquired, but the boy would not answer. So Daniel answered for him. "Good. We'll stay and help you!"

"Marvelous!" Maria replied, beaming. "Viktor, prepare for overnight guests!"

17

Stealing Petrol

Whatever Maria's exact plans were, she kept them to herself.
After lunch that afternoon, the boys helped Viktor plant and water
vegetables on a tract behind the greenhouse, and then pick, or in the case
of potatoes and carrots, dig up, those planted inside the greenhouse that
were now ready. Viktor seemed genuinely pleased to have two extra
pair's of hands and two extra backs committed to this labor. When they
were finished, the spring planting was largely complete, and they had
enough vegetables for weeks.

That night they slept in soft beds in a bedroom that was just
slightly smaller than the entire dormitory at St. Jude's. In the morning the
boys busied themselves playing football out on the lawn with a ball Maria
had found somewhere. It was smaller than regulation, but large enough to
pass for a reasonable facsimile. For a time Maria watched from the

veranda, her eyes fixed on the boys as if she were reacquainting herself with the movement of human beings. After several hours the boys tired of the various permutations of two-man football and spent the rest of the day going room to room, discovering the great uninhabited spaces of the estate. That day, except at mealtimes and for the brief period she'd been a football spectator, Maria seemed to vanish, leaving Viktor to occasionally check on the boys, like a schoolmarm.

On one of Viktor's missions of supervision, Josef conspired with Daniel to hide and surprise him. In the many lonely, deserted hallways of the estate, to be suddenly set upon and screeched at by something like a flock of mad crows would unnerve anyone. Viktor, while not a man who was easily frightened, reacted like any other person under such circumstances and nearly leaped right out of his skin, to the howling delight of the perpetrators. Nonetheless, guests were guests and Viktor tried not to appear bad-tempered, forced a quick smile, and went about his other business.

The following day Maria led a vigorous hike of the estate's grounds. She and the boys walked for almost an hour and a half to the property's farthest point and then returned. They saw no people or other buildings but glimpsed much wildlife, especially deer, rabbits, and grouse. In the afternoon, she had them ride horses. She watched them as if she were grading their abilities. Maneuvering the horse easily, Josef sat tall and confident in the saddle while Daniel was barely able to hold on.

On the third morning Maria left the boys alone to amuse themselves in the library, a large room with three walls of books and one wall with a cozy fireplace. This room delighted Daniel but left Josef whining.

"Why are we here? I'm wasting my time. I should be trying to get back to Zabreh."

"Just relax," Daniel replied. "We'll ask her at lunch what her plans are. Believe me, things could be much worse."

While Viktor kept Josef's attention by tending to the horses and working in the garden, Daniel asked for a few pieces of paper, a pen, and some ink and went about finishing the recopying his journal. By writing even smaller, he compressed the number of pages from fourteen to nine, rid the diary of any penciled entries, and altered the names and places. By folding the pages twice, they now fit neatly in his pocket.

The journal had Daniel reflecting on their recent improbable turn of fortune: meeting the countess, their fine lodgings, the incredible food, the chance for escape to Switzerland. And then he wondered, who among us can say what is improbable anymore? In an age where voices can be transmitted thousands of miles instantaneously over wires, where giant steel crates shaped like cigars with heavy steel arms can fly through the sky, where a small glass bulb, with the flick of a switch, can turn night into day. Just a few short years ago, all of these devices were utopian imaginings of a deranged mind. So who really is to say anymore what is and isn't improbable? In light of the crazy things he *knew* to be true, their circumstances seemed tame. And quite pleasant.

After another sumptuous midday meal, Maria led Josef and Daniel onto a broad balcony that overlooked a lush, green expanse of lawn rimmed by budding trees. In the distance past the forest, they could just barely glimpse the Danube and the cove where their boat was beached. They sat in high-backed wicker chairs as Viktor handed Maria a brandy in a glass that, to the boys' thinking, resembled a footed fishbowl.

"Sirs," he asked. "Would you care for a brandy?"

This was heady stuff. Brandy, they had heard, was a drink that would turn mere commoners into landed gentry. It would confer upon them the sophistication and social skills they were sadly lacking. At worst, they would get a little drunk. Disguising their eagerness, they replied yes.

Viktor returned to the sideboard in the dining room to fill their orders. Maria thoughtfully sipped her brandy, a rare Napoleonic bottling she was drinking up rather than abandoning it to the Nazis.

"It's so peaceful here," remarked Daniel, trying to make conversation.

Maria regarded the vista before them and said somewhat cryptically, "Looks can be deceiving."

Viktor returned, sans brandy, and announced, "Your Highness, your cousin Alexander is here to see you."

Maria bounded to her feet, exited to the dining room, and met Alexander as he swept in. He was tall, ruggedly handsome, with a sturdy build and the same regal bearing as Maria's. She smiled radiantly at her unexpected but welcome guest.

Josef elbowed Daniel, "Try and hear what they're saying."

Daniel crept to a window opening from the dining room onto the balcony and, crouching beneath it, listened intently.

Alexander sounded worried. "They are coming either tonight or tomorrow."

"Bastards," hissed Maria vehemently. "Well, I'll just have to move up my plans. Are you sure I can't persuade you to join me?"

"I must settle my affairs in Budapest first. But I hope I shall see you soon."

Maria called out, "Viktor, can you please come in here as soon as you can?"

Alexander and Maria hugged and she thanked him for his

warning. He said, "I must be off before they catch me here. Take care."
They embraced once more, and Alexander exited as Viktor came in.
Knowing Viktor could not sneak up on him now, Daniel relaxed some.

Maria began very businesslike. "They are probably coming
tonight. Or tomorrow."

This was not good news. Viktor was silent.

Maria continued. "Can you take the two boys with you?"

Daniel pressed closer to hear.

"Madam, please. It just doesn't make sense for me. Why not do
as we planned and leave them?"

Maria did not respond at first. Then, "I'm afraid the Nazis will
just kill them."

Daniel gulped.

Viktor asked, "And you cannot take them?"

"I don't think there's enough room. And the added weight. Plus
my abilities are ... limited. It's not good."

"Countess, my chances of making it safely to Hungary alone are
poor, perhaps one in five. With two boys, the odds drop to ... what? One
in fifteen? One in twenty?"

"If you wait for the odds to be in your favor, the grass will die
beneath your feet. We are looking down a gun barrel. You, they want in
their army. Me, they want my money and then they'll kill me."

Viktor countered, "But the odds are much worse for each of us
with the boys along."

Maria was in deep thought. Finally she spoke up, "I don't know
if I can live with myself if I abandon them." She took a deep breath. "So
I guess it's decided."

"But you said ..."

"I'll just make it work, somehow ..." she added.

Maria took a moment to think, then turned to go. Daniel hurried back to his seat.

"Well?" Josef asked, expecting a detailed report. But before Daniel could oblige, Maria returned. Daniel tried to appear innocent and, in so doing, looked guilty as sin. Fortunately, Maria ignored their very presence, and sipping her brandy, silently brooded, her mind hatching private plans.

Viktor returned with snifters for the guests. Smiling like dolts, the boys clinked glasses and took healthy swigs. By the time the brandy hit Daniel's stomach, he thought his eyes would explode out of his head. His mouth and throat were lined with liquid fire. He looked helplessly at Josef, whose eyes were filled with tears.

They tried to remain suave, but Maria's attention was alerted. "Is there something wrong?"

With strangled voices they assured her, "Oh no, nothing. Nothing at all." They had, however, discovered they didn't like brandy. They set their glasses down and afforded them the respect of arsenic. Perhaps it was an acquired taste. Maria calmly drained the last drops of hers.

"There's been a change in plans," she announced. "I will definitely need your help."

They shrugged in assent. She stood up. "Good. Now come with me." Her confident demeanor made it unthinkable to question her.

She rang for Viktor, who accompanied them to a small outbuilding. He brought out several coils of rope a half inch thick in diameter and dropped them on the grass.

"You're going to learn the craft of weaving," she explained with a mysterious smile, and set them to work fashioning the rope into a crude net. Once she was sure they knew what they were doing, she left them under Viktor's command.

The net took about an hour and a half to complete and was fifteen feet long and eight feet wide. It was not a work of art; its webbing rough-hewn, a tennis ball could easily pass through it while something the size of a football could not. Viktor brought a horse around, and they loaded their handiwork on its back. Maria, on horseback, led them down a narrow dirt road through dense woods. About a mile from the estate they stopped at a point where the winding road was cut perilously into the steep wooded hillside, which fell off to a precipitous drop on one side while rising almost as precipitously on the other. The road also turned sharply at this point creating a blind corner, making it extremely hazardous for drivers as well as imperative to slow considerably.

Here, Maria directed the unloading of the net and its placement on the slope. They could only make their way uphill by grabbing onto the small trees that had somehow established a foothold in the rocky soil.

About twenty feet above the road were two trees about fifteen feet apart. They securely tied the net between the trees. Next, they carried heavy rocks from all over the slope and placed them behind the net. It took two hours, but in that time and with much sweaty labor the boys filled the net until it bulged with the huge quantity of rocks straining behind it.

Once the net could hold no more, they walked back to the estate. After they washed up, Maria led them to a locked basement room. The cellar was dark and smelled of mildew and the corners were ensnared with cobwebs. It was like a dungeon and it sent visions of Frankenstein racing through Daniel's mind.

She opened a cupboard that held fourteen Mannlicher-

Schoenauer 6.5 x 54 rifles. The two boys' eyes grew wide with excitement. It made sense that an estate such as this, used primarily for hunting, would be well stocked with weapons. These guns had low recoil, excellent accuracy, decent killing power, and polished walnut stock that gleamed. Some would call the Mannlicher-Schoenauer the world's finest rifle. The boys also were tempered with some nervousness. Daniel warned Maria, "I've never used a gun."

"Me, neither," seconded Josef.

"No problem, my dear boys," Maria pledged with supreme confidence. "It's easy. Any idiot can shoot a gun. But a good Hungarian goulash—now, that's hard."

Two years before, Maria had gotten rid of several shotguns in her collection. She thought the spray of shotgun pellets rewarded lousy marksmanship and wasn't sporting. Now, with her needs no longer being to hunt animals, she was having second thoughts about that decision. She presumed she had two lousy marksmen and wished she had a couple shotguns.

They carried their rifles outside, and Viktor patiently demonstrated how to load and fire them. They didn't use any bullets in their practice for fear the noise would attract unwanted attention. Consequently, it was impossible to tell if they had, or could, hit anything smaller than a stalled bus at ten paces.

After each boy spent ten minutes at shooting practice, Maria took Josef and Daniel to an upstairs bedroom. There, she laid out a number of rustic hunting outfits in a range of sizes. The first one Daniel put on fit him perfectly, and he decided to stick with it. Josef was awestruck by the variety.

"Where did all these clothes come from?" he asked, calling into the next room where Maria was trying on outfits of her own.

"Silly child, this is a hunting lodge. On some autumn weekends I would have a hundred guests. Some would drive up on a whim, with the clothes on their backs. We couldn't have a duke dropping in after a party in Vienna and have him wearing his evening clothes to shoot grouse, now, could we?"

The rich were indeed different, Daniel thought, to have huge sums invested in clothes in the event some absentminded duke forgot his suitcase. She pranced back into the room wearing a jaunty number composed of a black boiled wool jacket and Tyrolean-style lederhosen. In the huge floor-to-ceiling mirror, she admired herself turning about and posing like a fashion model. She made a pouty face, rejected the outfit, and exited to try on another. She changed clothes at least a half dozen times before making the final, arduous decision.

Daniel and Josef enjoyed the show, and Maria in turn enjoyed having an audience. She seemed well aware that she had great-looking legs and an eye-catching derriere which more than made up for her lack of bosom. At last she cried, "There! This is it!" After all these changes of costume, Maria ultimately chose a pair of man-tailored navy blue trousers with a cream silk blouse, topped by a short Chanel jacket to match. Classic yet practical, she told herself, apropos for any situation, even potentially difficult ones.

"Now, what have you selected?" she asked eagerly.

They had picked dark brown pants that buttoned below the knees; the heavy socks covering their calves had been knitted from lambs' wool so fine that they did not itch. Daniel wore a pea-green shirt of heavy poplin, while Josef's was beige. They completed the ensemble with hunting boots. Daniel thought they somehow looked like thugs, but Maria was pleased.

Josef was impatient to know the purpose of all this; the booby-trap they had labored all afternoon to build, the odd clothes, the fashion show.

"Ask her!" demanded Daniel.

"Forget it! You ask."

At last, a puzzled Josef inquired, "Uh, Your Highness ..."

She interrupted, "Please, we're comrades now. Call me Countess."

"Countess, what's this all about?"

She didn't answer at first but was clearly having an internal debate as to how to respond. After a moment she said forcefully, "The less you know, the better off you will be."

Josef wished his teachers in school had followed that policy. She had answered in such admonitory tones that they dared not bring up the subject again. She returned to her narcissistic engagement with the mirror and then, after a moment, advised, "Better get some sleep now. It may be a very long night."

Exhausted by the afternoon's heavy labors, Daniel and Josef were quick to follow her suggestion. Bearing a tray with supper, Viktor woke them up as the sun was setting. They rapidly tore into roast beef on rye sandwiches, and swallowed tall glasses of fresh milk. They ate their dessert, tarts left over from lunch, as they hurried down to the front door.

Viktor met them with three horses—one for himself, one for the boys to share, and Maria's spirited stallion, who pawed the ground and sidestepped nervously.

Josef mounted first and took the reins since he had considerably more experience with horses than Daniel. They settled uncomfortably into the saddle, Josef complaining, "You're hanging on too tight!" as Daniel squeezed with all his might around Josef's waist.

Daniel retorted, "Move up, you're about to push me off the back end!" Their griping ceased, however, with one cautionary glance from Maria. Her demeanor had changed drastically, from that of a flutter-brained fashion addict to one of a no-nonsense commander in chief. Both boys sensed the danger and seriousness of whatever activity they were about to partake.

Viktor carried the rifles on the back of his saddle. By now it was quite dark, and they followed close behind him. The horses knew the way and sure-footedly loped down the narrow road. They returned to their afternoon work site. He gave the boys each a rifle, then led the horses around the curve into a heavy thicket, where they were tied securely. He then positioned himself approximately 150 to 200 yards further on up the road at a spot where he could see the valley below and thus any approaching intruders.

Finally, Maria explained her plan to the boys. "I have reason to believe the Nazis will be arriving to arrest me tonight. We can't have that, now, can we? The indignity of it all, the poor facilities. You can imagine."

Daniel and Josef exchanged looks, barely discernable in the pale moonlight. Both had tried to avoid imagining just what sort of "facilities" their own family members might be enduring.

Maria went on. "Viktor will signal us if and when they approach. Then" — she pointed to the rocks restrained by the rope netting — "we will let these rocks loose, surprising them and blocking their path."

"Why don't we just block the road with the rocks now?" Josef inquired.

Maria responded, "Surprise, my dear. And what if they don't come? We'll have barricaded ourselves in unnecessarily.

"If they do come," she continued, patting the stock of her rifle with anticipation. "The rifles will serve to detain our unwelcome guests. Perhaps 'disable' them if they prove troublesome."

She pointed to some empty gas tanks hidden in the brush. "While Viktor and I stand guard, you will siphon off their petrol. Do you know how to do that?"

Daniel shrugged hopelessly, but Josef eagerly replied, "Sure!"

"How could you?" demanded Daniel. "I didn't see a single automobile in Zabreh that didn't belong to a German."

"Believe me, I've seen it done," Josef assured Maria.

"Good." She smiled and walked off to confer with Viktor.

"Seen it done ..." repeated Daniel skeptically. "Where?"

"Father Benes did it once when we were on an outing and ran out of gas," Josef reported brightly.

"Oh, well, that makes you an expert."

"Any fool could do it."

"Well, that means you're qualified," Daniel fired back.

Josef dismissed the insult and began to play with his rifle, taking aim at treetops and dropping to a commando's crouch. He would have liked to have crawled on his belly with the weapon on his back, imagining himself singularly breeching the Kaiser's lines back in 1917, but he had too much fear of Maria's wrath should he soil his brand-new clothes.

Second thoughts continued to bounce around Daniel's head like balls in a mad billiard game. "Isn't it awfully risky to siphon petrol from a car full of armed Nazis? Couldn't we go into town and siphon it from parked cars there?"

Maria replied with swiftness and certainty. "Of course it's dangerous. It's terribly dangerous, but I don't know what else I can do. Viktor's already been into town three times at night siphoning petrol. That's how we got the fuel so far. But we don't have enough yet and there's no more time. The Nazis are coming tonight, most likely, and their vehicle should have more petrol than Viktor could ever find in town. Do you have any better ideas?"

"Why don't we just hide?" offered Daniel.

"Where, my dear?" Maria replied soothingly. "They have dogs; eventually they'll find us—or me at least. And this is a golden opportunity to get our petrol and get out. Now, do you have any *more* ideas?"

Of course, the boys did not. Resigning themselves to this precipitous gamble, based almost solely on the confidence Maria seemed to radiate, they threw their lot with her and waited.

Maria offered them cigarettes. Daniel's experience with smoking was nonexistent. However, he took her offer and called on his acting skills to avoid choking and appearing like a rank novice. Josef, on the other hand, smoked with such skill and grace Daniel was left envious and wondering where he had learned it.

After blowing some expert smoke rings, Josef asked Maria, "What if they don't come?"

"All the better," she replied, taking a deep drag. "But I can assure you, they *will* come." She put her hands on her hips, and surveyed the scene. "Have either of you killed a man?" she asked.

They shook their heads.

"Be prepared to. Those bastards would show you no mercy. Don't for a second show them any."

Daniel felt extremely uncomfortable. He didn't want to argue about it, but looked so uneasy that Maria couldn't help but notice. "Daniel, do you find this difficult?" she probed.

"Wouldn't God show them mercy?" he asked quietly.

"Not if He knew what was good for Him!" she returned. "Besides, you're not God."

An awkward silence reigned. Maria appeared frustrated, afraid that Daniel's misgivings might compromise their safety. She offered another argument with all the force she could muster, which was considerable. "Listen, my dear boy, the SS would kill you in a heartbeat and consider the world a better place for it. That's their plan, you know— to rid the world of Jews and gypsies and Catholics and anyone else not part of their master race. Don't you dare hesitate to protect yourself. If you can't hold up your end, get out of here now. You're of no use to me."

Josef stared at Daniel. "How can you care about them after what they did to your father and your family?"

"I don't want to be like them!" he blurted out, full of emotion.

"Look," began Maria calmly. "No one is asking you to become a Nazi. All I'm asking of you is to protect yourself, and me, if need be. If that means killing one or two of our dear German friends, so be it. Do you still have difficulty with that?"

Josef gave Daniel a menacing look, one he used prefatory to throwing a punch. Daniel gave in. "Well, if you put it that way ..."

"Good!" said Maria quickly, thus ending the debate. She dropped her cigarette butt in the dirt and ground it out with her boot heel, imbuing this mundane act with elegance and finality. She brushed some imaginary dust off the seat of her riding pants. "Let's get back to our positions," she urged, very businesslike.

Josef turned to his place below the road, while Daniel took the higher ground near the net. They waited. And waited. Maria nodded off against a large boulder shortly after midnight, but Josef and Daniel remained tense and fully awake a few hours longer, until sleep finally overtook them.

18

Taking Flight

Daniel awoke with a start at a sound incongruous with the usual forest noises, that of a distant motor. He glanced over to see Maria wide awake, gun cocked, ready, without a trace of fear. Josef was also awakened by the faint, yet distinct sound. Acknowledging his wakefulness, Maria looked down at Josef and nodded. Then staring intently down the road, she ignored them both.

Three pairs of ears listened acutely to discern the sort of engine it might be. What was it? A car? But on what road?

All speculation ended when they heard Viktor's signal, a bird call. This was it. Maria and Daniel began to hack furiously at the ropes restraining the bulging load of rocks. As the sound of the car grew louder, they worked even harder. The knives were either dull or ill-suited to this task for it was taking far longer than they anticipated or wanted. By the sound of it, the car was quite close now, perhaps as near as Viktor's hiding spot. They were close to panicking. Finally Maria broke through her end of the rope and a second later so did Daniel his. They both waited expectantly for the avalanche. Only nothing happened. Mocking gravity, the rocks simply sat there.

Mutely accusing him of the snafu, Maria glared at Daniel. By now the Gestapo's car was slowing to make the curve, less than fifty yards away!

"Push them, my dear boy!" she ordered imperiously.

Daniel jumped behind them and shoved, asking, "Aren't you going to help?"

She held out her hands, examined her manicure, and replied, "I supervise ..." Apparently, her birthright exempted her from any activity that might break a nail.

He scrambled on top of the rocks and madly stomped in an effort to elicit the help of physics, but they remained immovable. Just as utter failure seemed certain, the dam broke. The rocks began rolling down the hill—and carried Daniel along for the ride. Frantically clawing at one of the saplings growing out of the bluff, he pulled himself off the landslide before he got buried beneath it.

The majority of the avalanche hit the road just in front of a black SS car, which screeched to a sudden halt. Additional rocks bounced on top of the hood and crashed through the windshield.

Cursing, brushing off pebbles of glass from his immaculate uniform, the driver jumped out, brandishing a machine gun. Viktor, who had followed the car on horseback, aimed his rifle squarely at the man.

"Drop your gun!" he commanded. "Get out, all of you! Now!"

The car doors slowly opened and four other Nazis emerged, guns in hand. When confronted with Viktor, Maria and Josef, their weapons cocked, the troopers sullenly tossed their guns to the ground.

Picking up his rifle, Daniel stumbled down to the road and tried to look like the hardened killer he wasn't. Faking confidence, he stood next to Maria. Josef hauled the petrol tanks to the automobile, inserted a long rubber tube into the vehicle and, as promised, began to siphon away its fuel.

At Maria's quiet command, Daniel moved in close to the Nazis and grabbed their discarded weapons. He avoided any contact with their murderous eyes, which regarded him with reptilian coldness. He walked to a point along the road where the slope deepened into a ravine perhaps sixty to eighty feet deep, and threw their guns into it. He searched their car and found several more weapons; he disposed of them in the same fashion.

The plan was to completely disarm the Nazis, siphon all their fuel, and then leave them. Maria didn't have the stomach to kill them and honestly saw no need to. She, Viktor, and the boys were on horseback; the Nazis would be in the middle of nowhere, out of petrol, with no arms. She didn't even plan to tie the Germans up. Why should she? They could never outrun her horses.

Viktor commanded the Germans, "On your stomachs! On the ground! Now!"

They grudgingly obeyed, but as they did so, the sound of another car was heard in the distance.

"Are there more Gestapo coming?" Viktor demanded of the SS captain. The captain looked up confidently but uttered no words.

A second car full of SS men was *not* part of Maria's plan. Improvisation was now in order.

Although Josef only had time to fill one tank, Viktor said sharply to him, "Let's go!"

They capped the tank, and Viktor swiftly tied it to the saddle of Josef and Daniel's horse. The two boys climbed on behind the load, and kicked the overburdened animal into a reluctant canter.

The abandoned siphoning hose hung out of the car's gas tank, and continued to spill fuel onto the road. As Viktor and Maria leaped on their mounts and took off at a gallop, Viktor turned and fired his rifle at the gasoline puddling on the ground.

The SS troopers jumped to their feet, and their captain began to fire at the riders with a handgun he had successfully hidden in his boot. The small gun was only accurate at close range, however, and did not discourage Viktor from continuing to pepper the gasoline with hot lead until he had ignited it. The flames raced up the hose into the car's gas tank and exploded, engulfing the vehicle in a huge fireball.

A second car pulled up behind the blazing first one as the troopers already there retreated from the inferno. Troopers emerged from the second car with rifles and fired a few shots, but by now the horses were too far away and obscured from their view by the thick, greasy black smoke of the blaze. Immediately the Nazis started clearing away the rocks to make room for the second car to slip by the twisted, burning wreck.

Maria passed the slow-moving horse carrying Josef, Daniel, and the gas tank, while Viktor took up the rear. She led them off the main road and onto a narrow footpath. They raced through a labyrinthine maze of woods and brush, across a creek that flowed as high as the horses' bellies, then ever downhill until they reached the cove where the boys had first encountered the countess.

Viktor dismounted and pulled aside a curtain of branches to

reveal a small hydroplane tethered to a tree, its pontoons partially in the water and half resting on the sandy shore.

"The petrol!" he shouted.

Josef jumped off the horse, while Daniel fumbled with the knots that held the tank in place. Once he'd got it untied, he handed the tank down to Josef, who sprinted to the plane. Viktor began to fuel it.

The sound of an automobile approaching warned them that time was short. "They couldn't have possibly cleared those rocks this quickly," Josef exclaimed. In fact, the SS men had, and their car was now flying down the dirt road, leaving a choking cloud of dust in its wake.

Maria listened intently. The sound was getting closer. "They could be here in minutes," she concluded and climbed quickly into the pilot's seat, where she put on a close-fitting leather helmet, placed aviator's goggles over her eyes, and wrapped a long white silk scarf around her neck, taking painstaking care in knotting it for the most stylish effect. Under the stressful circumstances, Daniel marveled at Maria's cool-headedness. And her vanity. She motioned to Daniel and Josef to climb aboard. Daniel got into the back seat behind her.

"Come on!" Daniel urged Josef, who appeared to be helping Viktor fuel the plane. Maria began her pilot's checklist, turning and flipping switches, preparing the plane for take-off.

Josef showed no inclination to board. "I'm staying," he informed them flatly. "I'm going back to Zabreh."

Daniel couldn't believe what he was hearing. By some miraculous permutation of fate they had found a way to fly free of the Nazis, away from the war and all its horrors, and like a fool Josef was still intent on his suicide mission to Zabreh. "Don't be stupid!" he pleaded. "You'll be killed for sure!"

Josef nodded self-assuredly. "I'll stick with Viktor."

This was obviously news to Viktor, and unwelcome news at that. "This is not a good idea," he objected. "One man can hide; it's far more difficult for two." He might have added, especially when one of the two is a headstrong fourteen-year-old boy.

Deep in the forest the SS car screeched and whined as it negotiated the steep, circuitous path.

Maria commanded, "Josef, do what you must, but we cannot wait. We must take off."

"I'm staying."

Viktor finished fueling the plane, and Maria released the throttle on the engine. They were ready to take off.

"Please come with us!" pleaded Daniel. In the distance the auto abruptly went silent, evidently drowned in the troopers' attempt to ford the creek. However, on foot the Nazis would still be on the scene in a minute's time. The fugitives heard the Germans' angry shouts, their heavy boots pounding down the path.

"I cannot promise your safety," said Viktor, mounting his horse.

"I must find my family," insisted Josef.

Daniel tried again. "Don't do this! Anna didn't die for this!"

A shot spat forth from the woods. Viktor swung about in the saddle and returned fire. His horse pawed the air, and sidestepped nervously.

Daniel desperately strove to find the words that might change Josef's mind in the remaining seconds they had left, for if they took off without him, he would never get back to Zabreh—he would probably never leave the river's edge.

He considered betraying Tomas's confidence and telling Josef that the man he worshipped as his father was not his father. Would Josef even believe him? Or hate him?

He had to try something, so he began, "Josef ... your father ..." Daniel swallowed hard. "Your father ... he, he wouldn't want to see you die in vain."

Josef looked at Viktor, who nodded his head in agreement. A bullet hit the sand a few feet away.

"Go!" ordered Viktor, motioning to the plane.

Maria shouted, "Push us out!" She activated the propellers, which slashed a nearby branch into a flurry of splinters and mulch.

Josef shoved the pontoon off the sand. Viktor took off into the woods, the two riderless horses galloping close behind. The plane moved out into the river, slowly at first, but rapidly gaining speed. Just as they left the calm waters of the cove and entered onto the flowing Danube, the Nazis emerged from the woods and began firing at them.

Caught between the Nazi gunfire and the waters of the Danube, Josef had his mind made up for him. He was standing on one of the pontoons as the plane headed out of the small cove onto the wide river. As the plane gained speed, he climbed into the backseat behind Daniel. Since it was meant to accommodate only one passenger, it was a tight squeeze.

Bullets whizzed about them, yet Maria seemed utterly oblivious to the deadly projectiles whistling by.

"Duck!" Daniel shouted to her.

"I can't. Then I couldn't see where we are going," she replied sensibly. With that pronouncement, she gave the engine additional fuel and the plane became airborne. Her scarf flowed jauntily in the breeze, a banner of triumph to the Nazis she left frustrated on the shore.

Daniel stared at the back of Maria's head, amazed at her courage. Or was it supreme stupidity? Maybe there was a lesson here, he thought; courage is simply the action of someone too stupid to know any better.

The plane continued to climb, although not without some serious pitches, yawing, and hiccoughs from the engine. Daniel leaned over the bulkhead and shouted, "Is everything all right?"

"Perfect!" she replied. "We're on our way to Switzerland!"

The engine sputtered, and they experienced a serious loss in altitude. It caught, and they climbed again.

"Maybe one of those bullets hit us," suggested Josef, white-faced.

As best he could, Daniel looked all over the plane and saw no evidence of damage. "No, I don't think so," he replied.

That left open an even more alarming possibility: that Maria was not quite the accomplished aviatrix her fashionable outfit had led the innocents in the backseat to believe. The plane took another erratic lurch, and Josef shouted into Daniel's ear, "Ask her if she knows how to fly this crate!"

"Why am I always the mouthpiece?" he wondered, but his words were lost in the slipstream. Reluctantly he leaned close to Maria's ear, "How often have you flown this plane?"

"This one? Once!" she replied nonchalantly.

With a sinking feeling, Daniel repeated, "Once?!"

"Yes, of course," she answered, irritated with the utter irrelevance of it all. "Nothing to it."

She thought for a moment. "To be perfectly truthful, I've flown exactly six times. I've simply never *landed* one before. At least not all by myself."

Stricken, Daniel cried, "What?!"

"Relax. I'm sure it's a breeze." But for the briefest moment her eyes gave away the inner fear of her lack of experience. It only lasted a split second, though, for she would never knowingly let the boys witness such vulnerability.

The plane pitched and dropped. Pulling back hard on the stick, Maria over-corrected, jerking Josef and Daniel about like rag dolls.

"What did she say?" asked Josef.

Unwilling to burden him with the imminence of their deaths, Daniel lied, "She said she's flown one ... one hundred times."

"Good," Josef answered. "All this swerving and diving must be to avoid the krauts' bullets."

The fact was, they were well out of range of the krauts, yet the swerving and diving continued. Before long the boys were quite green in the face and consciously swallowing to keep last night's dinner from making an unwanted reappearance. Their queasiness, however, took their minds off Maria's lack of polish in the cockpit. In their cramped position, they remained silent praying for both their lives and their stomachs.

The morning Maria first met Daniel and Josef she had been checking on her airplane stashed in the cove. She acted even more imperious than usual that morning because she feared the craft would be discovered and wanted to get the troublesome urchins away from its hiding place fast. As her cunning mind spun like a roulette wheel and circumstances changed, the urchins become part of her plans. Those plans, while perhaps not working as flawlessly as a Kippelstein watch, had been effective, at least so far.

Daniel shouted out to Maria, "Where did you get this plane?"

Maria shouted back her answer, which was more detailed than Daniel ever imagined. Two years ago Maria had stumbled upon the aircraft at auction in Geneva. The story circulating at the time about the plane's history involved an American industrialist who had struck up a friendship with Glenn Curtiss, the namesake and head of the company that manufactured the Seagull, Curtiss-Wright Corporation. (Wright stood for Orville and Wilbur, who had two decades before ceased any interest in the firm. Nonetheless, the company, besides having quite a pedigree, was the second largest manufacturer of aircraft in the United States.) Glenn Curtiss had invented the first pontoon airplane in 1911. He'd built his Curtiss-Seagull expressly for the U.S. Navy. The American industrialist, however, had managed to get Curtiss to make him a Seagull as well. About the same time the industrialist's business fortunes began taking a tumble, he used his new Seagull to hop across the Atlantic via Nova Scotia, Iceland, and Scotland before landing on the continent, well ahead of his creditors. The creditors, though, caught up with the industrialist in France and sent him in leg irons back to the U.S. on a slow boat. The pontoon plane, an oddity in Europe, was auctioned off in Geneva, but no one bid on it. Except Maria. She had always wanted a plane but didn't want the bother or cost of building a landing strip. The river near her country château would serve as a fine runway for the Seagull.

Daniel had never seen Maria so chatty. She was rattling on seemingly without taking a breath. She certainly left no room for Daniel to speak. He was reminded of his mother, who, when she was nervous, could talk a person's ear off. He had once asked his mother if Christians made babies the same way Jews did. She responded on twenty different topics, none of which had anything to do with his question. Not allowing Daniel a word, she kept yakking until Daniel left the room in boredom. At that point he'd utterly forgotten the original question he'd asked. He wondered if something similar was happening here.

Maria kept chattering on. When Glenn Curtiss learned of the new owner of his plane, he flew a young U.S. navy pilot to Switzerland to teach Maria, or whomever she wanted, how to fly the craft. (Curtiss extended this seemingly unusual courtesy because he had been trying to sell Seagulls to European governments and he thought having one in the skies there might be good advertising. Furthermore, having some incompetent pilot crash one would be terrible publicity for the aircraft. Thus the special navy teacher.) Maria had Arne, her smartest and most trusted employee, learn how to pilot the plane, as she had no intention of learning to fly. However, after the Anschluss in Austria, the Nazis drafted Arne into the Austrian army and thus Maria was left with little choice but to learn to fly the craft herself. It wasn't particularly complicated; after all, nineteen-year-old U.S. navy boys could handle it. However, she had only taken off and landed once. And Arne had been there to back her up. She had never actually flown solo.

They flew low, just above the treetops, over tidy farms and majestic wooded hills. Neither boy had ever seen Austria before, and from their unique sparrow's-eye point of view, each found it spectacularly beautiful. In fact they thought it almost, but not quite, as beautiful as their homeland.

Maria had stopped talking long enough for Josef to shout to Daniel, "Ask her why we're flying so low!"

"Are we flying low to avoid the Luftwaffe?" shouted Daniel to Maria.

"No. It's so when we run out of gas we don't have far to fall."

Her cheerful tones did nothing to allay the sheer horror the boys felt at that news. They stared at each other, aghast. No more questions, they silently vowed, until they were safely on the ground, since Maria's answers did nothing but reveal yet more reasons to fear that by casting their lot with her, they had made a profound, perhaps life-ending mistake.

However, for a time Maria seemed to improve in competence and they began to relax ... until the plane took another terrifying drop. She turned to them and asked, "Are you having a good time?" Obviously, she seemed to be.

Too petrified to answer, they merely bared their teeth in a sickly grimace they hoped would pass for a grin.

The sight of any airplane, but especially one with giant bratwurst feet, was rare enough that farmers, cattle, and goats alike stopped and took notice. Maria spiritedly returned the waves from those mortals locked to the earth several hundred feet below.

The hills grew into mountains, leading to the wall that was the Austrian Alps and, beyond that, Switzerland. Maria's meager flying skills were yet more challenged. She had to fly higher due to the jagged peaks below, and the wind currents and downdrafts tossed the light aircraft about at their will. Worst of all, the frequent lakes and broad, lazy rivers that would have afforded an emergency landing area had disappeared, replaced with rushing torrents of white water and the occasional pond too small to be of any use.

Daniel had warned himself not to ask any more questions, yet he could not help but inquire, "Where are we going to land?"

"We'll find something," she promised, her voice slightly tainted with uncertainty.

He peered over her shoulder and saw that the gas gauge was below one-eighth of a tank. Several minutes later the engine began to knock, and Daniel glanced again. Now the needle indicated "empty." The plane dropped, the needle on the altimeter spun crazily, but Maria

managed to bring it back to level flight. Her face was grimly set, as
though it had only then occurred to her that even countesses are not
immortal. Josef worriedly chewed his nails to the quick and, despite his
acrophobia, glanced down frequently, as though calculating the odds of
surviving such a plummet.

The engine sputtered in its failing efforts to maintain altitude on
mere fumes. Maria warned, "We're going down!"

A deep blue lake beckoned in the distance, but it remained to be
seen if they had enough fuel to reach it. The engine coughed as though it
was in the terminal stages of tuberculosis, and twice stalled altogether.
Frantically Maria worked the throttle and managed to restart the motor.

Daniel and Josef were soaked in sweat blown cold in the
constant, onrushing wind. They concentrated on their goal, the lake, while
they prayed with all their might, willing the plane to remain airborne and
reach its welcoming waters.

The lake was only a few hundred yards distant, but the plane was
rapidly losing all power. They had to maintain sufficient altitude to clear
a stand of tall spruce that guarded the shore. Somehow the plane did it,
missing the boughs so narrowly that the boys could have reached out and
plucked off a pine cone.

As water miraculously appeared below them, Maria
demonstrated her landing skills were on a par with her flying abilities in
general. She came down bone-crushingly hard, and the plane's gigantic
feet bounced right off the surface of the water, as though the lake were
rejecting it and spitting it back into the sky. Gravity, however, proved to
be a stronger force, and the next time they touched down they stayed put.
At this, the engine gave up the ghost entirely.

This proved to be a blessing, since the shoreline was fast

approaching and Maria was unable to figure out how to brake. She randomly fiddled with buttons and turned knobs and, in so doing, lifted some flaps on the wings that slowed their forward momentum. They drifted to a stop about twenty yards from shore. Twenty yards of frigid alpine water that one short month earlier had been solid ice.

Maria looked at them. Words were not necessary. They knew what she expected of them and didn't like it. "I got us this far," she elaborated.

"The water is freezing!" protested Daniel. In vain.

She rummaged in the pockets of her jacket and produced a small mirror and a lipstick; she carefully repaired her makeup before responding. "Surely you don't expect a person of my lineage and breeding ..."

Josef shrugged, pulled off his shoes and outer clothes, and, clad only in his underwear, dove straight in. He came up for air and shook his head, flinging water droplets from his hair. "Whew!" he cried. His voice had climbed a few octaves. "Now I know how they get the sopranos for the Vienna Boys Choir!"

Daniel reluctantly followed Josef's example. Until he hit the surface of the mountain lake, he didn't know what cold was. It literally hit his chest like a sledgehammer, pounding all his breath away. He fought to the surface, gasping. Each boy took the rear of a pontoon and, kicking furiously, propelled the plane toward shore.

As they stood shivering on the shore, Maria stepped out of the plane with their shoes, clothes, and a suitcase, apparently packed and hidden in advance. She had thought of everything, even spare clothes for the boys. She opened the bag and tossed them pairs of fresh, dry underpants.

"Now change!" she commanded. They gaped. "Don't stand there

like dumkopfs!"

They scrambled for the dry clothes, made for the trees, and quickly dressed behind the underbrush in a dense stand of pines.

Maria threw her arms out wide as if to embrace the sky. "Ah, freedom!" she said to no one in particular. She called to the boys, "Welcome to Switzerland!"

A road ran close by the lake, and as the boys finished dressing, an armored scout car pulled up. Daniel grabbed Josef's arm. "Look!" he warned.

Three Nazi soldiers climbed from the vehicle. They should not have been there, unless Germany had somehow conquered Switzerland in the span of a few hours. The boys watched through the branches as the soldiers approached Maria.

"Heil Hitler!" one called out.

Maria glared at them defiantly and didn't reply. She never even glanced in the boys' direction, lest she give them away.

"Who are you?" the soldier demanded, his Luger drawn.

"I'm Amelia Earhart. Is this New Zealand?" she asked scornfully.

"You have no papers, no clearance?" he asked rhetorically. "You are under arrest. Take her."

A subordinate soldier roughly grabbed her wrist and pushed her unceremoniously into the scout car. But Maria kept her composure and dignity, and gave the soldier an utterly contemptuous glare. Daniel thought admiringly of Maria's fierce stare, and if looks could kill, three German heads would have rolled that very minute.

One of the soldier's gazed suspiciously about, as if he expected to find other fugitives. But all signs indicated that Maria had flown solo. So after one last look he joined his fellow troopers and the scout car sped off.

Once Daniel and Josef were sure that the coast was clear, they walked up the road in the same direction the German vehicle had traveled. About a mile farther on they reached a signpost that solved the mystery of the Nazis' presence; they hadn't made it to Switzerland at all, but had gone down in German-occupied Austria. It indicated that Innsbruck was seventy kilometers to the east, Switzerland fifteen kilometers to the west.

Josef and Daniel looked at each other grimly, thinking kindred thoughts. A mere fifteen kilometers. So close, yet ill chance had dogged them again, landing them in a Nazi-controlled Austrian lake instead of a friendly Swiss one.

Josef brightened quickly. "Good. We're only a few hours walk from the border."

"What?" Daniel responded, shocked. "We're going to Innsbruck!"

"But we're so close! Come on."

Daniel stood his ground. "We have to try and help Maria."

Josef grew indignant. "Now hold it! I couldn't go help my own family, but I'm supposed to rescue some spoiled Countess? With her breeding and royal blood she can take care of herself. Besides, how can we help her?"

"You're acting like all the people who didn't lift a finger when the Gestapo killed my father. Who didn't raise their voices when they took your family," Daniel accused him

For a fleeting moment, Josef's face reflected the inner conflict he felt. He knew they should do something, and he quickly cooked up a plan. "All right," he agreed. "We go to Switzerland, raise an army, and go back and rescue her *and* my family."

Obviously, he meant every ridiculous word. Daniel couldn't believe what he was hearing. "Raise an army? In a neutral country?! What are you, Josef of Arc?! That is the dumbest idea ..."

Josef sighed, reality being too hard to ignore. "Okay, but why do you need me? You don't even trust me!"

"'Cause I'm not sure I can do it alone."

Wistfully looking off in the direction of Switzerland, Josef wrapped his arms around his chest and kicked at the dust in the road. He wanted to plug his ears and tune Daniel out.

Daniel was all the more determined to be heard. "Look. No one helped our country when the Nazis took over. No one helped Anna." Daniel paused to let the weight of the truth hit home. "We've got a chance to help Maria. She helped us! I couldn't live with myself if I abandon her. I'm going to Innsbruck. You ... you go live in your dream world. Go recruit William Tell and the Three Musketeers and whomever else you can find to come back and storm Austria!" He then turned and resolutely began the seventy-kilometer trek. To hell with Josef, he thought.

He'd only gone about thirty paces when Josef called out, "Kip!"

Daniel stopped and turned around. Josef was standing in the same spot, still staring off toward Switzerland. Then Josef shook his head, as if to cut his dreams free, and wiped his sleeve across his face with disgust.

"You should really learn not to spit when you talk."

With that Josef wheeled about and began walking toward Innsbruck. No admission of defeat on his part. No validation whatsoever of Daniel's good sense. Yet, Daniel could not find it in his heart to be angry. Josef's actions were the only words necessary. Together they had a chance, albeit a slim one, to help Maria.

19

Lucky Thirteen

They walked until dark, a distance of thirty miles. By then their legs felt as heavy as marble columns. With almost no words, the boys ambled a short way into a pasture and fashioned crude beds out of hay from a haystack. They slept as shepherds have for millennia, beneath a thousand stars. An occasional cocoa-brown and chalk-white Simmental cow came by and, keeping a safe distance, checked out the field's newest boarders.

The following morning, rested but famished, they hitched a ride from a farmer driving a wagon east to Innsbruck. The lift spared them an arduous trek up and down the steep grades leading to the Tyrolean city. On the way they passed through the small towns of Telfs and Zirl. They were quite astonished to discover that Innsbruck was not a sleepy little mountain village, but a major provincial center of 80,000 people. The farmer dropped them at the Altstadt, the city center of Innsbruck's old town.

Within the constraints of the narrow Inn River valley, formed by the Nordkette mountain to the north and the Patscherkofel and Serles peaks to the south, buildings tended to grow up rather than sprawl horizontally. Most were five- or six-story walk-ups, their steeply inclined roofs designed to shed the alpine winter snow.

Josef and Daniel were impressed by the buildings in the Old Town Center. First to grab their eyes was the Golden Dachlor, or Golden Roof, a luxury porch built for Maximilian I so that he could observe the goings-on of the square. The roof was made of copper shingles that shimmered like rich gold in the sun's light. Next to the Golden Dachlor was the striking Stadtturin, the Old Town City Watch Tower. This narrow tower had a large clock facing the square with an onion spire the color of deep green. Opposite the Golden Roof was the most ostentatious building of all, the Helblinghaus. The Helblinghaus looked like a five story, salmon pink-colored wedding cake, with the most elaborate baroque-rococo decorations imaginable. It was like no building they had ever seen before.

The boys decided to venture forth from the Helblinghaus because they figured they wouldn't need bread crumbs, like Hansel and Gretel, to find their way back. Anyone in town could direct them back to this crazy, fantastic structure.

They wandered around the narrow streets of the old town, which dated to the Dark Ages of the thirteenth century. And it *was* dark; the streets were hemmed in like canyons, although the occasional broad square relieved the claustrophobic feel. The boys observed that many residents had brightened their windows with boxes of petunias and geraniums, which gave the Altstadt a head start on spring. Street vendors catered to the tourist trade. But the ubiquitous Nazi banners festooned flagpoles and buildings: a blot on the otherwise idyllic landscape.

Using the tips Tomas had given them, Josef and Daniel began looking for contacts with the underground Resistance. One block from the town center, they went to a rathskeller but were put off by the bartender's surly stare. They ventured a block further and found a beer hall, sat down at a corner table, and furtively cased the place. They saw no Nazis. But before they could approach the barkeep, three German soldiers walked in and were greeted jovially. The boys exited immediately. Promptly their heads swam with second thoughts. No bartender would treat soldiers of the Third Reich rudely, unless he wanted his place torn apart, or shut down, or burned down, or whatever the mood of the Nazis happened to call for. As a result, a jovial greeting might merely be an act of a clever, survival-oriented Resistance member. But then Josef pointed out something perceptive; in the kind of place the boys were seeking, the customers wouldn't want Nazis in their midst. So they kept going, trusting their instincts.

Three more beer gardens were checked out and found to be lacking in some key aspect. They wandered farther from Innsbruck's main streets, to progressively smaller and quieter drinking establishments. Eight more places failed to pass the test, whatever that ill-defined mix of intuition was. Secretly they each began to doubt the wisdom of this detour. Almost by accident they spotted a small bierstube down a narrow side street. It was the thirteenth stop, unlucky thirteen, cursed thirteen, and they thought of just skipping it and going on to fourteen, but they didn't. They would take a quick look and be gone. Once inside, however, they found the place had a feel reminiscent of Jan's in Bratislava, before the two young slaves appeared on the scene to clean it up. The windows were dusty to the point of near-opacity, cigarette butts and spent matches littered the floor, and there was an air of casual conviviality. No Nazis caroused within, and a young waitress, who was rather plain-looking but had a highly contagious smile, approached them moments after they walked in.

She did not look through them as if they were ghosts, like so many women do to young men who don't yet sport whiskers. She had auburn hair and smoky gray eyes that regarded them with a fiery, yet friendly intensity. Josef and Daniel were instantly smitten, for despite her somewhat average looks, her other attributes were outstanding—lush curves with slim, shapely legs revealed by her short dirndl.

"What can I get for you?" she asked, her voice welcoming and cheerful.

"A beer," answered Josef.

"Make it two," added Daniel. Maria had slipped some Austrian schillings and Swiss francs into their pockets, in the event they somehow became separated. But the amounts were not princely. Upon their arrival in Innsbruck they had splurged on three pretzels from a street vendor, each devouring one and splitting the third. Consequently, after paying for their beers, they would be nearly broke.

Money worries, however, were the farthest thing from their minds in the presence of this fraulein. As she turned to leave she flashed her smile again; it was a smile that could melt the coldest steel. After she left to fill their order, they avidly discussed her charms.

Josef, dreamer and braggart that he was, described in vivid detail the extreme pleasure he would provide for her if only he could get her alone.

While such delicious fantasies had crossed Daniel's mind, he hadn't lost sight of the serious matters at hand. The girl returned with the beers, and was off to attend to other customers before Josef could transfix her with his charm. The boys drank quickly, to quench their thirst as well as quell their jumpy nerves. The prospect of actually approaching the bartender and making contact suddenly seemed like an impossible ordeal.

Together, they summoned all their courage and walked up to the bartender. He was tall, slender, about forty years old, with light brown hair and a sparse mustache.

"Good day," began Daniel awkwardly, both because of his lack of skill at speaking German and his uncertainty over what exactly to say.

The man ignored him at first and continued to dry beer mugs. When the boys didn't go away, he looked down at them and said pointedly, "Good day."

"Is there a lot of mining in these mountains? *Underground*?" asked Josef coyly.

The man paused a beat in his polishing. They thought he had taken the bait, but instead he firmly stated, "No." Then he asked more conversationally, "Where did you get those accents?"

"We're from Prague," replied Daniel.

"How did you get here?"

"You wouldn't believe me if I told you," Daniel sighed, and changed tack. "Let me ask you this. What's the German word for 'resistance'?"

The bartender again stared at them appraisingly. "There is no word for that in German. Only in Austrian. And now, maybe in Czech." He put down his rag. "Come here. Let me show you something."

He went through a door next to the bar. Josef and Daniel looked at each other indecisively, then glanced around the beer hall. Perhaps they had found their elusive contact; or perhaps, a Nazi informer who would club them on the head, tie them up, and deliver them to the Gestapo. The odds were as good as the flip of a coin. They followed him anyway.

The man turned on a dusty overhead bulb that dimly lit a storeroom. He quietly shut the door behind them and then furiously seized both of the boys by their shirt collars and slammed them up against the wall. They struggled, but his slender build belied considerable strength. He got right in their faces and spoke in a hard, coarse voice. "What do you want?!"

Scared breathless, Josef managed to croak, "A friend of ours is being held by the Gestapo."

At this juncture the barmaid who had taken their order slipped inside. Their captor stiffened at the intrusion, but relaxed and nodded at her.

"Who is your friend?" he demanded of the boys.

"Her name is Maria von Hapsburg," said Daniel.

The girl intervened, "One of *the* Hapsburgs?"

Daniel nodded. "So she says." She certainly acted the part and had all the wealth and property of a Hapsburg.

The waitress nodded wisely. "Someone very important is being held here," she confirmed. "Brought in yesterday."

"That's her!" they exclaimed.

"She said the Nazis wanted her money," added Josef.

The bartender loosened his choking grip and the boys breathed easier. He and the barmaid conferred in whispers, but the boys could not make out a word of their rapid-fire German. When their conversation ended, the barmaid took Josef to another small storage room upstairs from the bierstube and locked him there. The bartender barked at Daniel, "I hear one sound out of you, both you and your buddy will be beaten to a pulp!" and then he left, quietly closing the door and locking it.

When Daniel's eyes adjusted to the near blackness, he could discern several chairs missing one or more legs and three round tabletops, completely without appendages, stacked like pancakes on the floor. Several wooden barrels, which either presently held ale or at one time did, further cramped the already constricted space. The room smelled so overpoweringly of stale beer that, he thought, if you could squeeze the wall and floorboards like a sponge, decades-old ale would come cascading out.

Daniel sat alone and waited. After some time he began to cry. He should have listened to Josef; this whole affair had been a terrible, terrible mistake. He cried at his own stupidity. What could an undersized fourteen-year-old do anyway? What a fool he was! Yet as the tears flowed, he cried in near silence, so as not to tempt the bartender's threat.

An hour and a half passed before Daniel heard a key turn in the door lock. He stood and in fear gravitated toward the shelter of one of the barrels. The man who entered was wearing a dark coat and a thick scarf wrapped around his face just beneath his eyes. A large cap covered his head and was pulled down close to his eyes. In the dim light, all Daniel could tell was the masked man stood about six feet tall and had an average build. He made Daniel sit down in a chair and began questioning the frightened, red-eyed boy.

"Who told you to come to this place?"

"No one," Daniel answered.

"Then why did you come and start asking questions?"

"We went to at least a dozen places first."

"Then why did you come here?"

"There weren't any Nazis here ..."

"What's your name?"

"Daniel Kippelstein."

"How do you spell that?"

While Daniel spelled it, the man wrote it down as if there was something highly sinister in those letters.

"What's your friend's name?"

Daniel spelled that too.

"Where are you from?"

Daniel answered every question and the man with the covered face took frequent notes. The questions were often repetitive; Daniel was asked to explain several times about their contact in Bratislava (without mentioning he was Josef's brother) and how he'd told them to try to connect with Resistance in other cities. After pressing for the contact's name, the man zoomed in two inches from Daniel's nose and yelled, "TELL ME! What's his name?!"

Daniel refused to utter a word, while shaking in his seat from fear. From this close encounter with the man, Daniel noticed he had blue eyes and light brown eyebrows.

Again questions were repeated and the man's notes were checked. After two hours of interrogation, the blue-eyed man abruptly left. Several minutes later a taller man entered, also with a scarf covering his face except for his eyes and a hat pulled closely over his head. He had dark eyes and black, bushy eyebrows. The taller man seemed to be more soft-spoken and less intense, but he asked nearly all the same questions the previous man had. The taller man also wrote down notes as Daniel answered, and he repeated questions to a ridiculous extent. Their clear intent was to try and catch the boy in a lie. Because of the near idiotic repetition of questions, Daniel began to suspect the taller man was a mental defective.

After two more hours of this rigorous yet, because of its repetition, mind-numbing questioning, the taller, dark-haired man asked Daniel again about his Bratislava contact.

"What's his name?"

"I won't tell you."

"What's his first name?"

"Alright, should I spell it?"

"Yes," the taller man eagerly replied, anxious for a break in Daniel's armor.

"H-I-T-L-E-R."

The taller man's eyes narrowed; he was not the least bit amused. Daniel recklessly continued, "If you're not going to help us, let us go! We don't know who you are, and all these pointless questions are wasting precious time!"

The tall man stood looking at Daniel and didn't say a word. Daniel, under the man's withering gaze, decided to back-pedal somewhat.

"I'm sorry. I don't mean any disrespect, but we really have important work to do and if you're not going to help ..." his voice trailed off, outracing his thoughts.

The tall man turned and walked out. Again Daniel was left alone in darkness.

Minutes later the door was unlocked and Josef was ushered back in by the bartender and the barmaid. The bartender said, "Go with her. Her name is Louisa. She will give you a place to sleep. We will talk in the morning."

"Are you going to help us?" Daniel asked.

"We will do what we can, but we guarantee nothing," the bartender replied bluntly.

It appeared, though, that the boys had convinced them of their authenticity. At first Daniel and Josef both felt it was incredible blind luck that they had found people willing and ready to help them. Yet as they discussed it, they realized common sense and self-interest played a much greater part in their discovery of comrades in arms than something as capricious as luck. First, as Tomas Czerny had noted without spelling it out, any establishment serving alcohol is a candidate for a Resistance meeting place. Josef pointed out that certain drinking venues attract, to varying degrees, angry, bitter people drinking away their anger and bitterness. In Nazi-occupied territory there was no shortage of such people. Daniel added that as liquor liberates and lubricates the tongue, it is natural that frustration with the fascists would arise in conversation, and that eventually some would begin discussing solutions to those frustrations, and then take actions to meet those solutions. Of course, not every bierstube was a Resistance cell, and in fact it took the boys most of a day and over a dozen stops before they found what they were looking for.

Second, the boys discovered that Louisa's brother, Kurt, had been arrested for helping several Jews get from Innsbruck to Vienna, where they were to be secretly transported to Palestine. Kurt had been detained in the Innsbruck Nazi headquarters for almost two months and was being slowly starved to death. During this time plans had been made and weapons gathered for Kurt's escape. Yet there apparently was a shortage of trustworthy and courageous coconspirators. Now Daniel and Josef presented the possibility of additional hands while in Maria lay the potential of reward money, if the Resistance could successfully free her.

Such advantages were not easily overlooked by Louisa and her comrades.

As for the suitability of Daniel and Josef as Resistance fighters, at this early stage of the war, nobody was particularly qualified; there were no advanced degrees in guerilla warfare, everyone's resume was essentially blank. Therefore, two intelligent, able-bodied, motivated fourteen-almost fifteen-year-olds were no more or less qualified than anyone else. So that is how common sense and self-interest, not blind luck, brought these disparate parties together in one united cause: to free the prisoners being held by the Nazis at their Innsbruck headquarters. And even if something as ephemeral as luck did play a role, considering the ill winds that had thus far buffeted the boys, one balmy breeze was more than overdue.

Louisa untied her apron and threw it on a hook as they walked out. She led Josef and Daniel to her apartment a block and a half away. It was small; they would have to sleep on the floor again, but it beat the cow pasture of the night before. Around a corner and out of view in her dining nook, Daniel noticed a picture of Hitler. Someone had used a heavy black grease pencil to give Adolf a pair of glasses, and a hole had been stabbed through his mouth, wherein a half-smoked cigar had been impudently stuck, so he now resembled Groucho Marx with a silly postage-stamp mustache. Daniel alerted Josef and they smiled appreciatively.

Once the boys were settled in, Louisa returned to work. They recounted for each other their interrogation experiences, which turned out to be practically identical except switched in order; Josef had been questioned first by the taller man, then the blue-eyed, light-haired one. They helped themselves to marzipan candies and cold sausages from Louisa's icebox and read the newspaper. Daniel worked to catch up on his journal, again careful to alter all names and locations.

As the day darkened into evening and writer's cramp set in, Daniel folded the pages and placed them back in Anna's copy of *Huckleberry Finn*. The fact that the book was the only tangible thing left of Anna's made Daniel feel terribly sad and lonely. She loved books; she had a sizable collection of them, yet it was this Twain novel, one of her favorites, that had somehow survived. Survival was so random. His watch, likewise, was all he had to show for his father's life. The tears began to well up, but he didn't want to cry, at least not in front of Josef. He would cry when all this was over; for Father, and Mother, Jacob, Anna, for himself.

To prevent a complete breakdown, he began to read, opening the book to the point where Huck meets young Buck Grangerford, whose family is embroiled in a bloody feud with another clan, the Shepherdsons. Reading how the Shepherdsons ambush and kill Buck only deepened Daniel's depression.

He thought about America. It was one of the many places where he wanted to travel. Maybe even first on the list. But what kind of place must it be where blood feuds go on and they kill each other's young people? Is this how they settle their disputes? Is this how they treat their neighbors? he wondered. It sounded so stupid and senseless.

Then it dawned on him—the butchery in Europe was simply one giant blood feud, and it was every bit as stupid and senseless as the one in *Huckleberry Finn*. Only it was on a much bigger, much more stupid and senseless scale. And it was real, not fiction. Daniel fell asleep with the book falling to his side.

Louisa did not return until the following morning, when she awoke them with great urgency. "They're taking her to Salzburg tomorrow. We must move quickly."

She drew some boys' clothes from a sack, outfits which would enable them to better blend into the Austrian mountain city than the country weekend hunting apparel Maria had given them. Being Czechoslovakian through and through, Daniel and Josef winced at the prospect of wearing knee-length lederhosen with a colored floral pattern embroidered on the bib and loose-collared white shirts. Reluctantly they changed into them, then accompanied Louisa to the beer hall.

She hustled them into the storeroom and removed several weapons from a wooden crate. The crate, which bore official German army markings, had evidently been pilfered from the enemy's arsenal. By now their uneasiness in the presence of firepower had diminished, though neither boy was eager to actually use one of the things. Still, Maria's kill-or-be-killed lecture was fresh in their minds.

Louisa held up a grayish green metal cylinder about the size of a soup can with two holes and a metal ring on the top. "This is a tear gas grenade," she explained. "You pull the ring here, out goes the pin, and you have five seconds before the gas explodes."

"What's the plan here?" asked Josef suspiciously.

Louisa looked at the boys. The moment of truth had arrived. "While we believe you, we don't trust you enough to risk our own lives. So the plan is this: We will create a distraction and cover you, but you will have to go in and free this countess, as well as the other prisoners being held."

"Wait a minute ..." began Josef skeptically before Louisa cut him off.

"If you won't risk your lives, why should we? Besides, you can't shoot well enough to cover us. So why shouldn't you be the ones to go in?"

"Go in where?" Daniel asked.

"Nazi headquarters, where they're holding the prisoners."

The boys stood silent. Before they could speak, Louisa jumped in again. "Let me explain the rest of the plan before you back out ..."

She rummaged in another box and presented them with rubber gas masks. They tried them on, each reflecting how much the other looked like an insect, their eyes swimming indistinctly behind the thick glass eyeholes. "You must wear these masks or you'll be very unhappy," she warned.

"What do you mean?" Daniel asked.

"You'll choke and cough, your eyes and throat will burn, you might heave your guts out, and while it won't kill you, you'll wish you were dead."

Josef noticed two additional masks. "Why do we need these?" he asked.

"One is for Maria. The other is for a prisoner named Kurt; he will unlock the other cells," Louisa explained.

She carefully detailed the escape plan, then made them repeat each step out loud to make sure they knew their roles. Daniel noted that Josef was a far quicker study in matters of guerilla warfare than he had ever been at math or geography.

In addition to the tear gas, she handed them a larger olive green grenade shaped like a lemon, with a black pin sticking out the top. They recognized it for the bomb it was, and handled it warily.

"And this is in case you get in trouble. Pitch it as far as you can and use it *only* in an emergency. Because after you pull the pin, you have five seconds before all hell breaks loose."

"How many others will be with us?" Daniel asked.

"Two."

"That's only five in total!" cried a shocked Josef, who felt it would take nothing less than a battalion to successfully storm a Gestapo prison.

"And two of them are us!" added Daniel with trepidation.

"The number of people is not as important as good planning and execution," she insisted.

"I don't like the word 'execution,'" said Josef dourly.

Two men entered the storeroom.

"This is Christian and Frederich," said Louisa by way of introduction. "Daniel and Josef."

As the two men spoke it became clear they were the boys' two interrogators. Christian looked to be in his thirties, while Frederich was perhaps in his early twenties. Christian was blue-eyed and nearly blond, as well as clean-shaven, his cheeks sunburned and ruddy from high altitude exposure to the sun. His hands were smooth and uncalloused, as though he was unused to heavy manual labor. The taller Frederich— black-haired, swarthy, with acne-scarred cheeks that had the texture of an orange—was a German national who had worked as a longshoreman in Danzig. He had come to the Resistance after the Nazis killed his girlfriend on the mere suspicion that she helped Jews escape the country. From their interrogation, the boys knew both men to be quite ruthless and tough, and they felt somewhat more confident knowing that such fellows were on their side. All four shook hands.

"So, are you in?" Christian probed.

The boys looked at each other. "How do we know we can trust you?" Daniel asked.

"You don't," Christian replied. "But then how do we know we can trust you? So I guess that makes us even."

"How do we know this is the best plan?" Josef countered.

"You just have to trust us," Christian returned.

Josef and Daniel eyed this threesome warily.

"We know the building and the area. And after all, you came to us," Frederich added.

"You're welcome to back out now. But once you're in ..." Christian didn't feel a need to complete the sentence.

The boys each thought a long moment. Finally Josef asked, "We do this tonight?"

There was no more discussion. They made a final equipment check, stowing the loose items in a leather-trimmed canvas traveling bag.

"Are you ready?" Christian asked. Louisa, Josef, and Daniel nodded.

They followed Louisa to a busy sidewalk café, sat down at a table, and ordered coffee. A huge Nazi flag was draped across the second-story elevation of the Gestapo headquarters, which faced the café.

Unlike most of the buildings in Innsbruck, it was a mere three stories high, with a sharply pitched roof adding additional height. All of the windows above the ground floor were obscured by black paint, leading Daniel to question just what acts the Nazis wished to hide from view. The arched entryway held a set of heavy steel double doors. An SS car pulled up, and a man in uniform emerged and went inside. They knew immediately this was someone important by the manner in which the other SS men stood erect and saluted with extra vigor. The high-level officer looked to be in his fifties, but had the trim physique of a much younger man. Even from their distant vantage point, Daniel could discern a deep scar down the left side of the officer's face.

"Who is he?" Josef whispered.

"Major Weissbach of the SS," Louisa answered.   "He's in Salzburg to deal with border problems between Austria and Switzerland. They call him 'The Torch.' He tells prisoners that if they confess, even if they're innocent, he'll let them go.   But once they confess he personally takes a flamethrower and burns them alive, until their fillings melt and run from their teeth like water."   She added in a grim monotone, "He did that to one of my brothers in Salzburg."

Rumors swirled, she continued, that Weissbach was the Nazis' ace interrogator, which meant he was no stranger to torture and a flamethrower was hardly his only tool.   He supposedly joined the Nazis early on, around 1931, in his hometown of Munich.   He had three significant promotions that, interestingly enough, all followed the discrediting and dismissal of his superior officer. It was never proven, of course, that Weissbach had used the Nazis' own rampant paranoia to destroy innocent and loyal superior officers, but after three such occurrences, the pattern forced a person to wonder.   Providing further irony, for all three occurrences, Weissbach was put in the difficult and uncomfortable position of interrogating the very officer he himself had unjustly smeared.   It came as no surprise, Louisa pointed out, that the talented and imaginative torturer elicited full confessions from the "guilty" officers before they unfortunately died from various causes during or just after their questioning.   Louisa repeated the story whispered among Weissbach's underlings that one of those superior officer's cause of death was listed as "hypertension," which was true but not quite a complete account.   Death occurred after electric prods with full electric current attached to the man's testicles were "mistakenly" left on overnight. *After* a full confession had been signed. Hypertension indeed.

For such sterling results, Louisa reported, Weissbach was highly regarded in Berlin, and thus put in charge of Operation Tourniquet, the Nazis' effort to stop the flow of refugees bleeding across the Austrian border into Switzerland. Maria von Hapsburg would be one of Operation Tourniquet's biggest trophies.

Josef began to fidget; he looked up and down the street for Christian and Frederich, who had slipped away after they left the beer hall. "Where are they?"

"Be patient," Louisa responded calmly. "Excuse me. I need to go to the WC," and she got up and left the table.

Josef had an excited look on his face. "We're going to be commandoes!"

Daniel was unmoved. "Josef, do you have any clue why we are going in?"

Josef looked uneasy and didn't answer.

"Do you think it's because of all our experience?"

They didn't have any experience, so Josef knew that wasn't it.

"Or that we're such good marksmen?"

Josef knew they were quite incompetent with guns. Again he didn't answer.

"We're going in because it's the most dangerous job and they don't care if we get killed."

Josef was stunned.

"That's right. We are of so little value, they don't care if we get killed."

Josef swallowed uncomfortably and looked off into the distance.

"So don't talk to me about being commandoes," Daniel said with finality.

20

The Mission

Inside Nazi headquarters Maria von Hapsburg was tied to a chair in a room devoid of any other furniture, its blank gray walls holding shadows cast by a single light hanging overhead. Her interrogation, which had started the previous day and had been on-going most of this day, had been physically abusive almost from the beginning. She had heard this was due to the Germans' belief that physical torture worked, and she was now witnessing their relish in the actual performance of such acts, which were spurred further by Maria's stubbornness and undisguised hatred of them. Up to now she had been quizzed and slapped and beaten by a low-level officer. Now it was time for an acknowledged expert; it was Major Weissbach's turn. He began pacing.

"Now, you know the sooner you cooperate, the sooner we can let you go ... So ... what is your name?"

"I told you ... Shirley Temple."

Stopping in front of Maria, Weissbach wound up and furiously belted her across the face with his fist. Used to it by now, she took the hit like a punching bag.

"We know you are Maria von Hapsburg. Why do you continue this foolish charade?"

"Why do you continue asking questions you already know the answers to? Who's foolish here?!"

Weissbach smiled a slight, twisted smile to himself, as if a particularly cruel thought had just alighted upon his mind, like a fly landing on excrement.

"Would you care for a cigarette?" he asked nonchalantly.

"Yes," Maria muttered.

Weissbach removed a cigarette from his pocket, lit it, and took a deep draw on it. Then he walked over behind Maria. He knelt down and, holding Maria's tightly bound arms, applied the burning end of the cigarette to the skin on the back of her hand. She tensed and screamed out as the cigarette slowly scorched her flesh. Her scream grew to a long, agonized wail as the major held the cigarette to her hand for half a minute or more, until it had burnt a deep hole into her hand. Then he pulled the cigarette away and took another long draw on it. He walked around in front of Maria and asked himself as he blew out a cloud of smoke, "I wonder why it always tastes so much better after I do that?" He began his questioning again. "Now where are your bank accounts?"

Maria, dazed but still filled with hate, looked up at him and answered, "The First Bank of the Reichstag."

Weissbach wound up and belted her face even more savagely. He turned away, took another draw on the cigarette. "You know this is hurting me more than it's hurting you."

Maria mumbled something in a very soft voice.

"What was that?" he snapped.

The countess lifted her head up, mustered some of her fast fading energy, and answered clearly and with conviction, "Rot in hell!"

Weissbach at first didn't react. But then he calmly walked over to Maria, reared one leg back, and viciously drove his boot into her face, sending her flying over backward. Blood began trickling down her nose and out one corner of her mouth.

"You have no idea how much this hurts me," he said, his eyes narrowing and that slight, warped smile crawling like a worm across his face.

Daniel, Josef, and Louisa sat at the outdoor café a good part of the afternoon and into the early evening, overdosing on strong black coffee, eating pastries, and growing more and more tense. They were rapidly learning that the hardest part of combat is the waiting. Louisa made small talk to distract them.

"I must admit, I think you two are very brave."

"Very brave or very stupid," Daniel said nervously, tending to think it was the latter.

"Speaking of stupid, I can't wait to change out of this outfit," Josef complained. "We look like yodeling sheepherders."

"Oh, I don't know," Louisa began. "That outfit shows off how attractive your legs are."

Surprised at her comment, Josef glanced down as if to confirm the fact that he did indeed have legs and that they could be described so by such a likable girl. He beamed with pride. It reminded him of Anna, but in a pleasing way, a way that made him happy.

Needless to say, the compliment irked Daniel. He didn't have to check out his own knobby knees and underdeveloped calves and thighs to know that lederhosen did not similarly flatter him. And why were girls always going out of their way to butter up the already conceited Josef? Didn't Daniel have any attributes himself that the opposite sex might find appealing?

But before he could debate or resolve this issue, Louisa nudged Josef and Daniel. Across the street Christian and Frederich were chatting casually, walking toward the Nazi headquarters. They turned into a vestibule one door south of the headquarters. Louisa stood up.

"I'll see you at the back door," she reminded them as she left quickly.

They rose, Josef carrying the valise with their tools, grenades, and gas masks. Daniel noted, "How come no one ever tells me I have attractive legs?"

Josef snickered, "Because no one wants to lie!"

Daniel set his mouth in exasperation and shook his head in resignation. How had he put up with Josef's vanity and hectoring for so long?

Major Weissbach dabbed sweat from his forehead with a handkerchief. The room was purposely warm, yet the oppressive stuffiness seemed to be taking more of a toll on him than its intended victim. The long drive from Salzburg had tired him; he needed a stiff drink, and decided to quit for the day. He opened the door and motioned to the guard stationed outside.

"Take her back to her cell." He then addressed Maria. "We have a big day planned for you tomorrow. You realize if you don't tell us what we need to know, you are of no use to us. You are like garbage. We will slit your throat and dump your body in the garbage."

Barely able to talk, Maria managed, "And if I do tell you, then I'll be no use to you anymore, and you'll slit my throat and dump me in the garbage. So what's the difference?"

"I hadn't thought of that. It's such a negative outlook. It's probably true, but how can you live with yourself and be so negative? It's not like you, Fraulein Temple ... not like you at all." He blithely tipped his hat to her as the battered woman was taken away. "Good night, my dear," he said with all the warmth of a gargoyle.

The boys mentally rehearsed their roles.Once inside the headquarters, they were to release the prisoners while Christian and Frederich kept the SS busy out front and Louisa blew open the back door. With the prisoners, Daniel and Josef would then escape out that back door.

The mountain night air was chilly, and short pants were not exactly seasonable attire. Goose bumps popping, they strolled across the street, up to Christian and Frederich in the vestibule.

"Do you think you can find the basement door?" Christian asked. They believed the prisoners were being held in the basement of the headquarters.

The boys nodded affirmatively.

"Stay low. We'll be covering you," Christian added.

Frederich pulled a black wool mask over his face. Josef opened the bag and handed Daniel a gas mask. They each put one on, then watched as Christian and Frederich approached the Nazi guard in front of the building.

Before the guard could react, Christian pulled a Luger out of his pocket, put it to the man's chest, and fired a muffled shot. He held him up briefly, so as to ease the Nazi's fall to the ground.

Daniel stared. The guard's face was just an arm's length from him. The man's eyes had gone black and vacant in an instant. It had happened so fast, yet Daniel had perceived it as if it had been occurring in slow motion. Fear gripped him like a vice; he felt paralyzed.

Their two comrades pulled the rings from tear gas grenades and lobbed them inside the Nazi headquarters, then waited just outside the doors. Moments later, two SS men stumbled out coughing and choking. Christian and Frederich each grabbed one and put a cloth over their mouths and noses. It had been dipped in chloroform, and momentarily both troopers went limp and unconscious.

It was time to move. Josef gave Daniel a hard shove to get him into gear, and they rushed into the headquarters as Frederich held the door open for them. The thick, acrid smoke billowed forth, but the masks proved to be effective. However, they could only see a few feet in front of them. The smoke prevented the Nazis from seeing them, but likewise they could not see the Nazis. The cloud also made it impossible to locate the basement door by sight. Crouching very low, they made their way along the appropriate wall described in the plans. At times the gas was so impenetrable that Daniel's only point of reference was the shuffle of Josef's feet just inches in front of him.

An SS man came running out of the fog, nearly stepping on Daniel's hand as he ran past. The soldier, however, never saw the boys. Shots rang out; more gunfire answered. Increasingly disoriented, Daniel could not tell if the shots were coming from Frederich and Christian or the Germans. Shouts, mostly German obscenities, added to the pandemonium.

The coughing had ceased, however, indicating their foes had managed to put on gas masks—and nullifying Josef and Daniel's advantage. The boys pressed on, crawling under a desk that impeded their progress.

They found a door on the other side, and according to the floor plan Louisa had described, they assumed it led to the basement. It was padlocked. Josef reached in the bag for a screwdriver, jammed the tool into the lock, and pried it from the wall.

A shot ricocheted close by as they pulled the door open. Inside, an array of cleaning supplies greeted them—brooms, mops, buckets, rags. Unbelievably, the compulsively neat Germans had padlocked the janitorial closet! The boys looked at each other in wordless disgust, and moved on. There was another door a few feet away.

It too was padlocked, but Josef quickly removed the impediment with the screwdriver. Just then four shots hit the wall to the right of the door. Josef and Daniel dove to their bellies. Dust and plaster fragments flew everywhere. The formerly padlocked door now swung open to a stairway that plunged into darkness. As he slowly uncovered his head (as if his arms would protect him), Daniel noticed a ring of keys on a small nail next to the door and grabbed them before descending. Josef scrambled after.

The only light in the basement was a dim bulb several feet from the stairs. As their eyes adjusted to the darkness, Daniel spoke just above a whisper, "Maria! Maria! Where are you?"

More shots rang out from upstairs. No response to his call could be discerned.

A waist-high steel slot in each door allowed meals to be shoved in and prisoners to be observed. Josef opened slots and called, "Kurt! Kurt! Are you here?"

At the third cell, Josef found him.

Kurt, though unseen, could not contain the surprise and unbridled joy in his voice. "I'm here! Who are you?"

"Louisa sent us. You are to free everyone else," Josef informed him. "Kip, bring me the keys!"

By process of elimination, Daniel was sure that he had located Maria's cell, though no one within responded to his call. He fumbled with the keys, unlocked the door, and walked into a small room, which smelled overpoweringly of putrefying human waste. A slight, pale form lay curled up in the corner. Daniel ran to it and pulled off a hood that covered the face. It was Maria—badly beaten, her eyes blackened, blood dried around her nose, her face pulpy with enormous bruises. But she was alive.

"Maria? It's Daniel."

She managed to open her eyes, trying to place the voice but sure she was lost in a dream.

"We've come for you!" Daniel informed her.

Josef joined them. "Can you get up?" he asked.

She could not rise on her own power, so they helped her. Daniel thought he saw a tear fall from one eye, perhaps out of pain, perhaps out of joy at this unexpected turn of events. She struggled to say something, but Josef hushed her. "Don't talk. Save your energy. We're not out yet."

When she draped one arm over Daniel's shoulder, the back of her hand was inches from his eyes, and he couldn't help seeing the ghastly cigarette burn that was now pus-filled and oozing a milky substance. He had to suppress himself from gagging.

Maria again tried to speak. She cleared her throat and rasped in a weak voice, "God bless you, my dear boys," and gave them a weak but heartfelt smile.

They were thankful to see that the Nazis hadn't broken her spirit. They helped her out of her cell and then freed Kurt from his. Kurt was rail-thin but in considerably better condition than Maria at the moment. He took the keys so that he could release the remaining prisoners. Josef, as instructed, gave him a gas mask.

"You'll need it; there's tear gas upstairs. There weren't enough gas masks for everyone. The back door should have been blasted open by now," said Josef, although they had heard no explosion. "Stay to the left when you get upstairs," Josef directed.

The boys tried to put a gas mask over Maria's face without unduly hurting her. She protested meekly, "Do I look that bad?"

Josef shook his head. "Tear gas."

She understood, and was relieved. Tear gas she could handle, but the loss of her beauty, never.

They put their masks back on and the three climbed the stairs, the boys half carrying, half pulling Maria along with them. The remaining six prisoners were left for Kurt to attend to.

Louisa's instructions were to wait exactly five minutes after gunfire erupted before placing a live grenade next to the key lock on the steel doors in the back of Nazi headquarters. She waited as the minutes seemed to inch by like a garden slug. As she was hiding behind some trash barrels in the back of the building, she was unable, of course, to see what was happening out front. This situation allowed her imagination to run wild, creating all sorts of dire scenarios at every brief pause in the shooting. She chewed on a large wad of gum to dissipate her nervous energy. Finally the second hand of her watch crossed the 12 for the fifth time and she sprung into action. She went to the back door. The lock was bolted tight.

When Maria and the boys emerged from the basement, there was still much gunfire and as much smoke as ever. They crawled, turning left from the basement door, the opposite direction from which Daniel and Josef had originally come. After about twenty feet they encountered a heavy steel door, the back exit Louisa had described. But it was locked solid.

"It should have been blown open by now," worried Daniel. He tried the door again to no avail.

"We're stuck," groaned Josef, his voice muffled by the gas mask.

The plan was going awry. It was anticipated that the boys would need at least five minutes, and probably ten or fifteen, to accomplish their tasks inside. In fact it took them just over four. And so at this moment they were on the other side of the door Louisa was now preparing to blow off.

The boys assumed there had been some foul-up in the plan and began to improvise. The only other route of escape was back out the front door.

"You stay with her," directed Daniel, amplifying his instructions with sign language. "I'll check the entrance."

Just outside Louisa pulled out a hand grenade from a bag she was carrying. Removing the wad of gum from her mouth, she placed it on the grenade. She then took a deep breath and pulled the pin. Quickly she stuck the grenade with the gum as adhesive to the lock and dashed for cover.

Inside, Maria and Josef huddled low to the floor next to the steel door. Meanwhile Daniel carefully scrambled back over the ground they had just covered.

Five ... four ... three ... two ... one ... Nothing happened. Louisa waited and watched. Still nothing.

Inside, the tear gas cloud was slowly dissipating, and before long they would be exposed to the view of the Germans. Daniel's hopes that they could make a run out the front door were annulled when, within eight feet of the door, he spotted the legs of a Nazi soldier standing next to it.

Furthermore, the gunfire was rapid and heavy, and Daniel had a sense that most, if not all, the Germans were at the front of the building firing at Christian and Frederich. If they tried to get out that way, they would either be shot by their friends or their enemies. Daniel returned to Josef and Maria.

Outside, Louisa cautiously approached the undetonated grenade. With each passing second it was more and more likely the grenade was a dud and would not explode. Nonetheless, there was something highly unnerving about the whole situation. She was now within arm's reach of the explosive. What could have gone wrong? In a flurry she pulled the grenade from the lock and threw it twenty yards down the alley where it bounced about like a harmless toy ball. She had two backup grenades but unfortunately did not have any more chewing gum to adhere the explosive to the lock. Thus are wars won or lost, on the supply of chewing gum.

Just on the other side of the steel door, Josef pointed to the front of the building. Daniel vehemently shook his head no, but noticed a stairway a few feet from the back door. Remembering Tomas's lecture about the high ground, he cocked his head toward it. Josef nodded, took Maria's arm, and they started up the stairs.

The stairway was poorly lit at the bottom and completely dark at the top. They had no idea what they might encounter—Germans or rabid animals or a dead end—but they had no other options.

Meanwhile, thinking fast, Louisa tipped over a garbage barrel, emptying its contents in the alley. She placed the barrel upside down right next to the door. Set on top of the barrel, the grenade would be within a foot and a half of the lock. Close enough, she thought, under the circumstances.

The interior of the second floor contained a narrow hallway lined with doors. As Daniel, Josef, and Maria groped along, they checked each one, but all were locked. The hall culminated in yet another stairway, to the third floor.

By now Kurt and the other prisoners had begun to make their way toward the back door. Outside, Louisa wanted to be absolutely certain she blew the door open, so she decided to use two grenades simultaneously. Firmly she pulled the pins—one—two—then hurriedly left the explosives on top of the barrel before sprinting for cover again. Four ... three ... two ... one ...

As Maria and the boys mounted the stairs to the third floor, a massive blast rocked the building. The force of the explosion threw them off balance. Maria crashed on top of Daniel, and Josef fell backwards onto his posterior, but they were unhurt. In the fall, a spare tear gas grenade and the large explosive grenade had tumbled out of the bag onto the floor directly in front of Maria. Josef quickly picked up the two devices and replaced them while Maria managed some rather unladylike expressions of displeasure, further reassuring them that the Nazis had done her no lasting harm. They continued on.

The stairs terminated in another padlocked door. Josef pried it open. The door gave on to a small room with a window. Daniel raced to look out and found it to be level with the roof. They opened the window and helped Maria through it—she gasped with pain at every touch to her battered body—then climbed out after her.

Unlike the flat roofs of Bratislava, this one was slanted a steep thirty degrees, making the going treacherous. Josef, afraid of heights as ever, concentrated on helping Maria, rather than visualizing his body splattered on the alley below. They made their way to the front of the building, where they set Maria down next to a chimney.

At the back of the building smoke and debris drifted everywhere. But the door lock had indeed not survived Louisa's assault. Fortunately, the steel door had, and was solid enough to protect Kurt and the other prisoners from the explosion. Louisa ran over to the door as Kurt and six others ran out. She quickly organized them to lead them back to the bierstube, where they would rendevous with Christian and Frederich. As they started their trek, Louisa was quite worried about the conspicuous absence of Daniel, Josef, and Maria.

Out front the gunfire was by now only sporadic. Carefully, Daniel slithered on his stomach to the roof's edge and peered down. Too frightened even to consider looking down, Josef stayed with Maria and stared at the sky. Aside from a few stray fluffs of tear gas floating out the front door, activity on the street below was at a standstill.

Daniel returned to the chimney and whispered, "Where do you think Christian and Frederich are?"

Before Josef could answer, Maria motioned for quiet. She was seated near the open chimney, which served as a conduit for voices traveling up from within. She silently indicated that they should listen too.

The German commander, Major Weissbach, had used a cast-iron stove and its open door as a shield during the attack. Crouched next to the stove, in spitfire German he barked out orders that traveled easily up the stove's chimney to the roof.

"You—check outside; bring me anyone captured. You—bring

everyone up from downstairs. You—get me my flamethrower."

Josef and Daniel could not understand the rapidly spoken and somewhat indistinct German.

But Maria heard and understood the orders loud and clear. Impulsively, she reached into Josef's bag and seized the large hand grenade. Before the boys could stop her, she pulled the pin and dropped it down the chimney. It was almost too big for the pipe and made an odd, rattling noise as it hurtled downward.

In a panic, they held onto the chimney for dear life and hid their faces in their armpits. They heard the grenade hit bottom; then, eerie silence.

On the ground floor the grenade hit the belly of the stove and popped quietly out the stove's open door directly in front of the major. It took him a moment to recognize just exactly what the object was. But recognize it was all he could do before the stillness was shattered by an enormous explosion. The detonation rattled and shook the entire building, nearly shaking Maria and the boys loose from their handhold on the chimney.

When the noise, smoke, and dust subsided, Maria raised her head and said wearily, "Enough madness."

"Why did you do that?!" demanded Josef, as Daniel simultaneously asked, "What were the krauts saying?"

Exhausted, she slowly repeated the Nazi major's orders. Grateful for her presence of mind, Josef and Daniel nodded with relief. Since they hoped all the other prisoners had already escaped out the back door, the only victims left for the commandant's barbecue would have been themselves, cornered on the high ground.

They retreated from their position on the roof and found a ladder, a sort of makeshift fire escape similar to that on Tomas's building, and slowly made their way down toward the alley below. Daniel went first, followed by Maria, who was still weak but somewhat energized by the disposal of her persecutors, and then a petrified Josef.

It seemed safe, since the firing had stopped. But when Daniel was about ten feet from the ground, a heavy German voice commanded, "Halt!"

Daniel turned toward the back entrance of the building, where a Nazi soldier, blackened from the explosion but very much alive, aimed his rifle at him. The boy froze.

A shot rang out. Daniel felt the impact and fell like a rock to the street below.

Blackness enveloped him. Not long afterwards, he awoke to find Christian leaning over him. The whole world appeared to be spinning with his head as the axis, and perspiration poured from his body.

"Where did they hit you?" Christian asked.

"My back," Daniel managed to gasp. He was deathly pale, and beads of sweat rolled off his forehead.

Daniel wiped his head and saw and felt warm blood covering his fingers. "My God," he whispered.

Christian carefully turned him on his side. He scrutinized Daniel's back in what light there was in the alley. He saw no bullet hole in his clothes, no blood marking an entrance wound. But blood was oozing from a wound in Daniel's hair above his right ear.

"It's your head," said Christian using his sleeve to absorb some of the blood. "Does it hurt?"

"No," Daniel replied. "But my back is aching."

His tailbone throbbed. It felt like someone had kicked his ass with a steel-toed boot. Maria and Josef finished their descent and rushed to Daniel's side.

"It's not a bullet," said Louisa examining his head, his hair matted with blood. "It looks like just a scalp wound. They bleed a lot. But it doesn't look serious," she concluded.

The Nazi soldier had evidently never got off a shot at Daniel, or if he did, he missed him entirely. The shot that definitely was heard and hit its mark was from Christian's gun, which instantly dropped the German. The spinning and sweating Daniel experienced was merely the aftermath of the fall when he passed out briefly. His wound was apparently caused by a stray piece of shrapnel at some point in the battle, but exactly when was anyone's guess.

Josef smiled in triumph. "Maybe our bad luck curse has been broken."

But his words were premature, as they would shortly discover.

"We need to get out of here now," urged Christian. He handed Louisa one of two Vz. 24 short rifles, the Czech-made version of the Mauser 98 rifle. He slung the other over his shoulder and moved ahead to make sure their path was safe.

Josef helped Daniel up and draped one of Daniel's arms over his shoulder. Similarly, Louisa supported Maria, and off they went as fast as they could, which turned out to be a fairly quick trot.

21

A Long Walk

They hurried to the bierstube as fast as Maria's and Daniel's injuries would allow. Their extraordinary escape had been marred by one deadly serious setback; Frederich had been mortally wounded. He had been felled by Nazi gunfire at the front of the building after Louisa's grenade had blasted open the back door.

Once Frederich was taken out, Christian wisely abandoned his now lone position in front of the headquarters, which accounted for the lack of gunfire witnessed by Daniel from his vantage point on the roof. Major Weissbach had survived the attack unscathed until Maria sent him to the infernal regions with her unnervingly accurate grenade delivery.

Christian and Louisa felt confident that none of the Nazis in the building survived. The operation was a success, except for the loss of Frederich.

But what a loss. There was no feeling that any curse had been lifted. They felt no sense of triumph, only an empty feeling that so much death had been necessary for their own survival.

There was little time to grieve the loss of their friend, for Christian knew there would be immediate reprisals and he was already a suspect of the Gestapo for other Resistance operations. The task before him was to help the freed prisoners as well as himself quickly escape to Switzerland. Louisa would remain in Innsbruck and maintain her cover as a waitress.

As they all gathered inside the locked and darkened bierstube, Christian was already hurrying to gather necessary articles for his trip. Louisa gave Maria a warm, wet cloth with which to clean herself. Maria asked for something to drink and Louisa instantly brought a glass of water.

Eyeing the fluid as if it was toxic, Maria said, "I was thinking more along the lines of cognac."

Louisa agreeably handed Maria a nearly full bottle and a small glass. Maria took only the bottle. She retired alone to the small room upstairs where Josef had been interrogated. A mirror the size of her face hung on the wall there, and she went to work repairing the damage done by the late Nazi major.

Meanwhile, Daniel and Josef ate some bread and cheese and greedily drank water as if they had spent the last week in the Sahara. The night's activities had left Daniel and Josef reeking of smoke and gunpowder. They shed their clothes (which, in their minds, were a fashion offense anyway) and dressed in the freshly cleaned garments they had worn when flying into Austria. They washed their hands and arms up to the elbows and scrubbed their faces. Their hair still smelled, but there was no time for a more thorough cleaning.

Ten minutes after her exit, Maria sashayed back downstairs, looking, and feeling, generally much better; her face cleaned up, hair pulled together, the burn on her hand wrapped in a bandage, the bottle of cognac a third lighter, and her spirits considerably improved. Except for some wicked bruises below her left eye, which water could not wash away, she appeared and acted almost like her old self.

"I must leave you now," Christian began, addressing the boys and Maria. "Louisa will see you to the border. Miss von Hapsburg ..."

Maria insisted, "Countess, if you please." She *was* her old self.

Obviously, Christian did not put much credence in this royalty business, but he humored her. "Countess, your escape was not easy. We lost our comrade Frederich and would appreciate ..."

"Say no more. I will not stand by silently while the Nazis rape my nation. I will arrange to provide substantial material support for you, as much as I possibly can. I am extremely grateful."

She held out her one good, unblemished hand to him. Christian took it; if not quite sure what to do at first, he did the right thing. He bowed from the waist and kissed it like a courtier of old.

"I look forward to seeing you again in happier times," said Maria sincerely, for once shedding her aristocratic overtones. After warmly shaking Josef's and Daniel's hands, Christian was off.

As the night dissolved, Louisa, who had borrowed a late 1920s model Austro-Daimler, drove the three of them far up into the mountains, where the road eventually dwindled into a muddy cow path. They could walk to Switzerland from there — a rugged hike, but not more than a day's journey.

Josef and Daniel each gave Louisa a healthy and heartfelt hug. Maria was not the hugging type, and again held out her hand for Louisa.

She had already seen the kissing routine and good-naturedly gave Maria's hand its due.

They all waved good-bye, then the boys and Maria began hiking up the steep slopes above the tree line. Once Louisa was back in the car and bouncing downhill toward Innsbruck, Daniel demanded of Maria, "Why did you treat them like that? They saved your life!"

Maria didn't have a democratic bone in her body, and thus hadn't the foggiest notion of what he was talking about. "Like what, my dearest one?"

"The hand-kissing, like you're the Pope or something."

"No, Daniel, my sweet little thing," she began. There was that word "sweet" again. Daniel repeated it to himself like it was poison. "I am not the Pope," she continued in her most condescending voice, implying that, if anything, she had a somewhat higher ranking. "But never forget that they are my subjects."

"Then why don't you treat us like your subjects?" Josef asked.

"You, my dear boys? You saved my life. That sets you above all the rest. In fact, I ... *almost* consider you my sons. So, act like royalty!"

Despite her bruised body, she threw her head back proudly and marched, as best she could, up the beautiful alpine slope.

Josef and Daniel's heads spun. They had both been as good as orphaned, and despite the experience and savvy they had gained during their wild flight to freedom, they knew they needed someone to look after them. Switzerland was not an end in itself, after all. They were still fourteen-year-old refugees without passports, jobs, family, or money. And now this impossibly haughty, rich, and brave countess had practically bestowed kinship upon them. While their gratitude was enormous, they said nothing, for no words could adequately sum up the torrent of feelings that rushed over them at that moment.

On his wrist Daniel felt the watch his father gave him for his thirteenth birthday. He looked at it with awe. A work of art, a monument to generations of refinement, the zenith of miniaturization, the watch could run forever, given a minimum of care. And there would be no shortage of that commodity for this timepiece, Daniel promised himself.

As they walked, Daniel shoved his hands into his pockets and felt the bullet casing. He pulled it out. The sinister reminder of his father's murderers seemed unnecessary now; it felt empty, spent, no longer of any use. He realized that he could never equate his father with such a grim memento mori. He looked at the bullet casing one last time, then threw it far down the hillside.

"What was that?" asked Josef.

"Nothing. Nothing important."

While the bullet casing weighed a fraction of an ounce, Daniel felt fifty pounds lighter. He trotted ahead of Josef and Maria, almost skipping. He felt liberated and the cool alpine air filled his lungs. He began to sing "Ave Maria," not too loud, because it was for his own private pleasure and he didn't want to be heard. The first phrases of the beautiful tune gave him goose bumps. But the crystal clear air carried the tune and Josef heard.

He called out, "Daniel? Are you singing?"

Daniel abruptly stopped and looked innocently at Josef.

"No."

"You were too. Sing for the Countess. He's really quite good. You must hear him."

"Is this true, Daniel?" Maria inquired.

Daniel rolled his eyeballs.

"Go ahead," Maria stated. "I demand you sing."

Daniel stared daggers at Josef and then finally, reluctantly began. He felt self-conscious and the first two phrases came out tentatively. But then he hit his stride and the glorious melody flowed. Maria stood slack-jawed. Josef beamed with pride as if Daniel was his great discovery.

When Daniel finished the first verse, Maria wrapped her arms around him.

"My boy, that is magnificent!"

She then kissed him on the forehead.

They crested the shoulder of the mountain and stood, gazing at the jagged peaks ahead of them and the spectacular valley below. Switzerland. They stared out at it. A great, dazzling, wondrous world—a world that has so frequently been brutalized and savaged; a flourishing garden turned into the most foul cesspool, in the wake of some brief, transitory human thirst for conquest. Here they stood face to face before something far more powerful than man's often absurd cravings.

Yet their journey was far from over. But for now, they had arrived at a place of refuge where they could rest, and mourn, and renew their hopes for a world where people might live together in freedom and tolerance. Perhaps that hope was a naive pipe dream, but in the presence of such alpine grandeur and striking natural beauty, it somehow seemed attainable.

Josef picked up a rock and began running through the green meadow. At last he launched the rock with the grace of an Olympic javelin thrower. Daniel admired the way he moved; with a natural athlete's poise, Josef seemed to float just above the ground, like Achilles with wings on his feet.

Daniel and Josef had become reluctant friends, bound by ties that made them as close as brothers. The hardships each had endured, the losses each had suffered had been played out in front of each other's witnessing eyes; yet they were not defeated. Their spirits were unbroken, their determination to make a better life intact.

Nevertheless, Daniel was still racked with questions: Why had he made it this far? Why hadn't hunger, or fever, or the SS silenced him? The answers only God would know. Maybe there was something that he would one day accomplish, something great, he just didn't know what, or when. That too only God would know.

Epilogue

The journey was rugged and took two days, but they made it across the border to Switzerland without further incident. Once safely in Switzerland, Maria talked a man into giving them a ride to Zurich, where her bank accounts were located.

The freedom of Switzerland wasn't as grand and exhilarating as Daniel had imagined it would be. The small, landlocked country was surrounded by enemies and dubious friends: the fascist Italians to the south, the Nazis to the east and north, and to the west, the French, who had not lifted a finger for either Austria or Czechoslovakia when they were overrun.

Inside Switzerland were thousands of desperate refugees. Prices were sky-high as were tensions between the native Swiss and people like Daniel, Josef, and Maria, who were viewed as interlopers. Among other things, apartments and houses were renting at a steep premium. Maria rented a small two-bedroom apartment for an exorbitant price and complained about both the cost and the accommodations every chance she could. This was quite a comedown from the villa she was used to, and she didn't let anyone forget it.

A couple weeks after arriving in Zurich, Maria got hold of a

Salzburg newspaper published two days after their escape. The following article was tucked well inside the newspaper.

Two Hurt as Ammunition Explodes
at Innsbruck Headquarters

At Nazi Headquarters in Innsbruck, several rounds of ammunition accidentally exploded causing minor damage and two injuries. The two injured German soldiers were treated by a doctor and released ...

On it went. No mention of escaped prisoners. No mention of at least four dead Germans and perhaps as many as seven. No mention of Frederich's death. No mention of tear gas or grenades exploding. No mention of a dead SS major. It was as if what they knew had happened never happened. Maria also had heard through a contact that sixty people in and around Innsbruck had been rounded up and shot as a reprisal for this minor ammunition explosion. She guessed that six Nazis must have been killed in the escape because, rumor had it, the SS usually shot ten people in retaliation for every dead German. But there was no report of these people being murdered by the SS. They just disappeared from the face of the earth with no mention.

Daniel wrote in his journal that it was like his mother and brother disappearing with no mention. And the printed lie about his father dying trying unsuccessfully to fight some fire. Eventually the truth would come out. Eventually.

Neither boy gave up on the search to find his family, but each went about it in his own way. Daniel, without relatives' addresses and with no idea where his mother and brother had been taken, vowed to bide his time until he could go and personally find them. When the Nazis invaded Poland in September, any such opportunity was dashed for the remainder of the war. Daniel did write to his grandparents on his mother's side who had emigrated to Brooklyn, New York. Without a street address, it was like putting a note in a bottle and throwing it in the ocean. He didn't know if it reached its destination, but he never heard back from them.

On the other hand, Josef was a proven letter writer of some skill and was undeterred by a lack of addresses. He wrote letters to any and all relatives he could think of. He expanded his correspondence to include Winston Churchill, Franklin Roosevelt, and Josef Stalin. He wrote to Charles Lindbergh asking the world renowned pilot to come to Switzerland and fly them out. He even penned a letter to Clark Gable in Hollywood, California. He thought if anyone would help them, it was Gable. He received no responses from anyone, which ultimately discouraged him. With the war raging all around Switzerland, he wasn't even sure if his letters made it out of the country. Seven months later, though, in January of 1940, he received an autographed photo of Clark Gable, and nothing else, from a place called MGM Studios. This reinvigorated and inspired him on a new letter-writing campaign, and gave him hope at a time when hope was an extremely rare commodity.

After the Germans surrendered in 1945, Daniel returned to Prague in search of his mother and brother. He joined an army of lost souls trying to grasp smoke that had long since disappeared up crematorium chimneys or find crumpled skeletons that had been buried in shallow mass graves scattered across a bombed-out continent. Like so many others, he uncovered no information on them; and they were never found. A year later he received a postcard from Josef Czerny postmarked from a place called Chicago on the shores of an enormous inland sea. Daniel wrote back but, as the Iron Curtain fell in 1947, it was the last he would ever hear from Josef.

Daniel tried to have his journal published, a project which ran afoul of the Czech Communist regime. The bureaucrats in charge of maintaining Marxist purity in all literary output did not feel his words gave sufficient glory to the state. So Daniel tried to smuggle his story out of the country to a publisher in France. The journal never made it, and for his efforts Daniel was sentenced to four years of imprisonment in Czechoslovakia's version of the Gulag.

Chastened by incarceration and the untimely death of his publishing contact in France, he allowed more pressing concerns to occupy his life — marriage, children, the daily struggle to get by in this "worker's paradise." He would wait for a more favorable time to publish and told himself he would reread the journal every year on the ides of March.

Before long, however, it became nothing more than an excruciatingly painful exercise in futility and self-recrimination. While he vowed not to forget, he couldn't bear to remember. And so he put the journal away for nearly forty years. Until one day in 1987.

It was a gray, blustery March 15th. Daniel, now sixty-two years old, peered out his kitchen window, the panes smudged with a long winter's grime. Snow flurries buffeted the shabby street below. Winter was tenaciously unwilling to resign its bleak tenure. Daniel's tenure was similarly dwindling. A cancer was found eating away at his stomach. The doctors had given him pain pills, that being the extent of the help they could provide. The irony, in a world overstocked with it, was that the pain pills upset his stomach. Death, his former enemy, beckoned now as a friend.

No longer enjoying the prosperous environs of his youth, Daniel now lived in one of Prague's poorest neighborhoods, impoverished further by the depredations of a world war and almost four decades of totalitarian rule. He held in his hands two of his proudest possessions—a watch and a portfolio of burgundy leather. The hour 3:15 was frozen on the watch's face, but it was not broken; he had stopped wearing it for fear of breaking it, and of theft, and truth be told, his arthritis made winding it a daily hell. But this day he managed to wind it, and the second hand jumped to life like a young boy just let out of school. He marveled at the small timepiece's ability to survive. He opened carefully the leather portfolio, handcrafted in the Parisian workshops of Hermes. The pages contained in the portfolio appeared utterly unworthy of their elegant cover. They were stained, dog-eared, creased, and yellowed. Scraps of paper for the most part.

An aged newspaper clipping fell out. It was Maria's obituary, bearing no date. Daniel recalled it must have been 1958 or '59. She died in Vienna, where she had lived since the conclusion of the war. Settling in Austria was a fortuitous circumstance for her. Communist Czechoslovakia or Hungary would never have agreed with her royal blood; in fact, living there most likely would have been lethal. Few days passed that Daniel didn't think of Maria in at least some fleeting way. She left a powerful impression, like a living, breathing tornado, that was impossible to erase.

He turned to the journal itself. The handwriting was Daniel's at the age of fourteen; the schoolboy's careful penmanship a far cry from his present arthritic scrawl. In many ways reading the journal dredged up memories that perhaps would be better left forgotten as he sat there dying. He recalled when his son, David, as a child had asked him about his travails during the occupation. He was too paralyzed with pain and guilt to speak of it then. But he couldn't help but feel now that what he had been through was important for the world to remember. He hoped someone, somewhere would find his experiences worthwhile. In his will he would leave the journal to his son to do with it as he saw fit. His son, now a security agent in a police anti-terrorist unit stationed in Eastern Europe, had through his work saved literally hundreds of innocent people from the hands of murderous madmen. Maybe that was what the grand design was all about; that he would have a son who would go on to save hundreds, if not thousands, of people's lives, adding them to the roll call of survivors, to the list of the fittest. And if that indeed was what it was all about, in some tiny way maybe, after almost fifty years, the purpose of his struggle on earth did make a small measure of sense. Perhaps, there was a reason why he survived when so many others more worthy did not.